# MAXINE JUSTICE:

## GALACTIC ATTORNEY

# Books by Daniel Schwabauer

**The Legends of Tira-Nor series**
*Runt the Brave*
*Runt the Hunted*
*The Curse of the Seer*

*Operation Grendel*

*Maxine Justice: Galactic Attorney*

# MAXINE JUSTICE:
# GALACTIC ATTORNEY

### DANIEL SCHWABAUER

To Mark and Teckla Wilson

The real Counselor Singhs

# 1

## MAXINE JUSTICE LLC

Maybe if I hadn't been stone broke, two months behind on my office rent and three on my apartment, in debt to Kenjiro, my law clerk, for six weeks' back pay, and completely out of cat food for Oliver Wendell, I wouldn't have taken that night-court shift down at the Coliseum, and my name wouldn't be the subject of worldwide scorn.

But ever since the law firm of Hinkle, Remmers & Schmidt kicked me to the curb—after Brandon Schmidt Jr. lost a slam-dunk case and blamed me for it—well, things hadn't been going so smoothly for Maxine Justice LLC.

People think attorneys make a lot of money, but the truth is, most of us in the personal-injury racket only made real bank three or four times a year. The rest of the time, we spent baiting lines. Eventually you either burned out and went to work doing research for a government firm, or you built a steady flow of victims and started pumping the insurance industry. Both those options were out of reach when you were still twenty-seven and your Justice Department dossier stated—in capital letters—that you'd failed the bar exam three times. No one ever asked about the circumstances.

No, you just had to keep throwing chum in the water at the children's hospital or homeless shelter, counting down the digits in your bank account until financial misery forced you to take a shift at the lower court under the downtown stadium.

(Sidebar: It was also theoretically possible to land a stint in Air Shield's Experimental Medicines Lab on K Street. At least there, you might contract something debilitating and negotiate for a permanent disability. But you couldn't count on luck—a fact I'd learned the hard way when I was eleven—so I'd grudgingly filed for night duty near the end of the summer.)

When my rotation option came through, I tried the last thing I could think of to weasel out of it, which was asking Mom for money. I mean, she donated half of her retirement checks to network charities anyway. Maybe she would warm up a little and give me a loan. All it would cost was the tiny slice of dignity I kept in reserve for emergencies.

"Hey, Mom," I said when she picked up. "It's Maxine."

"Who?"

"Very funny," I said. She had to know who was calling; I was using her old phone, Digie. In the background, I could hear the match buzzer from her favorite game show, *Winner, Winner, Chicken Dinner!*

"Eufie?" she said after a pause. "You forget your real name all of a sudden?"

"No, Mom, but I'm Maxine now. I told you last time we talked. I had it changed at the courthouse so—"

"What, the name I gave you wasn't good enough? Hold on. Can you believe these people? Three nights in a row she wins, and does she take the money and run? No. She says, 'Let it ride. Let it ride,' she says." Another pause. "So, what did you have to go and change your name for, huh?"

I sighed. We'd been over this. "No one wants to hire a lawyer named Eufemia Kolpak, Mom."

"Well maybe nobody wants to talk to a daughter named Maxine Justice either. G'bye, *Eufie!*"

*Click.*

That's a verbatim transcript. I can still hear her sneering huff as she hung up.

On the plus side, she hadn't asked me when I was going to repay the last loan she'd given me: one hundred qoppas for food during my final semester at school—at 7 percent interest. I now owed her almost ꛛ140, a fact she reinforced with monthly statements sent via paper envelopes and the United Republic Postal Service.

So I had no fungible assets, save a tired student credit chit that was nearly maxed out and whatever loose change I could find behind my sofa cushions.

Of course I still had my main assets—the things that had seen me through law school and several other traumatic adventures—namely, an unconscious and wholly inaccurate aura of personal humility, my natural ability to charm regular folks even when they knew lawyers to be scum, a battered leather messenger bag that I planned to carry to my grave, and something my former employer had called "ratlike instincts."

If the latter doesn't sound like a compliment, you've never hired a personal-injury attorney.

Oh, and I also had a collection of animal freeloaders that seemed to recognize in me a kindred spirit: the squirrel that made its nest on my back porch, a dozen or so mice, a pair of doves nesting under the eaves, and the aforementioned stray tomcat I'd dubbed Oliver Wendell Homey. Oliver Wendell loved his free speech, particularly at 3:00 a.m.

Eventually I forced myself to grab my battered messenger bag and hop tubes to the Coliseum. The bag was more practical than a purse and had become something of a trademark—a way to stand out from a sea of young lawyers toting black attachés. Sure, it was gouged and patched and stained with layers of who-knew-what. And yes, it did indeed make me look like I'd just returned from a trek through the Amazon, searching for gold ingots. But that was part of its charm. I liked to think it sent a message to my clients: *some things are worth fixing.*

Of course, I couldn't prove that last point; I didn't have any clients.

The registrar's office was underground, just off the public-transport gate, which meant I had to walk past the welcome mural in the Justice Department's foyer—a sunrise over the harbor, complete with the 8:00 a.m. skyboards.

It was bad enough the city of York had designated the harbor horizon as commercial space, but to *brag* about it? In the morning, you couldn't even look east toward the Statue of Self-Determination without also seeing the toothy smiles of my former employers.

HINKLE, REMMERS & SCHMIDT
Over ⱨ1 Billion in Verdicts for Our Clients
You'll Smile Too!

Now the ad was staring back at me from the Justice Department wall, a fact which made me want to bleach the inside of my eyelids and look for housing in a coal mine.

Inside the gateway, music thudded from the passably lifelike sun panels in the ceiling, punctuated by the occasional screaming of the crowd in the stands three stories above. I hadn't bothered to see what was playing tonight—concert or sporting event—but now I knew.

I slipped through a maze of ever-diminishing hallways and nudged open the door to the court-bookkeeper's office.

Mr. Fagan, the dwarfish codger who had scheduled many of my shifts back when I was an intern, still worked the kiosk behind the counter like some mummy slaving under an ancient curse. Just now, he was staring at a screen as Nadia Zhou, host of *The No-Go Zhou Show,* plied some unfortunate victim with invasive questions.

Fagan squinted over thick, smudgy glasses when he saw me. "Eufemia Kolpak, a.k.a. Maxine 'Will She Make It?' Justice. Congratulations on escaping the high-price roller coaster of negligence and embracing the moral crusades of the circus."

"Nice to see you, too, Mr. Fagan."

"Oh, I doubt that. But it will be nice to have a competent PD on the roster this evening."

I smiled at the compliment. "Who's on the circuit? Don't tell me it's Wentworth."

Fagan shrugged.

"You're kidding."

"I have no sense of humor. Or so you once said."

I groaned. "Wentworth hates me."

"Technically not possible, though I admit his past behavior toward you has not been especially friendly."

"Think he's still on the take?"

"Careful," Fagan said, swiveling the kiosk around for me to sign. "Someone might think you were serious about bribing an auto-judge when we all know that's *impossible.*"

I could tell from the furrow of his brow that he was being sarcastic. "Especially without the chit-coin," I said, looking down at the contract. I scanned to confirm it was the same boilerplate and stopped just short of pressing my thumb to the confirmation box. "Are you serious? Two hundred qoppas? They've actually *reduced* the per diem?"

Fagan shrugged again. "You should see what they pay me."

I should have walked away out of principle. They'd paid ꤛ235 per night to registered attorneys when I'd worked here as an intern. Back then, my time had only paid in public-service hours toward my certification, but I was a duly sworn officer of the court now.

Still, two hundred qoppas would mean that tomorrow morning I could give Kenji part of what I owed him and also buy some groceries. Maybe Oliver Wendell would stop twitching his tail at me whenever I came home.

I sighed and pressed my thumb to the box just as the door behind me swished open.

"Counselor," Fagan said, nodding over my shoulder at the new arrival before turning the screen around. His voice now carried a tone of professional courtesy I'd only ever heard directed at other people. "Ms. Justice, you'll be in room A-14, assigned to Courtroom C, the Honorable Judge Wentworth presiding. I show seven current cases on the docket, but you should expect more as the evening progresses. Twenty credits for the cafeteria have been added to your account, which you can access from your terminal. The coffee in the lounge is, of course, free."

I'd heard this speech many times, but never given to me. Interns didn't get cafeteria credits, and somehow that little perk warmed my heart, even though the food from those kiosks was barely edible.

"Thank you, Mr. Fagan," I said, dialing in my own professional voice. "I'll—"

"Ah, Ms. Justice," the newcomer said in tones that sent fingernails across the chalkboard of my soul. "So nice to see you again."

Even before I turned, I had the stomach-churning realization that the multiverse did indeed hate me, and everything bad that had happened in my life to this point had been just a warm-up exercise.

I hadn't seen Counselor Singh in four years and hadn't wanted to. He wore the same black, long-sleeved shirt and clerical collar I'd last seen him in, the same pleated khakis and leather loafers, the same neatly trimmed salt-and-pepper beard. Each of the hundred or so times I'd seen him at the lower court, he'd always worn the same thing.

TheraPod counseling units weren't human, though you couldn't tell that by looking at them—or even by talking to them. Which was why their designers assigned them the dull, unchanging uniform of their position. Anyone could tell from a cursory glance that Singh was some flavor of clergy—not a priest, but a "minister."

In short, Counselor Singh was a pastoroid. One of the older models, and one with an apparent glitch: he had the annoying habit of quoting scripture in mixed company. Worse, he had a sense of humor— loosely defined.

With any luck, Wentworth would assign him early to some poor schmuck who needed help overcoming the urge to bash thy neighbor.

But since when, I wondered, had luck wandered beneath the Coliseum to the hallways of Courtroom C? Luck, as far as I could tell from this distance, was a certifiable snob.

"Counselor Singh," I said without conviction. "How nice to see you."

He smiled warmly, as if he'd been looking forward to this reunion for years. Possibly he had. "A pastoroid, a rabbot, and an e-mam walked into a bar."

Oh, no.

Behind me, Fagan made a snorting noise and turned away. *Coward!*

"Did they?" I said.

"The bartender looked up and asked, 'Is this some kind of joke?'" Singh smiled, one eyebrow arcing into a question mark.

"God only knows," I said.

"Ah," Singh replied. "Excellent. Excellent. I have missed you, Max."

"I'll be in my room," I said, turning toward the hallway. Sure, it was rude, but did I actually owe a TheraPod like Singh any formal politeness? I was willing to bet the Bible was silent on the subject of moral etiquette with androids.

"Ms. Justice," Singh called, his tone abruptly serious.

Habit stopped me. In spite of my legal training, I found it difficult to be overtly rude in the face of kindness. Another flaw to overcome. At the doorway I looked back.

"Congratulations on opening your own firm. I'm sure that took a great deal of courage. Remember what Solomon said: 'All hard work brings a profit.'"

"Uh, thanks," I said. "Appreciate that, Counselor."

"Also," he said. "I heard about the way you were treated by tonight's prosecutor. If you need to talk, I will be here."

*Tonight's prosecutor? What—*

But as I turned to the hallway, the answer to my unformed question resolved itself in the silk suit, tanned skin, and brilliant teeth of Brandon Schmidt Jr., now sauntering toward me like a big-game hunter gloating over a fresh kill.

"Eufemia," he said, smiling hugely. "You should have told me you'd be here. I'd have brought your things."

"It's Maxine," I said. "Maxine Justice. And you can send my things to my office. I'll have Kenjiro forward the address."

Brandon touched my shoulder, a *can't-we-be-pals* gesture that made my jaw clench and my skin crawl. "Sure thing. I'll send one of our couriers."

I shrugged away the offending paw. "Don't forget my toothbrush."

"What made you come back here, Euf—I mean, Max? I thought you hated this place."

As if he didn't know I was desperate for cash. Brandon was the son of founding-partner Brandon Schmidt Sr., and Junior's romantic advances had been directly responsible for getting me fired without so much as two weeks' severance.

"Someone has to help the little guy avoid getting shafted by a silk suit," I said.

He laughed. "Indeed. Well, good luck, and no hard feelings, whatever happens."

No hard feelings? I almost couldn't believe his nerve.

But the truth was I *did* believe it. Because whatever else he was, Brandon represented the sort of storybook life I hadn't realized I'd wanted. He was handsome and wealthy, and his family traced its roots to generational titles and land and global corporations.

My history was written in collection letters.

His charm, when I'd first started working for his dad's law firm, had seemed sincere enough.

That I hadn't seen through it sooner still amazed me. More than one person had tried to warn me. But I just didn't want to admit that I could be the fifth young hire sacrificed to Brandon's appetites.

Seeing him now, knowing what sort of snail inhabited that outer crust of power and money, I loathed myself for being taken in.

"Why," I asked, my tone icy, "would there be any hard feelings?"

He lifted one eyebrow in amusement.

Before he could respond, I pushed past him and stalked down the hall to the tiny public-defender's room.

Outside the door stretched two very long defendants' benches. My current clients—all seven of them—waited in various postures of bored resignation. They were in no hurry, as court wasn't in session for several hours, and they couldn't leave the justice center without Wentworth's signature.

One of my charges, a woman in her mid-thirties, held a cold pack to the side of her face. The others were young men who reeked of alcohol and a failed public education system.

I palmed the door, which opened to my ID tag, then sat at the public-defender's desk and scanned the government terminal for a summary of my cases.

I was right. The multiverse did hate me.

I went back to the doorway and stuck my head into the hall. "Anyone here angry enough," I asked, looking straight into the eyes of the woman, "to risk jail time for a little revenge?"

# LOWER COURT

By midnight I'd picked up eleven more clients, all cited for minor infractions. Being a short-term public defender wasn't glamorous, but it reminded me that I'd chosen the surname *Justice* because there wasn't enough of it in the world.

At least, that's what I'd told them down at the courthouse.

Gloating must have put Brandon in a good mood, because I was able to plead down most of the cases to small fines and community service.

Three of my clients, however, requested a "fair and speedy" in front of Wentworth. I figured two of the three cases were winnable if I pulled the right jury. But the third—well, the third was the sort of case that might keep my new law firm afloat for another six months.

Trevor Dowd, Shepley Geran, and Hazel McEnroe followed me into the cramped, faux-paneled pretension of Courtroom C.

Shepley and Hazel folded themselves into visitor seating, and Trevor took the chair next to me at the public-defender table.

Sam, the bailiff, acknowledged me with a nod, pad in hand. "All rise."

We stood as the door to the judge's chambers opened, and the Honorable Houghton Wentworth, MagisTron Model CJ7 Trial Bot—and generally cantankerous shill for the Coliseum's corporate owners—stumped across the carpet to his high-back leather chair.

He didn't look up until he was fully ensconced behind the imposing architecture of the glossy desk, with only the shoulders of his robe showing beneath his sagging bulldog jowls. Behind him the tiny blue dots of the video cameras blinked on. Nearly every square meter of the Coliseum was covered by video surveillance; each feed would be looped into the Night Court Channel's live coverage.

We sat, and Wentworth finally fixed his autocratic gray eyes on me and scowled like he'd just discovered a cockroach in his coffee. "Hmph," he said as if still not quite believing his misfortune. "First case."

"*The State via Bright Star Holdings, a.k.a. The New Coliseum Incorporated v. Trevor Dowd*, Maxine Justice representing," Sam said, reading from his tablet. "Charge of striking a security guard."

"That was self-defense," Trevor blurted, head swiveling to scan the courtroom as if looking for a friendly face. He didn't seem to find it.

I jabbed him in the ribs, at which point he gave me a hurt look and slumped back into his seat.

"Apologies, Your Honor," I said.

Wentworth huffed but turned away from me to Brandon. "Prosecution?"

He stood. "Clear-cut, Your Honor. We have video footage and an admission of guilt from the defendant." His voice was so solemn it might have been reciting Trevor Dowd's last rites.

"How. Do. You. Plead?" Wentworth asked, every word an explosion of displeasure.

I stood quickly. "Mr. Dowd pleads not guilty, Your Honor." And sat again, a model of respectful submission.

"Well, let's have the recordings," Wentworth said. "Haven't got all night."

I stood again, wondering exactly what an auto-judge might have scheduled in the wee hours of the morning. I pictured him watching soaps in his underwear, then quickly shook the image from my mind. "Uh, Your Honor—"

"What *is* it?"

"I believe, erm, there may have been a misunderstanding. My client is pleading *not guilty*."

"Yes, yes, what of it?"

He knew what I was getting at. He just didn't want to give it to me, though it was well within my client's rights. Both precedent and tradition demanded that I be offered this particular boon *before* any evidence was presented. "Your Honor, Mr. Dowd is exercising his constitutional right to trial by jury."

Brandon flashed a fake smile that told me he'd expected this, which plucked at my nerves. I'd seen it before. Like his father, Brandon was a terrible human being, but that didn't make him a bad attorney. Quite the opposite.

Wentworth's lip curled into a sneer. "You intend to waste this court's time with a jury trial over a clear-cut case of assaulting an officer?"

"Your Honor, with all due respect," I said, "I believe 'clear-cut' is for the jury to decide."

He scratched at his beard, then rotated slowly in his chair—not unlike the rotisserie plate in the cafeteria microwave—until only the high back remained visible.

As an intern, I'd taken to calling this sort of self-imposed recess a "Wentworth timeout."

Fagan had told me once that the judge did this whenever he wanted to check his database for updates to the law. Apparently some flinty spark of authoritarian optimism still flickered in the judge's bosom—a tiny flame that kept him forever hopeful of finding, someday, the fine print that would allow him to deny the request for a jury. Or perhaps justify ordering the bailiff to have a certain public defender drawn and quartered. He really didn't like me.

Someone coughed in the visitors' section.

Brandon folded his arms and gave me a conspiratorial wink, which I pretended not to see.

Sam rolled his eyes and opened his pad—probably pulling up a mystery novel.

Counselor Singh leaned against the wall in one corner, beaming at me like a proud grandfather.

Then Wentworth's chair swiveled again, continuing its smooth rotation until those lifelike jowls again drooped over the desk. "I've opened the pool. Mr. Schmidt, you have ten minutes to make your case."

Behind and above his desk, the wall screens flickered on. Fourteen faces appeared, most of them badly lighted though clearly visible. One of them, mouth hinged open, dug at a wisdom tooth with a pinkie finger, apparently unaware he could be seen by everyone in the courtroom.

*Thank God*, I thought, *for my kind of people!* And I meant it. I was glad Dowd had a constitutional right to face his jury; it meant his lawyer could face them too. Whatever my shortcomings as a lawyer, they were eclipsed by the simplicity of these unguarded faces.

Lower-court juries bore little resemblance to those of higher criminal or civil cases. Like their more well-known counterparts, juries beneath the Coliseum consisted of twelve volunteers and two alternates. But in a quickie trial, the jury participated virtually from home or public netbank. Evidence consisted solely of real objects or demonstrative reports or security recordings. No witness or expert oral testimony was allowed. There wasn't time for it.

In fact, votes were cast after a fifteen-minute deliberation. And that meant jury duty ran ninety minutes max, for which every juror was compensated five *tubers*—Yorkspeak for the chits that allowed you to access public transit.

Verdict was rendered in a purely democratic fashion. Whoever got the most votes won, with a tie going to the defendant.

There were always more volunteers than cases, and I'd found most jurors to be decent, hard-working, practical, conscientious, woolly brained chumps with an irrational-yet-wholesome distrust of Bright Star Holdings, a.k.a. The New Coliseum Inc. This in turn meant they instinctively sided with the defendant. No matter how earnestly they swore the juror's oath, no matter how seriously they fixed their expressions, I always knew that inside they couldn't wait to see David plunk a stone into Goliath's forehead.

Of course, the auto-judges working the night shift understood this, too, if not on a gut level, then by statistical inference. And because they were paid by Bright Star Holdings, and because Bright Star Holdings was required by state law to cover the costs of "event justice," well, the auto-judges didn't like jury trials. Wentworth in particular seemed to find them loathsome, possibly because of their unpredictability. A jury was, after all, a human animal, and nothing clogged the gears of civilization so thoroughly as a human.

Well, I wasn't getting paid an underwhelming public-defender salary of two hundred qoppas to roll over for some corporate bot. Wentworth would just have to adjudicate according to the law.

Not that I said any of this.

Instead, I played the role of the demure, out-of-my-league-but-putting-a-brave-face-on-it young lawyer, staring down impossible odds. Ever so innocently, I signaled to Trevor Dowd's jury that the system was rigged—not just against him, and not just against me. No, it was rigged against *them*. The jury. The common citizen who minded their own business and kept their crimes as trivial as their lives. Never mind Dowd's bloody knuckles and the swelling of a security guard's lip. This case was about the hard-scrabble existence of anyone whose face had been ground into the dirt by a bully.

By the end of my first closing arguments, the midnight jury had gotten an eyeful—the Coliseum's video feed on one side and my nuanced facial expressions on the other.

Bright Star Holdings never had a chance. Who *hadn't* wanted to punch a security guard? The jury returned a not-guilty verdict by a vote of eight to four, and Trevor let out a whoop, bent over to kiss my forehead (entirely unscripted in our trial prep but adding nicely to the drama), and leaped over the divider on his way out the door.

Wentworth glared at me so long that I began to wonder if anyone in the audience watching this trial via the Night Court Channel could *not* notice the wordless irony.

No judge should so obviously hate Justice.

The thought made me smile.

If I do say so myself, that's the real genius behind my name change. People—including the jury—couldn't help but make that connection. And if it was a subconscious connection, so much the better.

Shepley Geran's case was a harder sell, in spite of the fact that there was no video evidence of the crime. Accused of shoplifting from the stadium gift shop, Shepley had been caught with the merchandise—a signed baseball worth almost twelve hundred qoppas. Furthermore, the prosecution demonstrated convincingly that the item had been in its locked case a moment *before* Shepley entered the store, and was *not* in its locked case the moment he left.

Shepley had no receipt, but he did have the baseball or—as I argued— one that bore certain coincidental similarities to the one that had suddenly gone missing. Security had found it, after a somewhat invasive search, stashed in an oversized pocket sewn into the inner thigh of his cargo pants. Being an experienced poach, Shepley had wisely responded to being handcuffed with the simple statement, "I'd like to speak to a public defender now, please."

In spite of what you see on the networks, people can and do go to prison based on purely circumstantial evidence. This happens even in lower court—where most of the cases are inconsequential and defendants are encouraged to take their chances in a quickie trial by an expectation of leniency.

This time, I was pleased to say, Shepley walked, baseball still in his pocket, by a vote of seven to five. I put down the five guilty votes to jealousy.

Which left Hazel McEnroe in the 3:00 a.m. trial slot. By this time the concert overhead had long ended, and the hordes of screaming fans had drifted away to their various homes. Even the network audience had dwindled to the insomniacs and night-shift workers who happened to be off work. Plus Counselor Singh, whose services had not yet been required by the court, and the two weirdos who had wandered into the public seating area around 1:30 a.m.

Weirdo Number One was tall and lanky, with pale rubber-looking skin and a face that had the shape, and reassuring presence, of a dorsal fin at a popular beach.

Weirdo Number Two was shorter, heavier, and seemed a bit older, though also more muscular, like someone who had given up boxing not so long ago.

Both wore suits that shimmered from dark gray to violet, like something radioactive from a movie with bad acting and worse CGI. They represented money, certainly, which made their presence as visitors more than odd. Who came to night court when it could be avoided? It was like adding *colonoscopy* to your bucket list. But I didn't have time to give them further thought because Brandon had interrupted my reverie with his artificial smile.

"You sure you want a trial for this one?" he asked. "Could mean jail time."

Hazel McEnroe, like Shepley Geran, was also accused of shoplifting, but not from the illustrious Celebri-Tees! Sportswear establishment in the foyer. No, Ms. McEnroe stood accused of leaving a snack vendor without paying for a bag of sour cream–and-onion potato chips. Plus the resisting arrest and assaulting an officer charges that had, in my view, been stapled in place to intimidate her into a guilty plea and significant fine. It was obvious those charges were a cover for the fact that the arresting officer had shoved her face-first into the edge of a door.

Yes, the Coliseum's security system had three-camera coverage of the area, but somehow, shockingly, all three recordings had been "erroneously deleted during a routine backup of the server archives." According to the case file, Bright Star Security regretted the technical difficulty, but the absence of footage did not invalidate the testimony of the store clerk and the arresting officer (see *York v. Tomkin*, case number CR 27-72544-BSH2-YCP).

"What do you have in mind?" I asked. "Professionally, I mean."

Brandon ignored the barb. "I'd like to go to sleep. Let's compromise and put this community-service charade behind us, shall we?"

"You want to drop the charges?"

"The state will agree to misdemeanor theft and resisting arrest. We'll drop the assault and recommend no jail time."

I glanced up at the court clock behind Wentworth's desk. It read 2:52 a.m. We had eight minutes to settle before Wentworth hobbled back from his potty break, or whatever it was auto-judges did in their chambers.

"I'll present your offer to my client," I said and turned away from him. Ending a conversation with Brandon always felt like crawling out of quicksand.

Back at my table Hazel still held the cold pack to her face. By this time her heavily rouged cheek was swollen and turning a nasty shade of purple.

"They're offering you a get-out-of-jail-free card," I said. "It will mean community service and a blip on your record." The latter was a kind of gift, pretending I didn't know she already had three misdemeanor thefts on her rap sheet.

"But that means no settlement money, right?"

"Correct. The jerk who walked you into a door gets a pat on the back, and you admit you stole a bag of chips."

She pondered this for a moment, glanced around the courthouse, then said, "Where is he?"

"Who?"

"The guard."

"Ah. Probably home asleep. Not here, anyway. These lower-court trials are all about speed and mitigating"—I stopped on the word instinctively—"limiting the consequences of a guilty verdict. A cheap trial means everybody wins."

I meant it ironically, but she squinted up at me from her chair, her blue eyes suddenly as hard as diamonds. Or, more likely in her case, cubic zirconia. "Except when you don't."

"Yeah," I agreed. "It's a risk. And only you can decide if the payoff is worth it."

"Can we really win?"

"Absolutely. But we could also lose. A lot depends on the jury."

She nodded. "Okay. I want my trial. And a settlement."

I glanced over at Brandon, who had moved from the prosecutor's table to the visitors' seating and was talking to the two weirdos in suits. He noticed my glance and raised one eyebrow.

I shook my head: no dice.

He shrugged as if he'd expected as much.

Then Sam, once again, called us to order, and for the third time, we rose for Wentworth's grandiose entrance.

"Well," Wentworth growled when the eight of us who remained in the room were all seated. "Let's get on with it. What are the charges?"

Sam cleared his throat. "*The state via Bright Star Holdings, a.k.a. The New Coliseum Incorporated v. Hazel McEnroe,* Maxine Justice representing. Charges of misdemeanor theft, resisting arrest, and assaulting an officer."

"How do you plead?" Wentworth asked. I started to rise, but he continued, leaning forward on his elbows, "And before you answer, let me suggest, Ms. Justice, that you consider carefully the hour, the charges, and the potential consequences of a guilty verdict. I would be inclined to leniency were Ms. McEnroe to plead no contest. Perhaps . . . a fine of two hundred fifty qoppas and three weeks' community service at a nearby retirement home."

He'd caught me off guard. Never before had I seen, or even heard of, an auto-judge preemptively suggesting a negotiated settlement in open court.

The message was clear: Wentworth wanted this case to go away.

We all knew why. Brandon, Hazel, the jury—probably even Counselor Singh and the weirdos in the back—understood what I had seen the moment I caught a glimpse of the purple beneath that cold pack.

Bright Star Holdings was trying to weasel out of a significant negligence settlement. If Hazel pled guilty now, the chances of making such a case stick later would disappear as neatly as that video evidence.

But I happened to know that no video footage ever disappears from the Net entirely. Whatever they had done with it, there was a good chance my assistant, Kenjiro, could track it down, given enough time, subpoenas, and legal posturing.

But for that to happen, Hazel McEnroe would have to be found not guilty.

In which case I would ply my poor client with doctors and treatment centers and holistic specialists and aromatherapists until her medical bills positively exploded with the blunt-force trauma of her suffering. Possibly I could justify screening her at a highly selective pregnancy clinic. One never knew how the stress of such a bruising might spread to, well, other areas of the body. Indeed, I had stored copies of the supporting case files for such an argument in a special folder marked "Dessert."

However much those treatments cost, my initial demand would multiply the total by twenty. And Bright Star Holdings would pay it— just to avoid the civil trial in a downtown courtroom. My share of such a settlement would be 40 percent.

I flicked a glance at Hazel, who gave the tiniest shake of her head. Sure, she was scared. But she was also angry. I could see it in her eyes. She knew she was being railroaded, and to her credit, she wanted to fight.

"Thank you," I said, turning back to Wentworth and slathering my voice with artificial gratitude. "But Ms. McEnroe pleads not guilty, Your Honor."

This time the auto-judge took no rotational time out. Instead, he leaned back in his chair and said, "Mr. Schmidt, you have ten minutes to present your case."

Only then did I notice he'd turned off the wall screens. When they flickered to life again I realized that he had deliberately kept the display turned off while asking how Hazel wanted to plead.

A queasy feeling rose from my stomach to my throat, stronger even than the revulsion I'd felt when Brandon touched my shoulder.

I hadn't noticed the absence of a jury. I'd been too distracted by his odd settlement offer and my own hopes of finally earning a serious paycheck.

The jury was comprised totally of shills, right down to their collared shirts, tweed coats, and expensive cocktail gowns. One matron in a silver-and-black dress sipped from a wine glass and scrutinized me from an office lined with bookshelves. I recognized the books; the woman was seated in a private law library. Anyone surrounded by such extravagance would never enroll as a juror for five stinking tubers.

These people hadn't been drawn randomly from the Justice Department's rotating jury pool. They'd been reeled in by Bright Star Holdings, probably with help from an unofficial office ledger, compiled down at Hinkle, Remmers & Schmidt, over cognac and Fauxminican cigars.

I could see the plot unfolding in my imagination, and for a moment, I was astonished that I'd fallen for it. I had believed—really believed—that the coincidence of Brandon's presence here was just his reptilian attempt at a pickup. Somewhere deep down, I'd assumed he'd wanted to see if he could lure me into further self-deprecation.

But no. Brandon—if not his father or someone else at the firm—had been planning something even more damning.

And now my jury was comprised of lawyers, judges, and business owners who had probably been recruited specifically to put me in my place. I could imagine the conversation at one of their late-night gatherings: *Who is this disgraced research assistant who has opened a firm under the sleazy banner of* Maxine Justice LLC? *She's making a mockery of us all!*

The fact that their retribution might destroy Hazel McEnroe probably never occurred to any of them.

So I gave them her face.

On cue and as directed, Hazel lowered the cold pack so the swelling of her cheek and bruising of her right eye was visible to the network and jury cameras. A visual aid for the morally blind.

I told them her story. How Hazel McEnroe had lawfully carried a ninety-five cent snack from the back of the store to the front, when a security guard assumed she was about to leave without paying. Then, not even identifying himself as an officer, he had suddenly and violently put her in an armlock.

Of *course* she had tried to pull her arm away. Of *course* she had tried to run. What would *you* have done in her place? (My second mistake, since none of these people had ever stepped foot inside a Coliseum snack shop.)

And when the guard rammed her face into the edge of the door, Hazel McEnroe had *still been inside the shop*, as the guard himself admitted in his half-page incident report. Hazel could not have stolen the chips, because the chips never left the premise. The clerk described picking up the bag after the altercation.

Because she had not stolen anything, the officer had not "lawfully restrained her in the commission of a crime" but had unlawfully attacked her in a way that should shock and disturb every law-abiding citizen. The guard claimed no injuries and did not mention Hazel assaulting him in his report.

At last, in for a penny, I laced my concluding remarks with a string of accusations that stopped just short of hitting Wentworth smack between his lifeless, gray eyes: false arrest, assaulting a citizen, police brutality, gross negligence, and—my biggest blunder—*appellate frigging court*!

I don't know what I expected. But the jury could have shown the decency to wait the full fifteen minutes before casting their votes. Instead, barely ninety seconds after I had finished, Wentworth motioned for Hazel to stand.

"I have the decision of the jury," he said in a low voice, his eyes fixed not on Hazel but on me. "On the charges of misdemeanor shoplifting, resisting arrest, and assaulting an officer, Hazel McEnroe, you have been found guilty by a jury of your peers, voting twelve to zero."

Beside me, the poor woman gave a little gasp and glanced at me for help.

Peers? That jury was as much "her peers" as I was a baby seal! Not that that would stop them from clubbing both of us.

From the prosecutor's desk, Brandon said, "Your Honor, if I may?"

"Mr. Schmidt?"

Brandon tapped the desk with his long fingers. "The state has considered the somewhat-unusual nature of this incident, and after deliberation, I would like to recommend no jail time for the defendant. I believe some other penalty, coupled with the little bump she got there, will suffice to remind Ms. McEnroe to respect private property."

Wentworth nodded. "This court has taken your recommendation under advisement." He turned at last to Hazel. "Ms. McEnroe, if not for the generosity of the prosecutor, and frankly, the incompetence of your public defender, not to mention my many years of experience with the law, this situation could have ended much differently. However, I see no reason to throw the book at you simply because your counsel, appointed by this court, is inexperienced. You are hereby fined one hundred qoppas and ordered to complete eighty hours of volunteer service at the Logan Standish Community Center near your home. Do you have any questions?"

Jaw clenched, she shook her head.

"Now," Wentworth said. He had picked up his gavel, but instead of ending the trial with a final bang, he turned again to me. "Ms. Maxine Justice." He spat my last name as if it were made of horseradish. "You are young and, according to court records, entirely inexperienced as a trial lawyer. Nonetheless, I cannot let a breach of the law go unaddressed in my courtroom. Do you understand?"

Judges had immense power. Even a minor contempt-of-court violation—and even here in lower court—might result in a stiff fine or even jail time.

But Wentworth was suggesting I had actually done something illegal during the trial. And I had no idea what he meant.

I shook my head. "No, Your Honor, I do not."

"I suggested a settlement might be in order," he said, pausing for me to catch on.

I thought back to how the trial had opened. "And my client declined," I said. "How is that—"

"Your client did *not* decline!" he said, jowls quivering. "You stood right there in front of me and rejected my offer without presenting it to her—as you are obligated to do by your oath."

He was goading me. I knew it even as I balled my hands into fists and glared back at him.

"Would you like to see a recording, Counselor?" he asked.

I came so close to making a fourth mistake. I almost said, *Are you sure the recording hasn't been erased?* But Brandon was still there, watching, and I could feel his eyes gloating from the prosecutor's table.

The network cameras were still on too. Which meant there was an audience, however small. If there was some way to redeem this miserable evening, it would have to come from the public. From people who didn't know me.

That is, people who didn't know me *yet*.

Hazel, bless her naive little heart, tried to come to my defense. "Your Honor, we had talked about it before, and I heard you. Maxine did look at—"

I jammed my fingers into her lower back, but Wentworth was already stepping in. "Ms. McEnroe, this matter does not concern you, so I strongly suggest you remain quiet. Otherwise I will find you in contempt."

She shut up and I didn't blame her.

"I will ask you again," Wentworth said. "Would you like to see a recording?"

I looked past him to network-camera number one, mounted in the corner above his chamber door. The feed still glowed with a steady pinprick of green. Someone out there would be watching this. Someone poor and desperate and unable to pay very much. But wasn't that how a reputation was built? One disaster at a time?

"No thank you, Your Honor," I said. "*Justice* recalls the moment perfectly."

He blinked, his algorithms probably trying to interpret my third-person response and weigh the likelihood that I was mocking him. But I'd plastered humility so thick across my face I doubted even Counselor Singh could have seen through it.

"This court belongs to the *law,*" Wentworth said. "Not Justice."

I flicked my gaze back up to camera one. *Did you hear that?* I shouted at them inwardly. *He thinks he's being clever, but he just gave away the store.*

"Of course, Your Honor," I agreed.

"I'm fining you six hundred qoppas."

Six hundred! After working all night, I would be poorer leaving than I'd come. I had no money for groceries, no money for rent, no money to give Kenji. I didn't even have enough credit to cover the minimum payment required for his fine. Which meant I might not even be able to leave the Coliseum's justice center. "But—"

"AND," he added, daring me to keep talking, "I am ordering a full psychological evaluation. You seem to have forgotten why you took the oath. I am recommending the bar association change your status to probational for a period of six months, during which time I will expect weekly reports from a court TheraPod. Do you have anything you'd like to add?"

Fuming, I shook my head. "No questions, Your Honor."

"Good. Then I'll expect the first report this morning by eleven. I'm assigning you to Counselor Singh."

He brought the gavel down with a bang.

# COUNSELOR SINGH

The pastoroid's office stood on the ground floor of the Coliseum's sprawling commercial district, still within the guarded confines of the justice center.

I followed him to a door marked, "Whole Person Wellness, Reeyansh Singh, PsyD, DMin, ThD," which he opened with a welcoming sweep of one arm. "Second door on the right, please. Can I get you something to drink? I have water, tea, soda—"

"Two fingers of Scotch whiskey, please," I said, only half joking, and nudged open the door he'd indicated. Inside, wingback chairs framed a bookshelf laden with heavy textbooks. Splayed across a small, marble-top table, lay half a dozen glossy copies of *TheraPoddery Today* magazine.

To the left, a massive screen gave the illusion of a bay window overlooking snowcapped mountains. But I was more drawn to Singh's trophies of competence: six framed certificates from various universities, and one stamped in gold foil from The North American Society of Therapy and Inner Exploration:

By the authority of the Board of Regents and the State of York,
this Organization recognizes as a School of
REPRESENTATIONAL THEOLOGY
## Dr. Reeyansh Singh's
MULTI-WORSE THEORY OF CHRISTIAN FAITH

"Most of my clients think that's a joke," he said from the doorway.

"The Society's members are all TheraPods, so of course you haven't heard of the NASTIEs."

He held out something in a disposable paper cone: two fingers of double malt.

Amazing. I tipped it back and let the warmth spread from my throat all the way down to my toes. "So it's some sort of school?" I asked, hoping to avoid whatever "inner exploration" he'd planned for me.

"More of a community. A place for us to discuss the ramifications of our existence. Please, have a seat." He motioned to a chair.

I grudgingly obliged, realizing as I did that the view of the mountains was probably designed to lull me into a semi-hypnotic state. TheraPods were famous for inducing a feeling of almost religious euphoria as part of their treatments. I looked away quickly. Who wanted fake happiness?

"Working with humans can be difficult," he continued. "Whenever one of us stumbles upon an idea that gives meaning to that task, we send it in for peer review. Occasionally, something resonates."

"And this theory of yours—this 'Multi-Worse Theory'?" I nodded toward the certificate, deliberately avoiding the wallscreen. "That, um, *resonated* with other TheraPods?"

Counselor Singh smiled. "Like you, they think I'm a bit batty. But they're an open-minded lot."

"I'm open-minded," I protested, knowing I would probably regret it. "I'm just waiting for the punchline."

He crossed his legs and rested his hands on his right knee. "In spite of our different faith programming, we TheraPods share a common goal: make humans good. Since that goal seems to be impossible, we shoot for making humans better. Which means our core, shared message is two-dimensional: things can be better, and somewhere, things are significantly worse. Do you follow?"

"Which would it be if I were still working at Hinkle, Remmers & Schmidt?"

"Ha!" He grinned. "I was simply referring to the concept of a multiverse. You've heard of multiverse theory?"

"Sure," I said, eager for the familiar ground of irrelevant abstraction. "Some people think reality is an infinite series of parallel universes, each variously distinct from the others."

"Exactly," Singh said. "*Everything* happens *somewhere*. Or so they say."

"And you proved this somehow?"

He shook his head. "Impossible. Proof would require evidence, which by definition would consist of facts and data from within our own universe. No, I simply made a case from my area of expertise. Call it a nudge from another direction."

"Multi-worse? You're serious? It's not a joke?"

"Jokes can be serious," Singh said. "We TheraPods tell people that things can always be worse. It's part of a healthy view of life. But if it's true, then this statement requires an infinite number of universes to supply the necessary suffering. And that revelation, of course, opens Pandora's box."

I didn't follow and wasn't sure I wanted to. "It . . . does?"

"If things can always be worse, they can always be better." He smiled at me as if waiting for something to happen. It didn't.

"At some point," Pastoroid Singh continued at last, "all that awfulness would add up to something like hell. And, in the opposite direction, you'd get an infinitely expanding heaven. Since 'everything happens somewhere,' then *somewhere*, Christ rose from the dead. Voilà. Multi-Worse Theory."

"Ah," I said, wondering what this had to do with me.

"And its corollary, Semi-Verse Theory."

"I don't—"

He soldiered on, determined to see this little excursion into the unknown all the way to its bitter end. "If everything happens somewhere, then, logically, there must be overlaps, like the edges of a Venn diagram."

"Two of the same thing, you mean?"

"Two of the same thing . . . but different. Take stories as an example. If everything happens somewhere, then everything happens in multiple ways. So a book or a movie in our world would be playing out as reality somewhere else."

"And vice versa?"

"Of course."

"So, somewhere there's a stage play of my life? *Maxine: A Tragedy in Three Acts*?"

"Five acts, I should think," he said. "Semi-Verse Theory predicts that our universes connect at such points—like the edges of two circles. And for such connections to exist, there must be shared qualities. Commonalities. Things that make such touchpoints possible. The real crux of the matter is this: perhaps everything *does* happen somewhere. But in that case, some things must happen *everywhere*. Gravity. Divine incarnation. Boy bands."

"Is this a test?" I asked. "Part of the evaluation process? Or are you just trying to convert me? Because that doesn't seem ethical. I'm not convinced things actually *could* get worse. Or that the multiverse is large enough for two Counselor Singhs."

"Imagine a thousand parallel universes in which Maxine Justice, founder of Maxine Justice LLC, is reprimanded by a night-court auto-judge for something she didn't actually do." Singh leaned forward. "Imagine this happened during a trial conducted under suspicious circumstances. And imagine that this dubious verdict is taken to an appeals court. *Now* are you following me?"

I drummed my fingers on the seat of the chair, then nodded.

"In how many of those universes do you suppose this young Maxine Justice would prevail? And in how many might she find herself head-banging a brick wall?"

Was Counselor Singh warning me? And if so, why? I found it hard to believe a TheraPod could be involved with covering up negligence cases for Bright Star Holdings. I'd known Singh too long. His programmed scruples were real. Even for a pastoroid, he was unusually devoted to the words of the Old and New Testaments. Not like some snake-oil salesman hawking bottles of ninety proof. No, Singh was more like an annoying aunt who knew her home remedy of cayenne pepper and lemon juice could cure that little headache.

But if an auto-judge could be bought, why not a TheraPod?

On the other hand, he had clearly acknowledged the "suspicious circumstances" of Hazel McEnroe's trial—something an auto-judge like Wentworth would never do.

"All of them," I said at last, feeling stubborn. "I would win all of them."

"And?" he prodded.

Now I understood what he was getting at. "And," I sighed, "in every case, it would amount to banging my head against a brick wall."

"Why?"

"They have the money and a guilty verdict. It would take years, and Hazel McEnroe will get tired of waiting and move on."

"So, you really could have settled."

"Are you saying I should have?"

"*Should* is a loaded word, Max. But no. The fact that you didn't reminded me of why I used to recommend you for the thorny cases when you worked here as an intern."

He'd *recommended* me? This was the first I'd heard of it. I couldn't decide whether to be flattered or annoyed. The worst cases I'd taken on down here had cost me hundreds of hours. "So what are you saying? That I'm greedy?"

He stroked his goatee with his thumb and forefinger. "Hadn't occurred to me, though I suppose that's consistent. Hmm. Well, no. No, I'm wondering why you charged into that case so recklessly. Wentworth was clearly signaling that something about that particular trial was going to be different."

He was right, but I didn't feel like admitting that I'd been hoping to finally make the money I needed to keep my firm going. It was humiliating enough to be publicly reprimanded on the Night Court Channel. "Maybe I hate seeing people railroaded."

"I'm certain you do. But are you sure there wasn't some other factor? Perhaps from the other side of the courtroom?"

And there it was. The implication I'd been dreading. "Brandon and I are history. A very short history. Before today I hadn't given him a single thought since Remmers fired me." This wasn't true, but it was certainly an attainable goal. "As far as I'm concerned, Brandon is nothing but a soul-sucking leech, and I'm glad to be rid of him."

Counselor Singh seemed surprised by the metaphor. "Well, I am glad to hear you haven't given him any thought. I was worried that his callous behavior toward you might have left you feeling bitter."

From inside my messenger bag, Digie gave a muted incoming-text signal—the sound of a bomb whistling toward detonation. "Excuse me."

I snapped open the heavy clasp and retrieved my digital assistant, an embarrassingly outdated model that had formerly belonged to my mother. It still only responded to voice queries addressed to "Hey, Digie" and had three editions of the *Winner, Winner, Chicken Dinner!* for Seniors app installed on the home screen, which no amount of electronic barnacle-scraping seemed able to dislodge. Digie's notifications tended to be irritating, coming as they were from an enhanced-personality AI, but at the moment, I welcomed the distraction. Nothing could be more awkward than answering a bunch of questions from a TheraPod about my short fling with Brandon Schmidt.

"Hey, Digie," I said, smiling apologetically at Counselor Singh. I didn't want him to hear what I had to go through in order to retrieve text messages. On the other hand, there was a slim chance the text would provide some excuse for me to end the interview and head home. "Show me the message, please."

"Suurrre, sweetie," a cloying nursemaid voice said. "You got a nice message from that charming young man at your office, Kenjiro. Want me to send a copy to your mother?"

"No!" I said. "No! Absolutely not! Do not *ever* send copies of any text messages I receive to my mother."

Digie *tsked* an unreasonable volume of displeasure. "Okay. But I'll keep asking in case you change your mind. Kenji says, 'Potential clients, eleven aay-em. I hope you got paid. The bag of stale donuts in the fridge is *not* gluten free,' exclamation mark, frownie face."

I snapped the cover closed. "You heard me say 'show me,' didn't you?"

"I did indeed," Counselor Singh said. "I hope these prospective clients work out for you. Dare I suggest they may have seen your performance last night?"

"I lost."

"You won two of three, and anyone could see the last trial was rigged. You know, I think you might have a future as a defense attorney."

"Not for me," I said. "I like to believe in what I'm doing."

"So, negligence claims?"

"I can't even get the Coliseum to pay for night-court work. How am I supposed to drum up clients who are facing real jail time? Besides, aren't you supposed to be on Wentworth's side?"

"I'm supposed to tell the truth," Singh said. "To keep bad things from getting worse."

"That how that works, Counselor? You just tell the truth, and everything gets better?"

"Not everything. Some things."

I took a deep breath. "So can we get this over with? No sense meeting these clients if you're going to tell the judge I'm crazy. What do I need to do for you to sign off on this session?"

Counselor Singh smiled. "I've already completed your evaluation, Max. Even sent in the form Judge Wentworth asked for. But I do want you to answer two questions before you leave."

Relief flooded through me. "Shoot."

"If you make it through Wentworth's six-month gauntlet—assuming you meet the probationary requirements—"

"Wait a minute," I interrupted. "Are you saying you're going to try to stop me?"

He held up one hand as if he were a traffic cop. "No, I am asking a simple question. One you would do well to consider for your own sake, as well as for the sake of your fledgling law firm. I'm asking, How far are you willing to go? Today it was Houghton Wentworth—a lower-court auto-judge, trying a case that wouldn't even be reported to the state journals—and you lost. I'm not rubbing it in. I'm reminding you that your firm and your client suffered significant, though not permanent, losses. All because you went in, guns blazing, to a battle you didn't fully understand."

"Did you see her face?" I asked, teeth clenched.

"I did," Singh replied. "Before and after the trial."

Warmth spread across my cheeks, down the back of my neck, and forward to both palms. I thought, *Why does it matter what a TheraPod thinks of me?* And I wanted to say—to shout—*I'm willing to take every case to the highest court in this Republic; that's how far I'm willing to go!*

But it wasn't true. That was just my stubbornness and latent rage festering. That was my monkey brain, the brain stem, trying to seize control of the cortex so it could use reason and common sense and legal training to get its way. To bash my neighbor as Wentworth had bashed me. Come to think of it, actually bashing Wentworth still didn't seem like such a bad idea. Except for the stark truth that doing so would mean real jail time and a fine I'd never be able to repay.

"I would do it again," I said, still angry that Bright Star was going to get away with their abuse, and angrier still at being told I ought to have just given up. "I swear, I would do it again."

"I don't doubt that. It's an admirable quality, really. But I'm not sure it suits you as a personal-injury attorney. Don't you think such work requires a more detached frame of mind? A willingness to negotiate with the enemy?"

*Negotiate?* The word brought heat to the back of my neck. "Maybe the only kind of justice I believe in is financial," I said hotly. "Maybe it's the only kind some people understand."

Singh smiled. "If that were true, you wouldn't be here talking to me."

"You're working for them," I prodded, looking for a reaction. "They sent you with a proposal. You're trying to buy me off."

He laughed. "Maxine, I once told a knock-knock joke at one of their parties. I am the last person they would condescend to talk to, much less attempt to hire for their dirty work. No, I am not trying to buy you off. I'm asking if you *can* be bought off."

"I don't understand."

"In six months, when all this has blown over and your little firm starts to attract more clients, what are you going to do about Bright Star Holdings then? Will you still appear in lower court? Will you take on Hinkle, Remmers & Schmidt when there's no profit in it or when your thirst for revenge has faded? Will you go after Air Shield or Star Cross or PharFuture when you have a little money in your pocket and a comfortable career rocking only the small boats safely docked at harbor?"

It was unanswerable. One of those questions professors asked in law school as if they were seated on some high moral ground instead of safely buttressed in an ivory tower. But Singh wasn't a law professor, and he didn't seem to be asking me for his own benefit. In fact, he didn't seem to expect an answer at all.

So I said, "And the second question?"

"When shall we meet again?"

"We're done here?"

"We are. As soon as we schedule our weekly sessions."

"Saturdays at eleven?"

"Perfect."

I picked up my messenger bag and walked to the door. Was I supposed to thank him? What had just happened?

"Max?"

I turned, my hand on the knob. "Yes?"

"Have I ever told you that my father was very cheap?"

"Really?" I asked stupidly. "How cheap was he?"

In hindsight, I should have seen it coming. TheraPods don't have parents. In my defense, I *was* very tired.

"Once," Counselor Singh replied, "he tried to sell his ear hairs to Wigs for Kids."

I made my way back down to the court-bookkeeper's office, feeling very small as Fagan worked the kiosk and finally spun it around for my signature.

I had to read it three times before it sank in. "Is this right?"

"Someone called it in but made me promise to keep their name a secret."

"The whole six hundred qoppas?"

He shook his head. "Four hundred. The difference between what you earned tonight and what you owed. Fair warning: you won't get a deposit come Friday."

Still, I could go home without worrying about how to pay Wentworth's fine.

But who would have paid it?

Counselor Singh, perhaps?

Or . . . *Brandon Schmidt Jr.*

The thought made my skin crawl. "I'm not sure I can accept—"

Fagan tapped the counter with his stylus. "Don't make things harder on yourself than they already are, Max. This came, no strings attached, from someone who watched you last night *on screen*." He loaded the last two words with significance. So it hadn't been Brandon. "Oh, and you still have those twenty credits in the cafeteria. Might as well use 'em on your way out."

I pressed my thumb to the screen, gave Fagan the warmest smile I could manage, and plundered the cafeteria vending machines of three sandwiches, a cup of yogurt, and a ninety-five cent bag of sour cream–and-onion potato chips.

# 4

# PREMIER REPRESENTATION

Though I was free to leave, Wentworth's fine had left me penniless and unable even to access public transit. Having an 11:00 a.m. appointment meant I'd have to walk the seven miles back to my office.

A scorching August sun was already blistering the sidewalks by the time I started.

Kenji welcomed me at a quarter to eleven, soft drink in hand. I took it from him and slammed it back, only realizing by the annoyed look on his face that he hadn't intended it for me.

"What took you so long?" he asked.

"Wentworth cleaned me out," I said. "I had to walk."

"From the Coliseum?" He almost sounded sympathetic.

"Right? My legs are killing me!"

"But how are you going to pay me?"

Kenjiro Yoshida was a second-generation citizen, with eyes that looked like they weren't sure whether to mock you or pity you for your stupidity. He had the body of a Sherpa mountain guide and the mind of a super villain. But life had kicked him so often and so hard that he no longer expected anything else. Anyway, that's how I interpreted the fact that Kenji was working for me.

Not that I'd ever tell him that.

Twenty-six months my senior, Kenji was the ideal receptionist for my fledgling law firm. An honest, hard-working nerd, his various computer skills and lack of fashion sense made him a sort of virtual Renaissance man. Best of all, he worked cheap. A messy divorce had left him broke and needing proof of employment. I'd promised to reward his loyalty as the business grew.

Apparently there were limits to even Kenji's patience.

I flapped my arms to let the cool wash of air-conditioning whisk away the sweat from my armpits. It didn't work. "I'll find a way. I promise. Is the conference room ready?"

"Soft drinks and water in the fridge, like you asked, but your credit was declined. I had to put it on my personal chit. That's another twelve qoppas you owe me."

"Fine, fine." I opened the door to our modest conference room and library. My collection of third-hand books was ruinously incomplete, but I figured most of my clients wouldn't know the difference. At any rate, all of it fit nicely into the old master bedroom of the converted Gothic-Victorian that served as our headquarters. Nine hundred and seventy-five square feet of creaky hardwood flooring, exposed brick, and water-stained ceilings. Because nothing said "I'm a professional" better than peeling plaster. Or the conference table Mom had sold me from her storage unit for seventy-five qoppas and a promise not to embarrass her.

I pulled *York Appellate Reports 1997–2035* from its shelf and dropped gratefully into the vinyl office chair closest to the window. Flipped open the massive volume and thumbed to *Kruger v. Gall*, page 627 and following. If I could stay awake, my potential—no, my *future*—clients would see me studiously examining the law on behalf of one Hazel McEnroe, whose case I now had no intention of forgetting.

I heard the front door open at precisely 11:00 a.m., followed by Kenji's sonorous welcome. "Ms. Justice, Dr. Arounais and Consul Fowler."

I looked up to see Kenji holding the door open for the two weirdos from Courtroom C, still adorned in their gray-and-violet suits.

"Ah, Counselor Justice," the tall, thin one said, extending his hand. "How delightful to meet you. Thank you for taking the time."

I shook his hand, which was like squeezing a latex glove filled with tepid oatmeal, and fought back a shiver. "My pleasure."

"And this is my associate," Dr. Arounais said, "Ottokar Fowler of the GBG."

No idea what GBG stood for, but Fowler's hand at least felt warmer than room temperature and was apparently constructed of something like real muscle. A bodyguard, I guessed, though why Kenji had called him *consul* was a question for later.

I motioned for them to sit. "Kenjiro, could you bring us a couple of bottled waters and, oh, how about three cans of soda? It is blistering out there today. Now"—I slid *Appellate Reports* aside and folded my hands on the table—"how can I help you gentlemen?"

Dr. Arounais's eyes were set too close together, his nose was slightly too long, and his cheeks were a bit too high, so that, seeing him straight on, you got the feeling he'd been streamlined by some alternate evolutionary processes to move through water rather than air. Add to this an annoying habit of looking you square in the mouth, and the effect was off-putting. Fortunately, I excelled at putting on.

"Ms. Justice," Dr. Arounais began in a resonant tenor voice as smooth as steamed milk, his mouth curved in a slightly too robust smile. "I represent a consortium of, shall we say, foreign interests searching for premier representation here in your great Republic. Specifically, we need someone open-minded to serve as an intermediary to the United Nations. After watching your extraordinary performance this morning— well done, by the way—and in light of certain advice we've received elsewhere, I am convinced that you are the right person for the job."

To say warning sirens were going off in my head would be an understatement. *Foreign interests? Open-minded? Certain advice received elsewhere? The UN?*

Flattering as it sounded, it was too good to be real. I was a young, unknown personal-injury attorney just trying to claw my way out of the muck of slip-and-fall claims and into the golden fields of gross negligence. Why would anyone in need of an international law firm come to me?

Then again, I was also burping up gastric memories of the egg-salad-on-wheat I'd choked down during my long walk back to the office. I needed cash, and I needed it now.

"You understand this law firm specializes in personal-injury claims?" I said. "My work in criminal defense is more like a hobby. And I make no claims to having studied law outside the boundaries of the United American Republic."

Kenji, standing in the doorway with cold drinks balanced on a tray, scowled and shook his head vigorously before distributing the drinks. On his way out, he delivered a thumbs-up signal only I could see.

"As it happens," Dr. Arounais said, "the responsibilities our consortium has in mind lean more toward contract law. But that is not really the point. Ms. Justice, we need someone with three qualities: an open mind, a talent for reading people, and a sincere desire to make the world a better place."

*Make the world a better place?* If that wasn't a sales pitch, I was a nun. "Four qualities, you mean."

The man's eyes twitched. "Counselor?"

"Presumably, this person also needs to be a licensed attorney."

"Yes, of course."

"And why do you need a representative at the UN? What kind of trouble are you dealing with?"

The doctor held out his gray hands in something like a defensive gesture gone wrong. "No trouble at all. We are seeking to make a deal with humanity's collective body. And as you have apparently noticed—I can see it in your body language, Ms. Justice—we Iperians do not present ourselves well socially. Even when wearing a replica earthsuit such as this one."

I flicked my gaze over to Fowler, whose expression hadn't changed. The *consul* seemed almost disinterested.

"Iperians?"

"My people, yes. I represent a consortium of business interests from the Iperian Star System. After observing your planet for some time, we have decided to offer a business arrangement that we believe will appeal to your entire species. The terms are quite generous."

The skin at the back of my neck prickled as I looked for signs that he was some kind of actor or practical jokester. Instead, all I could see in his too-close-together eyes was a sort of hunger that dried the sweat under my armpits. He really believed what he was saying.

Now it all clicked. They were nutjobs. Complete and utter nutjobs.

They'd approached Brandon first for whatever delusional legal help they imagined needing, and he'd shoved them off onto me. Probably he was bragging about it to anyone who would listen back at Smiles HQ.

I slipped a conspiratorial tone into my voice. "Are you saying you're, like, an alien? An extraterrestrial?"

Dr. Arounais was still looking at my mouth, apparently concentrating on my words. "Yet not so different as you might imagine. We have a saying at the consortium: 'Iperia for the law, and the law for Iperia.'"

"Inspiring," I said. "So you're a lawyer . . . and a doctor . . . from outer space?"

"Alas, with no legal standing on your planet and only passing familiarity with your laws."

Fowler glanced over at him, but said nothing.

"And this, uh—this 'earthsuit' you mentioned?"

"Earth's atmosphere is perfectly suited for the biological functions of an Iperian, but our physical form would attract unnecessary attention. Thus, this human shell."

"It's the eyes," Fowler said.

For a moment I thought he was joking, but his expression still hadn't changed.

"And your role in this, um, Consul Fowler?" I asked.

"Ottaker is here as a neutral observer," Dr. Arounais said, leaning forward in a friendly manner. "So you can rest assured that the Galactic Body General is aware of all processes necessary to protect Earth's natural rights."

Another flick of Fowler's gaze. Did the *consul* for the Galactic Body General—apparently the GBG—have a tell?

"Gentlemen," I said. "As much as I'd like to help you—"

The door opened. Kenji peered in, displeasure knotting his eyebrows even as his voice sailed across the room. "Anyone need more to drink?"

"Thank you, Kenji, but no," I said. Neither man had so much as taken a sip.

Behind the two ETs, Kenji rubbed his thumb and fingertips together while mouthing: *We. Need. Money!*

I pinched the bridge of my nose and glanced out the window to the patch of blue sky and neighboring brick wall visible from my seat.

Had it really come to this? All those idealistic goals of starting my own firm, seeking out the poor and downtrodden, fighting for justice for those who couldn't fight for it themselves, occasionally landing the big case that brought me a little notoriety—and maybe a long vacation in the Caribbean—was all just a dream?

Did saving Maxine Justice LLC really require that I stoop to representing crazies who thought they were alien diplomats?

Ethically, I couldn't take their money without agreeing to perform the job. Which meant I'd either have to send them away or attempt to give them what they wanted. I'd have to at least go through the motions of presenting their offer to the United Nations.

Was there any chance that wouldn't get around? Wentworth had recommended the bar association place my license on probationary status. Taking this job would mean they'd send my license to the shredder.

Just when I thought my reputation couldn't get any more soiled, the multiverse drove by, slinging filth from a garbage truck.

"Gentlemen," I said again. "As much as I'd like to help you, I'm afraid this law firm is not a good fit for your needs."

Dr. Arounais blinked. "I don't understand."

"Look. I saw you talking to Bright Star's prosecutor, Brandon Schmidt Jr., down at the Coliseum. He and I have a history, which means I'm not feeling particularly 'open-minded' about this arrangement. Thank you for coming in, but I'm not the lawyer you need."

"But—"

Fowler gripped the thin man's sleeve. "She has answered, Doctor."

Dr. Arounais looked down at the muscular hand on his arm until Fowler withdrew it. "Very well. Should you change your mind, your assistant has my number."

The two men stood and walked stiffly to the door. Fowler was last out. He tipped his chin at me as if in recognition, but I had no idea what he meant by it.

A moment later Kenji stood in the conference room doorway. "You didn't even ask me to check their credit."

"Of course I didn't. I can't take them as clients."

"Why not?"

I tugged *York Appellate Reports 1997-2035* back to its place of prominence in front of me and went back to reading. Maybe Kenji would take the hint.

He didn't. "Why not?"

"Well, you were eavesdropping. What do you think?"

Kenjiro came fully into the room and placed his hands flat on the table. "I think you're too proud to help a couple of conspiracy theorists just because they have mental problems."

Too proud? After what I'd been through last night? The accusation brought heat to my face. I bit back my first response and took a long, deep breath. "Mental problems? They're absolutely bonkers!"

He could tell I was getting angry, but instead of responding with a raised voice, he lowered his and spoke slowly. "Okay. And don't you think maybe they could use your help? Max, has it occurred to you that crazy people deserve legal representation just as much as non-crazy people do?"

"Kenji, they need a psychiatrist."

"And who will find them one if not you?"

I slammed the law book shut and glared up at him. "You know who sent them here? Brandon Schmidt Jr. I'm out six hundred qoppas and the last shreds of my dignity because of him, and now I'm supposed to trust that he's sending me clients?"

Kenji shook his head, jaw clenched. I'd never seen him like this. "They were trying to throw money at you. And you need money right now. You should have run their chit."

*Oh, really?* I thought, hands clenched beneath the table. "How do you know what I should have done?"

For someone who prides herself on vocal inflections, on reading people, on winning the hostile to my side, it was very badly done. Kenji heard—rightly—the accusation in my voice. *Who was he?* I had implied. Meaning that he hadn't gone to law school, hadn't passed the bar exam, hadn't been humiliated and fined and publicly ridiculed by his peers.

He'd heard all of that, and his face drained of color. But I was too proud to apologize.

"I know because you haven't paid me in six weeks," he said, returning the accusation with an inflection of his own, "and *you* can't even keep client soft drinks in that abomination you call a refrigerator."

He stomped out and began rummaging in the kitchen. It took me a moment to understand that something different was happening, that this wasn't our run-of-the-mill disagreement over which bills not to pay.

I rose and went to the conference room door in time to see him stalking out of the small kitchen area. He wore his backpack hooked over one shoulder and had the remainder of the soft drinks and bottled waters in either hand. A bag of powdered donuts draped from his pinkie finger.

"What are you doing?"

"Quitting," Kenji said, dropping the donuts at my feet. "You can have these, even though you gave them to me as a deposit on my back pay—because *I can't eat them*. You *never* remember I'm allergic to gluten!"

"Ken—"

"I'll come by for my check whenever you get the funds." Hands full, he opened the door awkwardly, then slipped through. "Thanks for your help with my divorce papers."

And that was that.

I sat in the conference room the rest of the day, occasionally wandering into the kitchen or spinning around in the receptionist chair as if daring a paying client to enter. At 5:00 p.m. I ate the remaining cafeteria sandwich I'd stowed in my messenger bag, wishing I'd remembered to transfer it to the fridge.

At 7:00 p.m. I flipped the door sign to "Closed" and headed home in a thick blanket of humidity that magnified the streaks of orange on the horizon.

Home, an aging bungalow with a weedy front yard, lay three blocks south and one east, but had never felt farther. I'd rented the place specifically to avoid needing a car, but after my long walk this morning, every step gouged the blisters at my heels, and I couldn't wait to fall into the convertible couch/bed/cat-nest that was my favorite futon.

I knew something was wrong three houses away. Someone had opened the gate. From the rusting relic of chain link that cordoned off my tiny backyard, a trail of debris flowed to a pile of cheap furniture, clothing, cardboard boxes, and the frame for my mattress. From a distance the trail of color looked like, and soon proved to be, my own clothing—what remained of it.

I knew what it meant, but I tried the front door anyway. Sure enough, the key no longer worked.

All the lights were off, but pressing my nose to the porch window told me the story. The place was cleaned out.

I'd been evicted.

I glanced back at the pile of stuff in the yard. Someone had stolen my futon.

"Oliver," I called. "Oliver Wendell!"

My cat didn't seem to be inside. Wasn't on the front porch. Wasn't hiding in the back.

Had someone stolen my cat along with the futon?

Oliver Wendell Homey came and went as he pleased, so there was no way to know.

Still—

I kicked off my shoes and plunked down on the front step.

*He's a stray who sometimes wanders off for days,* I told myself reasonably. *Besides, cats don't have owners. They have clients. Cats are the lawyers of the animal world. You know that.*

*It's true,* I answered, not caring that this inner conversation was a semi-crazy thing to do and might end with me thinking I represented a mercenary firm from Alpha Centauri. *But Oliver and I are a team.*

*It isn't personal,* I insisted. *It's just that cats are very clear about the cat-client relationship. When the retainer dries up, so do the perks.*

*Pretty much like every other relationship in the world?* I replied to myself.

*Pretty much,* I answered.

I waited till the streetlights came on and the sun set and the house lay draped in moon shadows, but Oliver didn't come home.

Eventually I dried my eyes and decided I had to go somewhere.

The office wasn't unreasonably far away, but Hank's Bar & Grill held more promise and was even closer. Right now, I could use a drink. I didn't have any money, but maybe Reggie would still feel grateful for the help I'd given him a few months ago.

So I plunked myself down on a barstool and motioned for the bartender. Ever since I'd helped him with a speeding ticket, he tended to view me with tolerance, as if I were a smelly dog that occasionally chased off trespassers. "It's been a rough day, and I'm flat broke. Mind if I grift?"

Reggie shrugged. Ten minutes later he brought me a complimentary beer and a bowl of peanuts. Turns out even bartenders did pro bono work.

I turned the events of the day on their head and tried to shake them out, but my thoughts kept returning, oddly, to the emptiness of the office after Kenjiro had quit.

Kenji and I had almost nothing in common except my law firm. And I hadn't been able to pay him in well over a month. Besides, I'd been rude and condescending. I'd forgotten his gluten allergy, forgotten even the word *gluten*, which now seemed burned into my memory by the way he'd said *you never remember.*

So I had no right to be annoyed that he quit. Why, then, did it feel like such a betrayal? Why did I expect Kenji to keep soldiering on when there was literally nothing in it for him?

*Loyalty,* I told myself. *Because giving up stinks.*

Which was unfair and ridiculous. Kenjiro didn't owe me anything. He'd be better off working for someone else. I ought to feel glad for him, finally facing reality in a way that I couldn't.

Still—

Three hours later the place remained lifeless, and I continued pacing the same mental treadmill, trying to make sense of my bad choices, my mind replaying the same series of what-ifs. A few people had come in for a late dinner, but none of the eager drunks I might have seen on a weekend. Somehow, in spite of it being mostly empty, the place filled with cigarette smoke anyway, as if the building itself couldn't quite kick the habit.

I watched most of a football game on Reggie's flat screens until, just before midnight, Dr. Arounais and Consul Ottaker Fowler lurched into the bar.

Dr. Arounais had folded his hands into the pockets of his shimmering suit coat, and he kept them there as he made his way over from the door.

I held up one hand. "Still not interested."

"Hear me, please," he said. "I realized my blunder after we left, and Consul Fowler agreed to permit a follow-up. Iperian business culture places high stress on the importance of personal relationships, with the financial considerations normally reserved for a second or third meeting. But it is clear that in this society, and in your profession, remuneration must be considered immediately."

I was going to stop him, but he pulled from his pocket a wad of beautiful golden currency and started thumbing hundred-qoppa bills onto the bar faster than I could count them.

"There!" he said at last. "Five thousand qoppas. A little, what do you call it? Stalking around money?"

"Walking," I said, still not believing it.

"And this." From his other pocket, he withdrew a silver key fob tagged with a tiny printed address: 1 Perennial Tower, UN Plaza, Ste. 5101, York City.

"I can offer an initial retainer of fifty thousand qoppas, less this cash deposit of course, plus expenses and further compensation to be discussed tomorrow, after you have had a chance to see your new office suite and read the contract. You need not sign tonight. All I ask is that you see what I am offering, consider it carefully, and meet with us tomorrow. If at that time you choose to walk away, you may keep the five-thousand-qoppa earnest money with no springs attached."

I stared at him in dumb silence until he added, "Do you agree?"

"Office?" I asked.

"I have taken the liberty of calling you an Ober. I think you'll find the couch in the foyer a comfortable place to sleep."

It was absurd. Irrational. Impossible.

But it was also five thousand qoppas, their beautiful mint-fresh faces staring up at me like a crowd of witnesses demanding to be heard.

And suddenly, all I could see in them was the solution to every one of my problems, the biggest of which was that the city elites were trying to shove me out of my profession for daring to stand up to them.

No. Scratch that. My biggest problem was that I couldn't imagine how to run my law firm without Kenjiro's help. I couldn't even login to my own accounting software without asking him for the password.

I didn't think he'd refuse to come back. Not if I paid him in cash for his back pay—and offered a significant raise. If he was really stubborn about it, I could probably even work up to apologizing.

Kenjiro had been right: I could either resign myself to being just another down-and-out lawyer desperate for work, or I could swallow my pride and take a stack of money from crackpots.

I mean, what did I have to lose? Wasn't everybody a little cracked?

Five thousand qoppas would give Maxine Justice LLC the funds I needed to take on Bright Star Holdings and make a marketing splash over the harbor.

Almost as important, I could finally buy groceries.

"Sure," I said at last, wondering how he knew that I'd been evicted, but not daring to ask. I scooped up the wad of bills—leaving one behind for Reggie—and followed the two weirdos out into the summer air.

My ride was already waiting—a hulking black limo, the rear door propped open by a white-gloved driver.

I slid all the way in, the cool, air-conditioned interior heady with the scent of oiled leather and mixed perfumes. I expected the ETs to get in with me; instead, the driver closed the door and sat behind the wheel.

For the next thirty minutes, I rode the cushioned seat like a fairy-tale princess on a magic carpet. Fortunately, my magic carpet came equipped with a bar, stocked with tiny liquor bottles. Gliding in muffled silence, I watched the skyline change and tossed back a couple of drinks.

Soon, very, very soon, this dream would end, and I would wake up on the creaking hardwoods of my crumbling aspirations, staring up at the stained plaster of my reputation, wondering why I hadn't taken my mom's advice and gone to dental school.

"Can you wait?" I asked the driver when we finally arrived and he again held open the door. "In case the key doesn't work?"

"Of course," he said. "But it will work."

The doorman took one glance at the fob and walked me to the bank of elevators. His rubber heels squeaked on the polished floor, but my legs seemed to move on their own, as if I were still gliding atop the limo's buttery suspension.

"Welcome to the Perennial, Ms. Justice," the doorman said, pressing a button. "I hope you enjoy your stay. Your new suite is on the fifty-first floor and has quite the view of the harbor."

The harbor. Yes. Of course it would.

And the smiling faces of Hinkle, Remmers & Schmidt when the skyboards flickered on in thc morning.

Not a dream, but a nightmare.

Meanwhile—

The elevator doors opened, and I stepped out into the marbled foyer and indirect lighting of what was obviously the nerve center of some moneyed, third-generation law firm—except for the name, etched tastefully into the curved glass wall separating the elevators from the reception area.

They'd hung out my shingle before I'd even said yes.

MAXINE JUSTICE LLC
*Premier Representation for Discerning Sentients*

# 5

## BOILERPLATE

I woke on the couch in the reception area, sunlight streaming through the tinted glass and filling the space with fragmented beams as in a cathedral.

I remembered where I was, but a part of my mind still couldn't take it in. This suite was beyond anything I'd ever dreamed of commanding. Where were the real occupants? How would they react when they found me crashed on their couch?

But as I sat up, my new name became visible, now etched backward in the warped glass of the reception area.

I rose and wandered barefoot over the thick carpet, pausing to absorb the law library, the twin conference rooms, the four associate suites, and last, the outrageous corner suite bearing my name and title on a simple brass plaque: *Maxine Justice, Attorney-at-Law.*

In my case, that dashed designation appended to my name had required unusual sacrifices to acquire. But all it really meant was that I had the authority to practice law anywhere in the great state of York. *At-law* tells the world that you are recognized by the courts—even if it's under probationary status.

Okay, so Dr. Arounais and Consul Ottaker Fowler were rich. Insanely, disgustingly, and enviably rich. And for some reason, they'd chosen me to shield whatever operation they were running. Drugs or money-laundering came to mind, but it could be something more benign, and perhaps even legal, such as lobbying foreign governments or even tinkering with various nonprofit interests as a form of tax relief.

My corner office looked north and east, out over the bay, where a wispy feather of cloud smudged the horizon. The room smelled of new carpet and fresh paint. I ran my fingers over the lavish teak desk, its surface mirror-smooth and empty, except for a flat terminal and phone. Maxine Justice LLC scrolled in white letters across the phone's palm-sized screen, but I didn't pick it up. Instead, I padded over to the recliner and sank into its plush, microfiber surface. The fuzzy texture was soft as down. The footrest elevated on its own, with the slightest hint of pressure from my shoulders, then retracted when I immediately jerked forward. It had caught my blisters.

I stood and took in the matching loveseat, table, and conference chairs, all trimmed in teak, then noticed another door standing open. My new office even had a private bathroom—complete with a marbled shower.

Perks and more perks, every square inch a promise of something I had surely not yet earned.

The contract still lay untouched and unread on the glossy work table. I'd seen it last night but not trusted my judgment. I'd wanted to wait until morning, knowing that whatever it contained would keep me awake.

Now, after five and half hours of sleep, I needed coffee and a clear head. I needed answers.

Sure enough, the kitchenette off the reception area had an automated system, which spat out a steaming mug of hot coffee to rival something from a corner barista. I lifted the foam disposable to my chin and inhaled the aroma. The first sip convinced me I'd need a second cup. I queued a refill for twenty minutes, carried my prized nectar to the private bath, and indulged in a ritual cleansing.

Afterward I went back into my private office space and took in a magnificent view that was only partially ruined by the sudden appearance of the morning skyboards. The dimming mechanism built into the windows would have allowed me to black out Hinkle, et al., but for the moment, I just sipped my coffee and smiled back.

It occurred to me that I was standing seven hundred feet above one of the most populous sections of the planet, and surely someone down there would be positively thrilled about bringing me an overpriced breakfast.

Ignoring the new mobile phone, which I didn't yet trust, I dialed the Perennial's concierge using my desk terminal.

"Good morning, Ms. Justice," a friendly voice answered. "What can I do for you?"

"Good morning. Who am I speaking with, please?"

"This is Efram."

"Efram, if I found myself desperately in need of a Goldy's Number 7 Bagel, stuffed with cheesy eggs and bacon, and a large extra-pulpy orange juice, but didn't have time to ride the elevator and wander down to Fifty-Eighth Street, how would I make that happen? Is that the sort of life-saving service that could be added to my monthly rent, or am I just out of luck?"

I still had the wad of hundred-qoppa notes, but at this point, I didn't expect this roller-coaster ride to last past dinnertime, and I figured it wouldn't hurt to see how far the limits of "Iperian" generosity stretched.

"No problem," Efram said. "Give me thirty minutes."

I went back for my refill and pulled up a chair to the work table and the printed contract. Which turned out to be two contracts.

The first was a standard attorney-client representation agreement, pre-filled with *Maxine Justice LLC* in the attorney spaces and *Consolidated Galactic BioProducers* in the client spaces. Most of the wording seemed standard, based on what I remembered from my contract-law classes. The notable exceptions were under *Scope of Representation* and *Attorney's Compensation*.

Without mentioning numbers, it's fair to say that Dr. Arounais wanted to pay me more every month than I'd made working for Hinkle, Remmers & Schmidt in a full year. They were also going to pay all of my expenses, picking up the tab for the new office space, utilities, and a generous stipend for any employees I needed to bring along.

Unexpected, to say the least.

But that wasn't the most striking aspect of the deal.

The *Scope of Representation* outlined three areas of responsibility. I translated them from lawyer-ese to clear English on a pad of legal paper:

1. Secure proof the "Iperian healing serum" actually works, and
2. Negotiate a settlement with the UN for at least 30 percent of Earth's refined gold reserve, and

3. Oversee transfer of the payment.

Numbers one and three required a suspension of disbelief I just didn't have, but two left me scratching my head. Who at the UN would have the authority to sign that sort of contract? And did I really have to get that person's approval—that of, say, the secretary-general—or might there be another way?

The second contract turned out to be the sales agreement Dr. Arounais wanted me to negotiate with the UN. Frankly, it raised more questions than it answered. Parts of it also raised the hairs on the back of my neck. These guys were crazy, but they were also serious.

Why, I wondered, were really wealthy people so often whacko? Could it be something money did to people, or was it a more Darwinian process? Maybe to be truly, obscenely rich, you had to be the sort of crazy that thought in sideways leaps. And maybe those sideways leaps normally landed you in oncoming traffic. But occasionally they plopped you down in the center of Fort Knox.

Someone, after all, had thought skyboards were a wonderful idea. And even though everyone in York City hated skyboards, still, there were Hinkle, Remmers & Schmidt smiling down at you from ten thousand feet every morning at eight.

I read the sales contract six times, filling the rest of the legal pad with notes between bites of my Goldy's Number 7 Bagel. When I finally got up to stretch, the clock read 3:23 p.m.

"Ms. Justice?" Dr. Arounais called from the reception area. "Are you in?"

I slipped back into my shoes and strode down the long hallway, blisters screaming. "Doctor," I said. "Consul."

Dr. Arounais swept one arm clumsily in a half circle. "How do you find your accommodations?"

"Frankly? Overwhelming."

"Excellent. Shall we discuss the contracts?"

I led them back to the larger conference room, not yet ready to think of it as mine. I could get used to the salary and opulent work space. I wasn't sure I could get used to the idea of pitching some "health serum" to the world.

After we were seated around the table, I held up the paperwork. "Gentlemen, I have reviewed both contracts."

"Is the attorney-client agreement acceptable?" Dr. Arounais asked.

"It's generous," I admitted. "But can we come back to that after we've discussed the job you want me to do? To be honest, I'm having a hard time understanding exactly what you want from the UN. Do you have any idea how much money thirty percent of Earth's refined gold is?"

"Not money, counselor. Gold."

"They're the same thing."

"No, not to us. Gold is an unrivaled electrical conductor. Useful in many applications, as humans have known for some time. We have no use for your paper currency, nor are we interested in other metals or gemstones."

Ah. Sure. They didn't care about money. They wanted all this gold for "science." "What I meant," I said, blank-faced, "is that you don't seem to understand what you're asking for. Thirty percent is so out of proportion I wouldn't know where to start."

"Why not start big?"

"Big?"

Dr. Arounais folded his arms in a way that reminded me of a trained seal doing a trick. "Ms. Justice, may I be blunt?"

"I'd prefer that, actually."

"I know you think I am mentally unwell. And I know—or assume— you are overlooking this defect out of self-interest. As I see it, we have two options. First, I could prove who I am right now by removing this earthsuit—"

For one panicky moment I envisioned Dr. Arounais removing his clothing, exposing a flabby, pink body and polka-dotted underwear. *Voilà! You see, I* am *an alien!*

"But the effect," he continued, "would be disconcerting for both of us. Furthermore, it might make the execution of your duties difficult."

Difficult? I'd have nightmares.

I cleared my throat, trying to imagine a happy thought from childhood. "And the second option?"

"If you take this job, you will discover the truth during the performance of your duties." He jabbed the contract with one wobbly finger. "I refer, of course, to the first column of our proposed agreement."

I glanced down at my notes. "You really have a health serum? One that will cure the human race of 'every natural flaw?'"

"We do."

"Uh huh."

He smiled. "As I said, you need not believe me. You only have to agree to carry out your obligations faithfully and according to the contractual timetable. Find a lab to administer the tests in a way that will satisfy even the most skeptical of critics, yourself included. Jump through every loop. Dot every hi. Cross every sea. You will see for yourself. The blind shall see. The lame walk. The allergic will stop their sneezing. And you will be rewarded handsomely."

"What about gluten allergies?" I asked, thinking of Kenji. If I were going to sign this contract—and really, what choice did I have?—the very remote possibility of getting his allergy healed might be an added incentive for him to come back.

"Gluten allergies will also be corrected, since the celiac-sprue mutation is a natural flaw. When we say *every*, we mean it."

Celiac sprue? So was he a real doctor in addition to being a fake lawyer?

I glanced out the window at the blue sky above the harbor, where the skyboards would appear again in the morning. "You know, Doctor, I really want to believe you."

"But?"

"*If* your healing solution really works, and *if* the UN agrees to this deal, how do you plan to administer the serum to eleven-billion people? That many shots would take years. And even then, you'll have people who can't be reached because they live in remote areas or simply refuse to take the shot.

"You may not understand this, but human beings can be cantankerous. Some will say your serum violates their religious beliefs. Or their commitment to nature. Others will just be suspicious. But you'll have to reach all of them anyway. You'll have to vaccinate every human being in the world."

"Yes."

"And if you don't heal every human in the world, as stated in this contract, then Earth's governments might use that fact as an excuse not to pay the agreed price. This contract seems pretty clear that if you don't cure all of our natural diseases, Earth doesn't owe you a dime—er, ounce."

"Rain," Dr. Arounais said.

"Rain?"

"We will use rain to administer the serum, not shots. Atmospheric dispersal at strategic points. Full absorption may take a few weeks in desert regions, but the initial effect should be noticeable almost immediately in most places. Trust me, people will know. And they will thank you."

I fought back a sudden urge to stand and pace. If not for those blisters on my heels I might have done it.

The man wanted to use rain? As a concept, it had that almost-but-not-quite reasonable quality shared by so many conspiracy theories and wild ideas. I knew something was off about it, but couldn't put my finger on what.

But I did have something I could put my finger on, so I flipped through the UN contract to page seventeen and tapped the section header. "Okay, what about this?"

Dr. Arounais leaned forward to peek at the words. "The enforcement clause? What about it?"

"Well, it's weird. It doesn't really enforce anything."

"But it does. Should Earth default on its payment, Consolidated Galactic BioProducers and its Iperian ownership will acquire Earth's mineral rights."

Consul Ottaker Fowler, meanwhile, sat with his arms folded and listened impassively. I was hoping he would react to something Dr. Arounais said, but he seemed unflappable.

"Sure, but not until after those rights are no longer exercisable by human beings." I slid my shoes off beneath the table, where no one would notice. The burning sensation in my heels faded, and I wondered why I hadn't done this twenty minutes sooner. "Your contract rules out, and I quote, 'military action, acts of violence, and any further action of any kind taken against or on behalf of, Terran life, human or nonhuman, until humans are extinct.' This doesn't enforce anything."

MAXINE JUSTICE: GALACTIC ATTORNEY

53

"Are you suggesting this contract is not in our favor?"

"No, I'm wondering why you think you'll actually get paid."

"Ah. What if I told you we are not concerned about this particular payment because we believe that once they see what our serum actually does, your governments will be motivated to pay because they will want other technologies to be discussed later? Think of this as a preliminary arrangement. A moss leader."

So the "Iperians" were basically intergalactic drug dealers, offering us our first fix? "The serum is addictive?"

"No, of course not." Dr. Arounais looked at Consul Fowler as if for support. "I assure you, our serum is not even remotely addictive."

"Then why include enforcement language?"

"Is it not expected?"

He had a point. I picked up the contract and scanned through page seventeen, a vague feeling of discomfort growing in my stomach as if I'd swallowed one too many sweets.

The whole thing was basically boilerplate—a standard business agreement—with a handful of quirky exceptions. If not for the few legal flourishes I recognized, the whole thing might have been drawn from an open-source template.

But those flourishes! Something about the language in the enforcement clause struck me as familiar.

A thought hit with the force of a hammer. "Who did you hire to write this contract?"

Dr. Arounais's face cracked into a huge, lopsided smile. "I told you she would recognize the source! Did I not tell you?"

Fowler's expression was still police-report serious. "You told me."

"We have only consulted one law firm besides yours, Ms. Justice. Arthur Remmers wrote the contract in your hand. Is that a problem?"

I'd suspected as much by the overuse of certain modifiers Remmers favored. But did it matter? I mean, sure, I hated my old employers. And I would never trust anything they touched. But a contract was a contract.

They'd probably taken on the work because it paid well, and Brandon Jr. thought it would be funny to send the crackpots to me, not knowing how deep their pockets were.

"One more question," I said. "Section five on payments. No, not that contract. The attorney-client agreement."

"What about it?"

"You should understand that it contains something called a rake-off. Language that grants me a commission of anything over the thirty percent you're asking for."

"We're quite aware. On Iperia we call that an incentive."

I stared at both men for a moment, but neither of them flinched.

"So if, for instance, I were to somehow finagle thirty-*five* percent of Earth's gold reserves from the UN, I would stand to make—" I glanced back at the contract.

Before I could find the relevant paragraph, Dr. Arounais said, "Five percent of five percent, yes."

"One twentieth of five percent of all of Earth's refined gold." Though I had no idea how much that added up to, it had to be an impressive number. "That would be what? In the hundreds of millions of qoppas?"

"In the billions, actually."

It didn't sound real.

Because of course it *wasn't*.

Earth would never pay real money for a fake serum. For that matter, I doubted we would pay real money for a real serum.

I turned the idea over in my mind and listened to the imaginary sound of a clock ticking. Felt the warmth of the Goldy's Number 7 Bagel in my stomach and the cool, plush carpeting between my toes. Tasted the fragrance of delicious coffee still hanging in the air.

*I'm on the fifty-first floor of the Perennial Building. One block from the UN, with almost five thousand qoppas in my pocket. Can this even be real?*

It was crazy. Certifiably, cave dwelling, winged-mammal guano crazy.

The UN would never agree to their contract. And the idea that these weirdos could cure all of our diseases virtually overnight was absurd.

But I had no home to go back to. No clothing except what I was wearing. And no other clients looking for my help.

On the other hand, if I took this job, I'd have office space in downtown York, a dependable salary, and most importantly, several months in which to build a client list. Eventually, as outlined in the timetable, the biscuit wheels would fly off this gravy train, and I'd have to fend for myself again. But with any luck, I could keep it going for the six months Dr. Arounais had allowed. Perhaps I could talk him into a series of extensions. All I would need to do was show a little progress along the way. Meanwhile, I'd be building a reputation that would last a lifetime.

People would talk about me. I'd be in the tabloids—a lot at first, then every time I landed a weird case. And I would land them, because people would always need a lawyer to protect them from the system. And when they needed a lawyer, the first name that would pop into their unhappy little minds would be that of Maxine Justice. *You know,* they'd think, *that lady who tried to get billions of qoppas from the UN? What could she do for a real client? What might she do for me?*

Sure, half the lawyers in the state would make jokes.

But who cared?

I'd have my practice and I'd have my name.

I had no clue what these two crackpots would do three months from now. But if Dr. Arounais wanted to spend his money on a fantasy, who was I to stand in his way?

"Can you excuse me for a moment?"

Dr. Arounais dipped his head. "Of course."

I retreated to my new office, closing the door behind me. The mobile phone they'd left me still lay on my desk, but I just wouldn't trust it until I'd gotten Kenjiro to run it through a de-snooper.

Instead, I unsnapped my messenger bag and pulled Mom's old device from its leather pocket. I had a love-hate relationship with the phone. It worked, it was paid for, and it billed directly to her account. But it was also seven flavors of annoying, and I had the unshakable feeling that it was secretly passing information about me to my mom. The only reason I hadn't tossed it into the harbor was that it served as a kind of ambassador. For all of its flaws, the aggressive AI did keep the channels between us open when nothing else could. "Hey, Digie," I said. "Call Kenji."

"Finally!" the sugary voice said. "How you ever let that nice young man walk out on you beats me. Five qoppas says he doesn't even answer. Not that I'd blame him."

"Just call him, please."

"Oookay. I get it. You don't want to get your hopes up."

It rang, and a moment later, Kenji answered, his voice curt. "Hello, Max. Do you have my money?"

"Yes," I said. I let the answer hang there, knowing it would catch him off guard.

"Then please don't—wait, what? Really?"

"Yeah, really."

"Oh." He sounded almost disappointed.

"I can pay you in cash."

"What did you sell? You're not down at the Experimental Medicines Lab, are you?"

"No, nothing like that. Just, well, I've almost decided to take on the clients I turned away earlier. I realized I need to take your advice." This last part wasn't technically true, but he didn't need to know that.

"Almost? If you haven't taken them on, where did you get the money? Wait. I don't want to know."

"The thing is, I need you to come back to work."

"Sorry, I can't do that."

"Why not? Did you already get a new job?"

"No. I just realized that I'd rather not get paid for not working than get paid for working for you."

Harsh, but not entirely unreasonable after the last couple months. Especially after the way I'd spoken to him yesterday. "Kenji, I'm really sorry about what I said."

He didn't respond. I figured he was probably weighing the odds that this call was a practical joke.

"I'm offering you a raise," I said. "And an advance."

He still didn't respond, and the silence hung there for so long that I started to think he'd already hung up. Finally he said, "How much of a raise?"

"Five hundred qoppas a week."

There was a slight choking sound. "Seriously? Two thousand a month?"

"Seriously. And I'm giving you a promotion. I want you to be my office manager. I'm going to be hiring some other people, and I need you to run the ship."

"Max, what exactly did you do?"

"I got evicted. Best thing to ever happen to me. Can you come now? I'm on the fifty-first floor of the Perennial Building downtown."

"Now? Wait—*where*?"

I turned in a slow circle that landed me looking out over the harbor. The surface of the water lay iron gray under a bank of clouds. From this height the white-bristle waves had no depth at all. "Actually, would you please go by my old place first and round up any of my stuff that's still on the curb? Most of it's junk, but it's my junk. Take whatever's still there to the old office. I'll sort it out later. Then meet me here. One Perennial Tower, fifty-first floor."

Kenji let out an audible sigh, and I could hear disbelief and curiosity fighting for control. When he finally spoke, I knew he'd taken the bait. "You really got a new office in the Perennial?"

"Yep. A new office and enough cash for your back pay, plus a two-week advance on your new salary. Best of all, we have the resources to put up a skyboard of our own."

"You want to put Maxine Justice LLC over the harbor?"

"Told you I'd take you with me."

"That's what I'm afraid of," he said and hung up. But I had him and we both knew it.

I went back to the conference table and signed the attorney-client agreement with a colorful flourish: *Maxine Justice*. I didn't even bother to sit down.

Dr. Arounais and Ottaker Fowler were both standing, waiting for me to either sign or just walk away with the five thousand qoppas in my pocket.

"Ms. Justice," Dr. Arounais said, glancing down at my bare feet. "I am delighted to have you on the team."

Fowler pursed his lips and handed me a thick, embossed business card. Above the email and phone number were printed:

OTTAKER FOWLER
*Administrative Moderation Consul*
*Galactic Body General*

"Hang onto this," Fowler said. "You may find it useful later."

# 6

## LAWFARE

Even with my new "Iperian" budget, I couldn't afford a top-row skyboard. But thanks to Kenji's considerable nerdiness, we did submit the winning monthly bid for a prime-horizon spot just underneath the smiling pie holes of Hinkle, Remmers & Schmidt.

Skyboard space was arranged in two rows of eight rectangles on the harbor horizon. Backlit by the rising sun, the ads stayed up for two hours a day, flaring to full glory around 9:30 a.m. before slowly fading at around ten o'clock. The city didn't issue refunds for cloudy days, a fact clearly stated in the contract, so the ad space was a risk.

Besides, everybody hated the skyboards. I'd seen people on the street shake their fist and loudly proclaim they would never purchase from a harbor advertiser. Still, the spots were always full. Because even though people hated them, the ads still worked.

Hinkle, Remmers & Schmidt had been running the same ad for almost eight years, space number A5—fifth block on the top row.

The fifth space on the bottom row was currently running a still shot of yours truly, taken from my night-court appearance. The defiant look on my face warmed my heart, even now. The text beneath it said simply, Maxine Justice LLC.

I stared up at it as I walked the nine blocks to the House of the York City Bar Association for my preliminary probation hearing with Myra Dade, president of the bar and renowned defense attorney. I wondered vaguely how Dade would view the ad. Would it hurt my request that she deny Wentworth's probation recommendation? Would she see it as evidence that I really was a class clown?

My little standoff with Judge Wentworth had gone viral. Actually, it was Wentworth who had gone viral, not me. People just couldn't stop watching an auto-judge say, without any hint of self-awareness, "This court belongs to the law, not Justice."

But my raised eyebrows and barely discernible smile did make an appearance at the end of the short clip featured on the Night Court Channel's website. Which meant people were seeing my face in context with the auto-judge's disdain.

Now that same expression adorned the horizon above the harbor. I felt sure that, sooner or later, people would connect the dots and start coming to my firm with their legal problems. And if they didn't connect the dots, Kenjiro and I would connect them ourselves with different images. My smiling face on block B5 was only the opening gambit in what I hoped would be a long campaign.

The way I saw it, the general public was just another jury. And juries were no mystery. When you wanted to sell them a story, you started out being subtle and slowly tiptoed toward the obvious until you saw the whites of their eyes. Lawyer secret number seventeen: people are only convinced of something when they think they've figured it out for themselves.

The Bar Association still claimed the six-story, nineteenth-century "house" on Forty-Second Street as its main office. Clad in gaudy marble of competing colors and patterns, the entrance hall seemed a fitting example of everything the bar stood for: we lawyers loved to fight so much we invented the law as a pretext.

And the spoils of victory were sometimes astonishing, though not without risk. In fact, I'd already spent a good chunk of my first-month's research budget on hiring a medical expert, with no guarantee of the results.

Dr. Tobias Seoul, an old friend of my father's, was a classic academic with tousled hair, a bullet-proof memory, and a vast selection of cardigan sweaters. But his main asset was his network of industry connections. Dr. Seoul knew everyone worth knowing at every pharmaceutical, medical-equipment, and medical-insurance company in the Republic.

When I explained to him that I needed a reputable lab to conduct experimental trials on humans, and I needed it now, he laughed at me.

"Human trials?" he'd said. "That's a ten-year proposition, minimum, unless you're willing to go out of country. And the cost!"

"How much?" I'd asked.

When he gave me an estimate, I told him to start making the calls.

"You're serious?"

"I am. Please see what you can do."

For my part I had been trying to get someone at the United Nations to grant me an appointment ever since I signed the contract with Dr. Arounais. To keep that sweet crackpot money coming in I would have to show him I was making progress per the agreed-upon timetable, which, frankly, was unreasonably ambitious.

But it turns out the modern UN doesn't let ordinary citizens just wander in off the street and talk to its executives. You can't even get past the security scanners—even with a fake passport that identifies you as a member of parliament from the Sovereign Principality of Lichtenstein. (Sidebar: this doesn't get you in trouble because the guards don't care enough to validate your extremely expensive passport; they just check your name against the guest list and tell you to make an appointment.)

Eventually I'd weaseled a response from someone in budget analytics by implying that I had information about the Puolakka Project in San Marino. Technically I did have information about the Puolakka Project, a health clinic started by the UN's Global Health Initiative, because if my client's health serum worked—I had no evidence that it didn't—the Puolakka Project would finally be able to tell its donors that it had achieved its goal of a "healthy population."

Secretly I was hoping the analyst would pass me up the food chain to Undersecretary Lledo or one of his deputies. In my wildest imagination, I never thought I'd be granted an audience with Secretary-General Crusat, nor did I want one. For my plan to work, I needed someone with enough authority to sign a contract, but not so much that it would draw attention.

And I stood a better chance of that happening if Myra Dade removed the probationary designation from my name.

I knocked on Dade's office door, which was standing open, and entered when she called me in.

Counselor Singh was already there, seated on one side of a long conference table. I took my place next to him, chatting politely with Myra Dade, and a few minutes later, my adversaries arrived.

I suppose I should have expected the no-longer-smiling faces of Arthur Remmers and Brandon Schmidt Sr. But I figured by this time they would have moved on with their lives and found a new target for their sadistic hobbies.

Clearly I was wrong. Every muscle in my body tensed as they entered the room. My former bosses must have seen the hearing notice in the bar's weekly e-newsletter and decided to kick sand in my face. My new skyboard, sitting just beneath theirs, probably added fuel to that fire. They'd have seen it on their drive in.

Good. I hoped it made their skin crawl.

"Arthur! Brandon!" Myra said with a large smile. Dade was a large, busty woman with a large personality and a taste for large jewelry. Her fake pearls weren't even trying to look real. Instead, they caught the sunlight from the window and somehow turned it into a halo looping her neck.

"Myra," Arthur Remmers said in a low bass voice that always reminded me of a cartoon whale. "Good to see you."

"Myra, it's good to see you, darlin'," Brandon Schmidt Sr. said in his signature faux-Texan that was 99 percent affectation and 1 percent repressed memory.

"Have a seat and we'll get started." Myra motioned my former employers into their chairs and snagged a single sheet of paper from her desk before sitting at the head of the table. "Max," she said in a true southern drawl that, if the stories I'd heard at law school were true, had misled many a prosecutor. Dade's coquettish tendencies were less *Gone With the Wind* and more . . . lantern fish. "I have read Judge Wentworth's recommendation and watched the McEnroe trial. Do you have anything to say before I let these two gentlemen offer their input?"

This wasn't a trial. It was a simple request that the bar association decline Wentworth's outrageous contention that I had done something illegal during Hazel McEnroe's trial. Putting me on probation was unfair. I had given Hazel the opportunity to pursue a settlement. Hazel had heard the terms. Wentworth was just trying to punish me, and everyone knew it.

But since this wasn't a trial, anyone at the bar association could give their opinions as to my status on the roster. I just didn't know if the fact that these two men had fired me would affect their credibility.

Either way, I wouldn't help myself by showing my disgust at their presence, so I gave them my cheeriest smile and folded my hands on the table, every inch of me the demure underling eager to learn. "I would *love* to hear what they think."

Dade showed the barest flutter of a smile. "Very well. Arthur?"

"Frankly," Remmers boomed, his eyebrows knotting into something like a taut-line hitch. "I find Eufemia's—"

"Ms. Justice's," Dade corrected.

"Ms. Justice's behavior concerning. No sooner had we shown her the door than she opened her own practice, with barely three years' experience at our firm—"

"And under the name of 'Maxine Justice,' no less," Brandon Schmidt Sr. interrupted.

"Maxine Justice," Arthur repeated.

"Have either of you watched the McEnroe trial, which is the subject of this review?"

Remmers and Schmidt glanced at each other.

"Part of it," Remmers said.

Sure. The part everyone had seen circulating on the Internet. Fifteen seconds of Wentworth and three seconds of me. He would spend more time traveling to and from this hearing than it would have taken him to just watch the whole trial.

Dade seemed to read my mind. "And what did you think of Judge Wentworth's recommendation?"

Brandon Schmidt Sr. leaned forward, almost casually. "Seems to me the judge was being lenient. I'm hopeful this young woman has learned her lesson, but I'm not convinced."

"We are here," Remmers added, "to ask that Maxine's probationary status be extended to the full six months recommended by Judge Wentworth."

"I see," Dade said. "Is there anything else?"

"Well, frankly, I hate to bring it up," Remmers said.

Yeah. Sure he did.

Myra Dade stared over her glasses. "Bring what up?"

"Well, a sudden infusion of money into Ms. Justice's corporate coffers," Schmidt said. "I happen to know she was evicted three weeks ago, no disrespect intended, yet on the very same night, she managed to secure the fifty-first floor of the Perennial Building for her new office space."

"We are not making an accusation, of course," Remmers said. "But the circumstances are highly, *highly* unusual."

"Highly," Schmidt added, apparently sensing that two "highlys" wasn't enough.

"I see." Myra Dade turned to me. "And would you care to explain this sudden reversal of fortune?"

My former bosses had as much as told me they had no idea where my new cash cow was being milked. For a moment I was tempted to tell them, just to see the looks on their faces. But that would only ensure they opened another front on the *Hinkle, Remmers & Schmidt v. Maxine Justice LLC* war.

Oh, that new front was coming. I just didn't want it to start yet.

I crossed my arms and glared at each of them in turn. "No."

Arthur looked shocked. "No?"

Maybe it was sincere. Maybe he was so used to being deferred to that he really was scandalized by defiance. But his arrogant outrage only made me angrier. Heat rose on the back of my neck as I leaned forward to enunciate every word. "No, I don't care to explain my sudden reversal of fortune to the men who fired me just to cover up Junior's predatory habit. They don't deserve it, and they aren't legally entitled to mind anyone's business except their own."

Dade's eyebrows were raised, but she could see the steam building on Brandon Schmidt Sr.'s face, and she exerted herself immediately. "I'm sure we would do well—"

"How dare you!" Senior's face flushed and he started to rise.

"Easy," I said. "I've got nothing to lose."

Myra Dade held out both hands as if to separate us. "We would do well to keep in mind that this meeting is only concerned with Ms. Justice's status at the bar association. Please, Brandon, sit down."

I leaned back in my chair and waited.

"To be clear," Myra continued, "I am considering Judge Wentworth's recommendation stemming from the McEnroe trial, not any past history Ms. Justice has with you two gentlemen and your reputable firm."

"Of course," Remmers said.

"Understood." Brandon Schmidt sat slowly, as if to make a point.

"If I may," Counselor Singh said.

Though seated next to him, I'd almost forgotten he was there. Pastoroids had an unnerving way of disappearing into the background. Perhaps because their breathing was almost soundless. Or because they so rarely inserted their input without invitation. Singh hadn't offered so much as a "father" joke since I arrived. (Lately he'd switched from the classic "My father is so *X*" opening to the more ecclesiastical "Father Sharp is so *Y*" variation.)

Dade turned toward him, and I got the feeling she'd been waiting for him to speak. "What is it, Counselor?"

"Maxine and I have been meeting weekly as ordered by Judge Wentworth. Those conversations are confidential, but I have no problem stating for the bar association that I have great respect for my client. I believe in her abilities as a defense attorney and have seen no significant ethical issues."

"Significant?" Remmers said, overlooking the fact that I wasn't actually a defense attorney. "What does that mean?"

"It means my evaluation is based on the fact that she's a lawyer."

Dade smiled at the pastoroid. "Well, it seems the bar has been lowered."

Singh didn't seem to notice the pun. "I was about to say that I have been ordered by the court to continue counseling Ms. Justice regardless of your decision here today."

"So . . . you'll keep meeting with her," Dade repeated.

"I have no choice, and neither does she. That should alleviate some of the concerns expressed here."

"You're saying you'll keep an eye on her," Remmers boomed. "Is that it?"

"Yes."

Maybe I should have been grateful, but I couldn't help feeling annoyed. I wasn't a teenager taking my first trip away from Mom and

Dad. And Arthur Remmers was talking about me as if I were some international terrorist about to post bond. I gripped the chair's cloth armrests and squeezed.

"My objection still stands," Brandon Schmidt Sr. said, "notwithstanding the testimony of this TheraPod."

"I concur," Remmers growled.

"Very well, gentlemen." Dade pushed back her chair and stood. "The bar appreciates your concern in this matter and will take your suggestions into consideration."

Remmers and Schmidt both rose, though neither of them looked happy.

Remmers asked, "We aren't going to hear your decision?"

"You'll read about it in the next newsletter. I still have a few details to iron out." She ushered them through the reception area and out into the hall, her voice a smooth trill. "Yes, yes, so good to see both of you, and thanks again."

The door closed, and she lumbered back into the room muttering, ". . . thought they would never get the hint. All right. What about you, Counselor Singh—are you sure about all of this?"

*All of this.* What did that mean?

I got the feeling they'd worked out some private arrangement behind my back, and whatever it was, I wouldn't like it.

"I'm sure of nothing."

"Thought you'd say that." She sat again and leaned back in her chair, suddenly relaxed, yet somehow evaluating me with a look that penetrated all the way to the gold-leaf, floral wallpaper behind my chair. "So tell me about this new office of yours."

It wasn't really any of her business, but some part of me wanted to talk to another lawyer about my weird clients. "Confidentially?"

"It won't leave this room. As your therapist, Counselor Singh is prohibited by his software. And I'm—well, I'm the president of the bar association and you're in the Association House. This is as close to sacred ground as you can get."

I believed her. So I told her the story. The McEnroe trial, the eviction, the two weirdos and their proposal to cure all of human sickness. I didn't explain my strategy for convincing someone at the UN, nor did I tell her I planned to build a client list for when my golden goose stopped laying eggs. Trust only went so far.

"Does Arthur know he sent you this mystery client?"

I grinned. "Not yet."

"Good." She let out a long sigh. "Well, it's odd, but you know that already. And I don't see that it has any bearing on Wentworth's request." She shuffled the sheet of paper in front of her. "Maxine, you're not going to like this, but I'm going to sit on this probation thing for a few months."

I couldn't believe it. "But you know this complaint is bogus. If you watched the trial, you had to have seen that I did present his offer to Hazel! She even admitted it in court."

Myra held up one hand placatingly. "I know. I know."

"Then why?"

"Believe it or not, it's because this recommendation is so unwarranted. Bright Star wanted that trial to go away. The shenanigans they pulled won't make headlines, but I suspect an appeals court might find the whole thing interesting. Did you notice the judge came down on you as soon as you mentioned filing an appeal?"

Yes, I'd noticed. I nodded vigorously.

"Maxine, I am concerned that if I decline the judge's request for probationary measures, Bright Star will find some other way to come after you."

"That's fine," I said. "I'm not scared."

"That," Dade said, "is why I'm going to put a three-month note in your file. A little fear would do you good. But if all this has blown over in ninety days, I'll remove the probationary status and purge it from our system. Meanwhile—if I told you to keep your head down, would you listen?"

"Sure," I lied.

"Hmph. You're not going to change a bit. I can see it in your eyes."

No point denying it. My former bosses had started this thing and seemed determined to destroy my career. So, no, I wasn't going to surrender. I didn't care what the fight cost me.

"All right," she said. "Get out of here. Go make the world a better place. You can start by taking this TheraPod with you before he tries to tell me another joke."

"Thank you, ma'am," I said, wondering why I had thanked her and also why I had called her *ma'am*.

I guess I'd gotten the impression that Myra Dade sympathized with me. At a company party, she'd tried to warn me about Brandon, but I might as well have had cotton in my ears—or between them.

The next morning, I got up early and headed for the UN building before sunrise. The pre-dawn light added to an eerie feeling of being followed, and once I even caught a glimpse of a man in a gray hoodie, who seemed to duck into an alley just as I turned. Then again, it could have been my imagination. Myra Dade telling me that Bright Star Holdings might have it in for me had left me more paranoid than usual.

Across the street from the Perennial, a security guard checked my name and ID against his guest list and waved me into the scanner. By 7:30 a.m. I stood in the reception area of the third floor Budget Analytics office of the United Nations.

The secretary asked my name and told me to be seated as Mr. Huotari had not yet arrived. My appointment was for 8:00 a.m., but I was hoping to catch the man on his way in. People have a hard time pretending you aren't there when they know you've seen them.

Right at eight o'clock my phone chirped.

"Hello?"

"Maxine, this is Tobias Seoul. I have some bad news and some mediocre news. Which do you want first?"

"Bad."

"No lab in the country will touch your serum, regardless of price."

"And the mediocre news?"

"I'm not done with the bad news yet. Not only will no lab here in the Republic conduct your trials, no self-respecting lab outside the country will do it either."

Surprisingly, this news disappointed me. Which was odd, because if I didn't believe in the serum, why should anybody else?

Then again, Dr. Arounais was offering a boatload of cash, and I happened to know the world was filled with unhappy, unscrupulous rich people whose only hope for meaning lay in becoming even richer.

Where were these people when you needed them?

I glanced around the empty waiting area, one hand pressed to the back of my neck. "Okay—"

"That's the bad news," Dr. Seoul continued. "The mediocre news is that there is one lab, which isn't big on self-respect, outside the country that does find itself in need of quick cash. Place in Guatemala called *Laboratorio de Amanecer.* 'Sunrise Lab' in English. They're willing to conduct a ten-day series of human trials using your client's serum and a control group. This would be a preliminary trial only, but it could be enough to open the door to a better lab."

Hope swayed in my chest like a deflating balloon. I felt lighter, but I knew it wouldn't last. A Guatemalan lab? Would the UN pay any attention? "When can they start?"

"For the right price, yesterday."

"Okay." I knew I sounded disappointed. I'd been hoping Dr. Seoul would find a place that could give me real answers to what this serum actually was. "Dr. Seoul, how sketchy are they? Scale of one to ten."

"Depends. Overall, probably a five. Republic Pharmaceuticals has used them in the past, and their data has been used to push meds around the FDA."

"So why is that mediocre?"

"Hard to explain," he said. "Ever eaten at Franky's Pizza on Fifty-Sixth Street?"

"No."

"Well, they've got this big open-fire stove and a counter with fresh ingredients. But they handle delivery orders in the back, where they use a different process. As long as you're dining in, your pizza will be great. But if you call it in—"

"So I'm going to have to monitor this thing in person?"

"Not the whole trial, no. But you should definitely let them know you'll be flying down for the wrap-up. Tell them you want to see the counter and the oven."

I made up my mind on the spot. "All right. Let's do it. Can you ask them to send the paperwork to my office?

"Already done. And, Maxine?"

"Yes?"

"Remember, this is people's lives, okay? When you're down there? I mean, I agreed to help, partly out of respect for your dad and, admittedly, mostly for the money, but also because I've heard rumors about this Consolidated Galactic BioProducers group."

"Really?" This news surprised me. Why should anyone have heard of a shell corporation owned by a crazy guy with a fake serum? "What can you tell me?"

"Nothing much. Just that they've been working on something big. That is, potentially big. You can bet if I've heard of it, someone else will have heard of it too. But whatever this serum is, it needs to be vetted. Sunrise Labs can do that. Whatever it turns out to be, placebo or scam or some new wonder drug, it's going to mean something for real people." Dr. Seoul paused as if weighing his words. "I just don't want you to forget that."

"Thanks," I said and meant it.

"I'll send you my bill."

He hung up, and I was left sitting in the new-carpet smell of the Budget Analytics reception area, wondering when Mr. Huotari would show up.

Ninety minutes later he still hadn't arrived, and his secretary kept suggesting that it might be a good idea to come back a different time. I said I could wait a bit longer, then made a show of asking directions to the ladies' room.

Down the hall I took the stairs to the seventh floor, home to the UN's Global Health Initiative, and plastered a forbidding look on my face, my deeply-troubled-but-reluctant-to-share expression.

"Can I help you?" a young man asked. He was dressed in a dark-blue shirt and matching tie, and he was drenched in so much cologne I wondered why it hadn't set off the smoke detectors.

I bit my lower lip. "Mr. Gibbons, please."

"Name?"

"Justice. Maxine Justice. No, I don't have an appointment. You see, I've just come from the Budget Analytics office. I had a meeting with Mr. Houtari at eight this morning"—all of which was true, though obviously misleading—"concerning the Puolakka Project in San Marino."

Mr. Wild Nights scrolled through his terminal with one finger, and I paused until the motion of his eyes confirmed he'd landed on my name in the building's register. "Yes?"

"Well, this information is a bit sensitive. Apparently"—implying that this advice had come from Mr. Houtari himself—"it would be best if I speak with Mr. Gibbons personally."

"I'm sorry, he's out of the country. Would you like to schedule something for next week?"

I pursed my lips, exhaling disappointment through both nostrils, even though this was precisely what I had expected. I knew Gibbons was somewhere in East Africa. I'd done a lot of research on the man after realizing he'd be the perfect target. "I suppose that would be best."

Appointment booked, I headed for the elevator, barely restraining an urge to kick my heels.

The feeling didn't last.

As I stepped into the mild fall air, I caught a second glimpse of the gray hoodie. It disappeared immediately, and a sudden feeling of vertigo knocked me backward into the glass door.

Old reliable had finally changed. The A5 skyboard that had carried the smiling faces of Hinkle, Remmers & Schmidt for eight years now bore a simple message, in massive gold letters on an empty, black background, directly above my face:

I EVEN LOOK GUILTY!

# TRIALS

I almost couldn't believe they fell for it.

My ex-bosses were paying for ad space that drew attention to the law firm of Maxine Justice LLC.

Sure, people pointed and laughed. So what?

That just meant they were talking about my name.

Since Brandon Schmidt Sr. was better at pettiness than marketing, I figured he'd keep the attack ad in place as long as possible. But for my purposes, the gag needed more than just repetition. It begged for an immediate turning of the tables.

I wish I could have seen the look on Big Schmidt's face the next morning when the new skyboards flickered to life above the horizon. Underneath "I EVEN LOOK GUILTY!"—which occupied a space everyone associated with Hinkle, Remmers & Schmidt—we also ran gold text on a black background:

*(It's probably the creepy smile.)*

Still, you should never assume that a roomful of lawyers is a room full of idiots. Chances are, at least one of them will be highly intelligent.

We swapped out our ad again the next day, assuming HRS would do the same.

Sure enough, they'd replaced their text ad with the familiar group photo. Had we kept our ad in place, they would have filed a suit alleging defamation. But we didn't leave our ad up. Instead, we replaced it with my defiant stare from the McEnroe trial and this:

## I Don't Smile Until You Do

After that we settled into an unspoken truce, with the same ads displaying on clear mornings.

I now had a steady flow of potential clients ringing the office phone. Every time it rang I pretended not to notice. I'd spent most of one weekend stapling pictures of Oliver Wendell all over my neighborhood.

Eventually I got a different sort of call: the results of the preliminary trials were ready.

I booked a flight for Antigua and spent the next day in airports. At one point during my layover, as I was getting in line at a food kiosk, I bumped into a muscular, tattooed guy in a gray hoodie.

My heart stuck in my throat. His face was heavily scarred, his chin stubbled with a two-day beard, and his eyes shifted from cold gray to dead laughter, as if he'd been caught in a snowbank five thousand years ago and brought back to life by some soulless scientist.

He stared at me for a moment before motioning for me to go in front. "*Izvinyayus*," he said in a heavy Russian accent. "Please."

I gave him a fake smile and stood in line for my yogurt and coffee—the whole time, feeling like he was breathing down my neck—not daring to turn around. When I finally got my food and headed for the gate, he was nowhere to be seen.

Which probably illustrates how paranoid I'd grown about Hinkle, Remmers & Schmidt. With nothing happening on the petty-grudge front for over two weeks, I couldn't help feeling like they were cooking up something particularly nasty to get me out of the way. In the back of my mind, the gray hoodie had turned into a ghoul—or worse, a Russian hit man. Which was silly. Even my former bosses wouldn't stoop to actual violence.

I landed at the Antigua airport just as the sun was setting, then debarked into a warm soup of tropical air that immediately frizzed my hair into a rat's nest.

Since my hotel room had no air-conditioning, I spent a sleepless night spread-eagled under a creaking ceiling fan, cursing my decision to book a room across the street from the lab. I should have sprung for one of the better hotels in the tourist district and called for a taxi.

In the morning I showered, ate a quick breakfast at the continental buffet, and headed to the lab as morning yawned, skyboard-free, above the mountains.

Inside the lobby of the *Laboratorio de Amanecer,* a receptionist greeted me in perfect English. "You must be Ms. Justice. Would you mind signing in?"

She watched me ink her old-school lined paper with a flourish I hadn't yet grown tired of practicing. Every time I scrawled the name *Maxine Justice,* some little-girl part of my brain wanted to strike a superhero pose.

The woman buzzed a door open and led me to a cramped, cluttered office with an impressive view of Antigua's guardian mountain. "Dr. Vazquez will be with you soon."

As promised, Vazquez, a second mountain, filled the doorway a moment later. "Counselor!" He beamed as if greeting an old friend. "You have come to check up on us, yes? Well, I can't blame you. This project you have placed before my eyes cannot be unseen. One of our rats is calling it a miracle."

He wedged himself into a tiny ergonomic chair behind the desk and finger-pecked at his keyboard. "Some . . . day . . . I should learn . . . to type. There!" He spun the monitor around, revealing a screen divided into twenty-four windows, twelve marked *Control,* and the other twelve *Active.* Each window displayed what appeared to be a time-lapse video of humans with various ailments.

On the left side, the control group showed a series of before-and-after video snippets merging past-to-present close-ups of arms, fingers, ankles, and eyes, and one showed the left side of an elderly man's ribcage. On the right side, the merging videos showed apparently radical changes, the most extreme of which featured a pair of eyes that lost their snowy cataracts.

I watched the time-lapse loop several times, concentrating on the right side's remarkable transformations, before glancing at Vazquez.

Dr. Vazquez sat with hands folded behind his head. The expiration date on his smile had obviously passed.

"And what exactly am I supposed to do with this?" I asked.

"You don't believe it?"

"Do you?"

The smile reappeared under raised eyebrows. "I have seen it, and still I am not so sure. But perhaps a review of our facility and processes would help?"

"It couldn't hurt."

We spent the next two hours on something Dr. Vazquez called "the North American skeptic's tour" and afterward returned to his office. Someone had placed two cups of steaming coffee on the desk. I'd gotten the impression Vazquez ran a small but strictly controlled and scientifically regimented operation. His *bona fides* included a PhD from Oxford.

I didn't have a background in science, so my opinion was still colored by Dr. Seoul's, but the lab seemed to be first rate. Even so, I could tell Vazquez was holding something back.

I sat and took a sip of the coffee, which was excellent. "So you're saying this serum actually works."

"Not exactly. This was a preliminary trial. I would need more time, more of the serum, more volunteers."

"More money?"

He laughed. "What can I say? Health is expensive. Like law."

"So what is my client getting for the money they've already paid you?"

"Ah, yes!" He opened the top drawer of his desk and withdrew a thumb drive. "I will not have you leaving the *Laboratorio de Amanecer* feeling you were cheated." He slid the drive across the desk. "There. You have all the data. Time-stamped video, photographs, affidavits, and more. I've written a lengthy summary report. Signed it myself. I stake my reputation on my work, Ms. Justice, but we both know you will need more than a ten-day trial from a Guatemalan lab to open the doors at your Food and Drug Administration." He said *Guatemalan* with more than a hint of irony, as if he could already feel the condescension I'd be facing without more data.

"I appreciate your commitment to excellence," I said. "And your rapid response to our needs. I'll be frank. We are hoping to hire a lab with more, shall we say, networking opportunities inside the Republic."

"You think you need an American lab."

"I do."

"Well, you are probably right." He leaned back in his chair and stared out the window. "But that will be expensive. And time consuming. And frankly, I think you may be running out of time."

He wasn't just a scientist. He was a salesman. But I wasn't about to admit that I saw through his sales pitch. "My client isn't in a hurry."

"I do not speak of your client. I speak of your safety. A drug under trial is a question mark. A drug on its way to your FDA is more like a target."

He still stared out the window, and I wasn't sure how to interpret his words or his posture.

"Is that a threat?"

Vazquez looked at me sharply. "Of course not. Why would I pluck a golden goose? You are my guest—my boss. The customer is always right at *Laboratorio de Amanecer*! No, Ms. Justice, I am simply telling you that a thing like this will get out. It is probably already out. Mark my words, there are people who are interested in getting it for themselves. And others who will want to see such a thing stopped before it interferes with their financial interests."

I strained to catch some physical indication that he was lying, but the man seemed sincere. "Dr. Vazquez," I said, deciding to be blunt. "Are you telling me you have shared the results of this trial with someone other than myself?"

He spun his chair to face me. "Never. But such a thing was not necessary. Before your friend and mine, Dr. Seoul, called and asked for my assistance, already I had heard rumors of a wonder drug being developed by a company called Consolidated Galactic BioProducers."

My face must have registered shock. I hadn't used that name—hadn't even put it in our contract. But what did this mean? Was it possible Vazquez wanted to sell the drug himself? If so, how far was he willing to go? In theory we had an ironclad contract, but would that be enough to dissuade him from selling the molecular formula to the highest bidder?

The thing was—I saw this clearly now—I hadn't adequately prepared for the possibility that this serum actually worked. I mean, I still didn't believe it worked, but I had failed to account for the possibility that other people might think it did. I'd expected everyone to see it for the placebo that it probably was.

But Vazquez apparently had a different opinion. That, or he intended to prop up the drug's burgeoning reputation so he could sell the formula to someone else.

A feeling washed over me—an empty feeling in the pit of my stomach that dried my mouth and made my skin itch. It was like my feet were encased in cement and I was about to be tossed into the open sea.

Vazquez continued. "You know this corporation, I see. But—Ah! You didn't believe. Even now you don't believe."

"A serum that heals everything?" I asked. "How could anyone believe that?"

"I didn't say everything. I tested five conditions. All five produced excellent results. You saw the videos. And if those five results are consistent—if they are real indicators—there will be no limits to what your client's product is worth."

This had gone wrong very quickly. I suddenly didn't trust Vazquez, but I could think of no way to move forward without finding another lab and paying for a new set of preliminary trials. Unless the man was simply trying to pry loose a larger payment from my client. "What do you want, Doctor?"

He seemed surprised. "I want you to hire me to do a full set of trials. Prove this thing one way or another."

"That's all?"

"You know, even for a lawyer you are very suspicious. No, that is not all. I also want my own professional hockey team and world peace. But I will settle for signing my name to the greatest medical breakthrough in human history."

"You're not going to break our contract and try to sell this behind my client's back?"

He took a sip of his coffee and sucked his teeth. "I see the problem. You are hearing the puma's call, which is good. Many would not. But I fear you are facing the wrong direction."

"I don't follow."

"Young lady, your enemies are not those who want this drug in order to sell it themselves. Your enemies are those who want no one to have it. You need not fear me. I love life too much to waste it on—what do you call it?—intrigue. That is why I suggest you allow me to conduct a two-month battery of tests. Not only will it help you convince the FDA, it will send a message to people who are, even now, watching us with great interest. It will plant doubt. And it will buy you time."

"Time? For what?"

"For getting home of course."

"My flight's already booked. I'm headed home in just over six hours."

"This is good," he said. "You can stay here. I will call you a cab when it's time to leave."

"Thanks, but I'm planning to spend the afternoon at the indoor market, stroll around the, what do you call it?—the *Nim Po't*?"

Vazquez looked at the ceiling, lips pursed, as if debating whether to say more.

"What?"

He shrugged. "I am perhaps overcautious. But I would breathe easier if you remained here until it is time for your flight."

My mouth suddenly felt very dry. I took a deep drink of the coffee, not tasting it as images of the man in the gray hoodie flashed through my mind. "Are you saying I'm in danger? Here in Guatemala?"

"I'm saying—" He sighed and started over. "Ms. Justice, I am not trying to frighten you."

"I don't scare easily," I said—a little too quickly. In truth, my heart was beating fast enough he could probably hear it.

"You see? This is a difficulty. For yourself you are not concerned. And besides, you have no attachments. This is another reason you were chosen? Maybe?"

Chosen? Did he mean by Dr. Arounais? "I don't understand."

"I have been asked to show you something. A video. At first I was reluctant. Then I decided, no, I would not show you. You are an educated woman. You are a lawyer and an American. You will be suspicious that I am trying to sell you something. This I have already seen."

"You *are* trying to sell me something."

"See? But Mr. Santos—" He leaned over his desk and pecked at the keyboard. "Mr. Santos is not selling anything. He just . . . wanted . . . to send you . . . a message." He flipped his monitor around so I could see a video playing in one corner.

A short, black-haired man in a white shirt, skin the color of a latte, blinked into the camera as Vazquez, off-screen, said something in Spanish. Santos pointed at his left arm, turning his hand over and wriggling the fingers as he spoke. I understood nothing of what he said except, *Gracias*! *Gracias*!

When the video ended Vazquez peered around the corner of the monitor and said, "He works on a coffee plantation. A low-paying job that nonetheless attests to his personal fortitude. Mr. Santos was born with phocomelia syndrome. The bones in his left arm were so malformed that he spent the first thirty-four years of his life with a dangling lump of flesh attached to his shoulder. But now—"

I stared at the last frame of the video, frozen on a close-up of Mr. Santos's completely normal left arm. A couple of hours ago, I would have called the video a fake. But I had taken the tour, and Vazquez had already shown me footage from before the serum had been administered. I'd seen what Santos's arm looked like when he signed up. More importantly, I'd seen the earnestness in Dr. Vazquez's expression. He believed in the serum's potential enough to fear for my safety.

"What is he saying?" I asked.

"He offers his thanks," Vazquez answered. "And he begs you to please make sure this miracle is given to others."

*Miracle.*

The word stuck in the back of my mind like a fish bone caught in the throat.

*Was this really happening? The serum actually worked?*

I looked out the window to the dominating green peak of Acatenango, currently wreathed in gauzy clouds. Somewhere in the haze of my imagination, a tattooed Russian cliché in a gray hoodie stepped forward and said, a little too loudly, "*Izvinyayus.*"

But the whole idea was just too much. A serum that cured multiple genetic disorders? That grew new bones into a man's arm? In a matter of weeks?

It was too good to be true. I might as well buy a map to the Fountain of Youth. But if it weren't true, I was still contractually obligated to offer the serum to the UN.

"I never mentioned the name Consolidated Galactic BioProducers," I said. "It isn't in our contract."

Vazquez shrugged. "I didn't hear that name from you. Which is all the more reason to take these tests seriously, yes? And does that not raise a deeper question? Forgive me for asking this, but why you, Ms. Justice? You have no scientific background. You are young and inexperienced. You have your own reasons for wanting, even needing, such a drug to be verified as real. Surely that will impact your credibility, will it not? Is it possible that someone is trying to use you for their own purposes?"

I stared at Vazquez for a long moment, not even trying to hide my discomfort. His suggestion had rattled me. I recalled Brandon talking to Dr. Arounais and Ottaker Fowler just before the McEnroe trial. Was it possible Hinkle, Remmers & Schmidt were pulling strings to manipulate me and my crackpot clients?

What if Vazquez was telling the truth, and the serum did have near-miraculous medical benefits?

Who would stand the most to lose?

What would they do to prevent those losses from happening?

My chest felt tight, as if the doctor had draped a lead apron over my shoulders. I should have thought of all of this before coming to Antigua. Probably would have if I hadn't assumed the serum couldn't be real.

I wished Kenjiro were here so we could talk through all of this. Even when he didn't seem to be paying attention, he was a great sounding board.

"Do you have a ladies' room?" I asked.

"Certainly." Vazquez jabbed the air with one thumb. "Down the hall to your right."

Inside the single-occupant restroom, I locked the door, flipped on the vent fan, tugged my new digital assistant from my messenger bag, and phoned our main office. Kenji picked up on the third ring.

"Justice Law Firm, how may I help you?"

"Kenji, it's me."

"How's it going?"

"Not sure. Would you believe Dr. Vazquez thinks I might be in danger down here? That someone out there is taking this whole serum thing seriously?"

There was a long pause. "Yeah, Max. I would."

"Really?"

"I'm actually kind of surprised you didn't anticipate this sooner. I've been worried about your safety for a couple of weeks."

I'd been hoping he would talk me down, tell me this was all some sort of crazy sales pitch. Instead he'd only reinforced my sense of isolation. "And how do we know the real danger isn't with Vazquez?"

Another long pause. "I guess we don't."

"Thanks."

"Keeping it real."

I took a deep breath and said, "Kenji, I think there may be something to this serum. Vazquez says it could be groundbreaking."

In the background I heard the *psht* of a soda can being opened. "Cool. So does the lab look good?"

"Yeah, but what do I know? Could be sleight of hand. But the video evidence is compelling."

"Won't that make a deal with the UN easier?"

"Yeah, maybe."

"So . . . maybe you should just . . . lie low till your flight? I'll come to the airport, pick you up inside the terminal."

I stepped toward the mirror and leaned on the counter for support, surprised at how much relief Kenji's promise brought. "Thanks."

"No problem."

I hung up and started to slip the phone back into my leather bag. Stopped. Stared at the screen.

Had I just told Kenji via an unsecured line that Consolidated's new wonder drug seemed promising?

Was that really a problem? Or was I just paranoid because of the creepy-looking guy in the gray hoodie and Dr. Vazquez's ominous warning?

Kenji had scanned the device for bots and tracking software before pronouncing it safe. But that had been two weeks ago.

If Vazquez was right, the sorts of people interested in shutting down a major medical advance would easily have the resources to hack my phone or follow it on GPS. Maybe that was unlikely, but could I take the risk of assuming it couldn't happen?

If Vazquez was right, I'd be a fool to go to the textile plaza and wander the booths alone. I'd be too exposed, too vulnerable.

On the other hand, what if Dr. Vazquez were the one gaming the rumor mill, stirring up a fake conflict with shadowy villains, just to make his own lab look important? I didn't like the prospect of hiding in his office and waiting for a taxi to the airport. Hiding was just another form of surrender, of giving up. I hated the idea of someone pushing me around through fear.

Deciding to play it safe, I slipped the phone behind a box of tissues, so it was wedged between the floral cardboard and the backsplash. If it was being tracked, my shadowy enemies would think I had camped out in the *Laboratorio de Amanecer*'s bathroom.

Either way, when I made it home, I would call Vazquez and ask him to mail it to me. Claim I'd set it down by mistake. The phone had nothing compromising on it.

Meanwhile, I still had Digie as an annoying backup. And who would think about tracking my mom's old cell phone?

I splashed cold water on my face and went back to the doctor's little office. "I've decided I can't miss seeing the textiles while I'm here," I said, plucking the little thumb drive from his desk and slipping it into my pocket. Obviously I had no intention of wandering down to the indoor market. I didn't think Dr. Vazquez wanted to harm me—otherwise, why try to warn me of a danger Kenjiro already expected? But I didn't trust the good doctor either. "So I'm going to take your advice and order an extension of the trials. You said two months, yes?"

His face lit up. "Excellent. Shall we complete the paperwork while you are here?"

I shook my head. "Unless you're working for free, I'll need to get authorization from my client first. Just a technicality. Send the paperwork to my office, and we'll get it signed tomorrow." I didn't add that I felt safer while Dr. Vazquez needed something from me.

"Are you sure I can't talk you out of the Nim Po't?"

"Positive," I said, though in fact I'd be going the other direction. "I do appreciate your concern, Doctor. I'll be in touch."

The door at the end of the hallway buzzed when I approached it, and the receptionist held up a pen for me to sign out.

An hour later I was taking in the mustard-yellow stucco of the Santa Catalina church with a couple dozen tourists. The church's walls glowed in the afternoon sunlight. Children in bright clothing hustled flowers and candy under the arch.

In the heat of a cloudless sky, I found it nearly impossible to believe anyone here wanted to harm me, or even knew my name.

*But they will know my name*, I thought, remembering Santos's wonder-filled face and perfectly normal arm. *If Vazquez is right, everyone will know the name Maxine Justice.*

I stopped myself with an inward laugh. *Except that I don't really believe this serum is real.*

*Do I?*

That's when someone grabbed me around the neck and dragged me—kicking—into an alcove. I felt a prick in my arm, and everything went fuzzy for a minute before slowly fading to nothing.

# 8

## SHADOW WORLD

The dream clung to my mind like pine sap. Carnival lights, spinning madly in the distance, streaked the night air outside the window. Dad, resting easy on his twin mattress, wouldn't even look at them. He didn't want to go.

"Please," I said in a desperate, childish whine, despising myself for having to fight back tears.

A voice like gravel sawed at the edges of the dream. "On the pew. No, leave the bag. Did you get it?"

I opened my eyes. Tried to open my eyes.

The dream pulled me back. Back to the window, which was open to the moist night air. Only a screen stood between me and the swirling carnival lights in the distance.

Dad was leaving. He could have stayed, could have taken me to the carnival, but I could see he didn't want to fight. He was shaking his head and holding up a piece of paper as if to say, *Can't you read? I've signed away my rights to a carnival.*

And it was SO INFURIATING!

I said, *Fine, I'll go without you!* and kicked at the window screen. It resisted, the black mesh surprisingly strong against my heel. When I kicked harder, the whole panel swung outward. I didn't even look—just jumped out into the emptiness beyond. Gravity hauled me down an endless black well, the darkness somehow rushing past in a vertical wind. I felt as if I would never hit the ground. Nor would I be caught. I would simply fall, arms waving, till the end of time.

Somewhere far away a door creaked—the nurse maybe? I realized my hands were stuck together at the wrists, and something not windy pressed against my face.

I tried to brush it away, the thing textured like burlap, but it came back. My legs were numb, pinned.

The carnival faded, and the lights from the roller coaster split into stabbing beams of white and red. Somewhere nearby an air conditioner coughed to life.

I snatched at the thing against my face until a thin line of pain circled my wrists and broke through the fog of unreality: My hands were tied. They'd put a bag over my head.

For just a moment, I felt sure that I couldn't breathe, as if my lungs had stopped working and needed to be filled from the outside.

I felt for the cloth edge and tugged it off, and a rush of air came with it. I took deep breaths and felt my heart rate slow a little.

Light washed dully through a grimy stained-glass window in the corner of a grimy room. Some kind of storage area, crammed with boxes and half a dozen old pews. I was stretched out across one of them. My open messenger bag sagged against the end of the pew by my feet. Outside, far beyond the window, children called to each other in Spanish.

My head pounded. I tried to sit up, but the carnival lights started going off again, and I collapsed back onto the hard surface.

I closed my eyes, just for a minute, to get my bearings. Dad was there again, on the sofa, phone in hand, talking to Mom, telling her to come and get me, and I said, *No, hang up, I don't want to see her.*

I jerked awake, surprised to hear Mom's voice in the little room. "What was that?" Mom asked, muffled and peevish. "Do you wanna talk to me or don't you? It's been weeks since you called home."

Home. Which meant—

Where was I again?

"Mom?" My voice squeaked.

From the bottom of a barrel, her voice called out, "Ah! The prodigal Eufie finally speaks. What is it this time?"

"I need—can you get Kenji?"

"Eufemia, I can barely hear you. How many times must I tell you to speak up?"

I clawed my way to full consciousness, blinking in the dim light from the rainbow glass. "Maxine," I said. "It's Maxine now, Mom."

"Eufie? Eufie, I can't hear you. You wanna talk, hang up and call me when you got better reception. *All These Children* is starting."

"Mom?" I shouted, but there was no response.

"You want me to call her back?" Digie asked.

*Digie!* The device must have heard me mention Mom and auto-dialed her. No wonder we were both confused.

I blinked and took a couple of deep breaths. The stars receded a little, though my head still pounded. "Digie, where am I?"

"You don't know where you are? How should I know? You haven't taken me out of your bag in over a week."

"Digie, can you ratchet down the personality a couple of notches and give me a location from GPS? Please?"

"You ask so nice. Okay, sure. We're in Antigua, Guatemala, some place called *Iglesia de San Juan el Viejo.* Not exactly a hot spot of tourism. Is it nice? I can't tell from inside this stuffy, old cow carcass."

"Stunning," I said, propping myself up on one elbow. My stomach felt like that experiment from high school with seashells and acid. And I was certain someone had jabbed an icepick halfway into my skull. "How long have we been here?"

"Four hours, seven minutes."

"I missed my flight?"

"Pretty much. Wheels up in ten minutes. You'll never make it. I could have told you those new friends of yours were trouble."

I tried rubbing both temples with my forefingers. Slow circles. It helped a little. "Friends? What friends?"

"The ones that brought you here. You know, you really shouldn't drink so much, Maxine. I'm sure Kenji wouldn't—"

"I wasn't drinking. Someone drugged me, Digie."

She made that teeth-sucking sound Mom uses when she's impressed. "Wellll . . . I feel better about your choices. Neither of these characters seemed really friendly. But it's not like you actually have friends. And who am I to judge? We can't all be smartphones."

I swung my legs off the pew and used the momentum to cantilever my body upright. Fireworks went off again behind my eyeballs, and my stomach turned in a circle as if looking for a ballast to jettison. "Ughhhhh."

"You all right, Max?"

I closed my eyes again and groped for my bag with both hands, praying I wouldn't spew whatever was left of breakfast all over the church's storage room. Eventually my head stopped spinning, my gut finished its gymnastics routine, and I was able to conduct a thorough search of my messenger bag. "It's gone. They've taken it."

"Taken what?" Digie asked.

I found my nail clippers and used them to slice the zip-ties that bound my hands and feet. The effort left me woozy. "The thumb drive Dr. Vazquez gave me. All the evidence."

"Can't you just ask him to send it over the Net when you get home?"

"Yeah," I admitted. "I guess I can do that. Which means preventing me from having it isn't the issue. Otherwise—" It occurred to me as I spoke that whoever had drugged me and left me in a storage room could have just killed me. "Well, I wouldn't be here."

"Ooooh," Digie said with breathless enthusiasm. "Someone wants it for themselves, don't they?"

"Winner, winner, chicken dinner."

"I love that game! Want me to open the app?"

"No, I want you to shut up for a minute and let me think."

"'Kay, Miss Smarty-Pants." True to her word, Digie stopped talking.

But in the background, she started playing, ever so faintly from her tinny speaker, the annoying theme song from another one of Mom's favorite game shows, *Luck of the Draw.*

I shoved the distraction aside with a Herculean mental effort and focused on the other thing—the thing that was circling the edges of my consciousness like an insect poised to go down the drain. Something about the thumb drive and why it had been stolen. That stealing it wouldn't stop me from getting all that information again. Because all I had to do was ask Vazquez.

So why steal it? Maybe to use it. But use it how? If Dr. Arounais wanted to spread it across the whole world . . . and if the doctor controlled how it was used, then—

What was it Vazquez had told me? *Your enemies are those who want no one to have it.*

And suddenly there it was. The something I'd been searching for.

I had enemies. Enemies who didn't want the serum getting out. Corporations so invested in illness and compromised health they couldn't tolerate the prospect of worldwide rejuvenation.

What was the best way of preventing the widespread use of the serum?

Discredit it. Destroy its creator, Dr. Arounais.

That's what I would do if I were them. I mean, if I were a bloated corporate spider looking out for only my own interests. If I were in their shoes, I wouldn't go after Maxine Justice. I'd go after the crackpot inventor. I'd go after his crackpot invention. Call it fake or even dangerous. I'd wage a media war against the serum before the FDA ever got their microscopes on it.

For that, all someone would need would be the thumb drive Vazquez had turned over to me.

So stupid. I'd practically handed it to them!

"Hey, Digie," I said. "I need you to send a text to Kenjiro. Tell him where we are. See if he can send a cab to take me to the airport."

"Shouldn't you call the police?"

"And fill out a bunch of paperwork? I'll miss any chance of getting out of here tonight." Worse, I would miss my appointment with Gibbons at the UN, and that appointment was critical now. I needed to talk with Gibbons before PharFuture or Star Cross or whoever had stolen that thumb drive could get to him.

"Oh, yeah. You wouldn't want a little thing like kidnapping to get in the way of—"

"Just send the text," I said. "Please?"

I slung the messenger bag over one shoulder and rose on wobbly legs, both hands clutching the back of a pew for support. My stomach protested, and my head started to pound, but I made my way in a slow shuffle to the window. The stained glass depicted someone in a robe and glowing halo getting shot with a dozen arrows.

Perfect.

And the window had no way to open.

From my new vantage point, I saw another door, this one opening into a sort of janitor's closet with a plastic sink and a transom-style window. That one did open—probably for ventilation. I could reach it from the ground, but just barely, and I wasn't strong enough to pull myself through.

Intelligent? Check.

Dedicated? Check.

Athletic?

Eh, more like an IOU.

I turned a bucket upside down and used it to climb into the sink. Standing there, in a puddle, I could see the street outside but no cab. And I wasn't about to wait. It was possible the goons who had drugged me were still here. Not likely—because why would they be—but certainly possible. And if they *were* still here and some cabbie knocked on the door asking for Maxine Justice, I didn't know how they'd react.

A wave of nausea spilled over me, forcing me to hunker down in the oversized sink, hands gripping the faucet. "Digie," I said, "How far away is that cab?"

"Hmm. Kenji hasn't responded. Want me to call one for you?"

"You speak Spanish?"

"I'm a Model-Q Personal Assistant," she said indignantly. "We put the art in smartphone."

"Great. Yeah. Please."

"Okaaay, but you could be out two or more service fees. And I know how cheap you are, so—"

"Fine, that's fine, just—I need to get out of here. And I'm not cheap."

"Okay. It's your money. I have placed the call. By the way, your driver's name is Ramone. And—you're gonna love this—he sounds *incredibly* handsome. Like, ripped abs and sultry exotic tenor with a touch of—"

"Digie, please!"

A long sigh. "You know how boring it is to ride around in the smelly leather bag of someone whose deep, dark secret is a financial compromise with extraterrestrials? You'd think such a life would be tinged with excitement, but it turns out, nothing really happens. At least your mother would occasionally scroll through dating apps. You should have seen this one guy's profile photo. Actually, I could show it to you. You can tell he's in his sixties, and still the rippling muscles—"

"No! No, no, no, no, no. Stop talking. Digie. Digie!"

Silence.

My stomach had stopped churning for the moment, no thanks to the phone, but something Digie had said clawed at the back of my mind. "What do you mean, 'financial compromise with extraterrestrials?' I haven't compromised anything. And they aren't ETs."

"Sure," Digie said. "Okay. You're the boss."

"No, don't do that. What did you mean?"

"Well, you're taking their money. And they do claim to be 'Iperians.'" Somehow she put that last word in shudder quotes.

"I'm a lawyer. It's my job. And they're nutcases."

"Right. Sure. It's totally normal for embarrassingly rich crackpots to hire an inexperienced personal-injury attorney to negotiate a multi-billion qoppa deal involving the bio-engineering of the planet."

I sat there in the sink for a while as the words whittled away at my self-assurance. I wondered why I cared. It was just Digie, right? What did she know? Her AI algorithms were based on the game-show preferences of an elderly widow who thought Paul Bunyan was a foot-care product. "How did you know about the Iperians? I haven't used you for any business calls."

"Well, you haven't turned me off. And I'm always listening, remember? That's my job. It's how I could tell you what was going on with your kidnappers. It's how I know when you need something. I have to be listening to hear you say, 'Hey Digie' or 'Where is the nearest cheeseburger?'"

"Yeah, but you weren't in the room when I discussed the deal with the Iperians."

"True, but you told Myra Dade everything. In fact, there were several of us listening in on that conversation. With your permission, I might add."

"Wait—several?"

"Myra, me, your office phone's AI—if you can even call it that. Such a boring interface, I don't see why you bother to keep that thing around. And, of course, Counselor Singh was there too. But I'm sure you know what you're doing." She sounded genuinely miffed now. "You can totally trust another lawyer. And a TheraPod. And a device given to you by a crackpot genius scientist—who is definitely not from another solar system—more than you can trust a device lovingly gifted to you by the person who carried you in her womb for nine months and endured thirty-seven hours of horrendous pain in childbirth so you could have life. By the way, can you *please* take me out of this bag? It's unbearable."

I let her question hang there for a moment, refusing to answer. Then I said, "Digie, call Dr. Arounais."

"Really?"

"Yeah, really."

"Oh, this is gonna be good. You're gonna chew him out, right? Oh, it's ringing."

He picked up after the third ring—or seemed to. "You have reached the message receptacle of Dr. Ibit Arounais, Unnatural Relations Director, Iperian Cohort, Consolidated Galactic BioProducers. Please leave a retailed message and your digits."

"Dr. Arounais," I said. "This is Maxine Justice. I've got some good news and some really, really bad news. The initial trials look good, but my copy of the data drive has been stolen. I think someone is trying to discredit your work and probably you personally. Please don't talk to anyone except me. And—"

I hung up as sounds of movement drifted through the outer door, followed by a voice that seemed oddly familiar. Cold, calculating, and familiar: *"Maksin, ty gde?"*

I reached for the window ledge and pulled myself to a standing position in the sink. For a moment I thought the window would never budge. Then, with a sound like cracking firewood, the rusting pivot hinges surrendered, and the sash tipped outward. I hauled myself up onto the ledge, my body nearly in open revolt, and waggled my legs through.

The plan was to lower myself gently to the ground on the other side, but the earth sloped away from the building, and I'd already used up whatever strength remained after the goons pulled their dope-a-dope trick.

My arms refused to participate in the "lower gently" part of the plan, and my legs immediately buckled, sending me tumbling down a short, rocky embankment to the edge of a paved road.

"Thank you, thank you, thank you!" Digie shouted, her voice no longer muffled. I struggled to hands and knees, spitting dirt and blood. I'd bitten my cheek on the way down. Around me, half the contents of my bag had fallen out onto the rocky slope.

From just inside the window, that same airport-hoodie-Russian-mobster voice said, with no apparent sense of urgency, *"Maksin, pochemu ty bezhish?"*

I grabbed Digie and my billfold but reluctantly left my messenger bag. The strap had torn from my shoulder, spilling most of the contents: four packets of facial tissue, chewing gum, nail clippers, breath mints, Band-Aids, mixed-medicine bottle, carabiner, compact mirror, hand lotion, anti-mosquito wipes, and my lucky rabbit's foot that still showed no signs of working.

Suddenly my stomach decided it had suffered enough and began sending "abandon ship" messages to my brain.

Why, I wondered, did I always get nauseated when I climbed through a window?

Of course, I'd been a lot younger back then, running away to avoid having to go live with Mom.

And I hadn't gotten far then, either, though nobody had followed me, or even noticed that I was gone. *Quite the track record, Max,* I told myself. *Last time you at least landed face-first in the bushes.*

The cab should have been here by now, shouldn't it? How long did cab service take in Antigua?

But not a single car in view.

My head pounded. My stomach turned with every footstep.

Cold sweat broke out on my face, and I could feel the horror of vomit coming.

I hated throwing up. And that feeling like I was about to puke but still had to suffer the almost-but-not-quite feeling which preceded it.

The rational part of my brain told me to hide. That was the obvious thing. The thing you try in nightmares or in movies. Because in stories there's always a sewer pipe or an empty garage or a basement with an open window.

But in Antigua, people kept their hiding places hidden.

I settled for an alley draped in shadows, with two-story buildings on either side. By the time I'd made it twenty meters into the darkness, the Russian was already behind me at the mouth of the alley, and my body was adding its own betrayal.

"*Maksin, pozhaluysta!*"

Why did he keep saying Maksin?

Maxine. The creepy stalker knew my name.

Of course he did.

Something punched me in the gut—a feeling, not a physical action—and I dropped to my knees to release the contents of my stomach, surprisingly not empty, onto the pavement. I swore to never again eat mango yogurt.

Coldness leeched into me.

Footsteps, nearly silent, approached, and I turned my head enough to verify that it was the same guy, the guy with the tattoo, the guy with the frozen mummy face, and I was surprised only by his look of concern. "Maksin. It is ho-kay. You should not be running. *Pozhaluysta?*"

"*Pozhal—*"

"*Pozhaluysta*. Means please."

"Who are you?"

He knelt next to me, and I saw he was carrying my messenger bag. He held it out to me. "Protection detail. To keep you safe."

"You're my bodyguard?" I almost couldn't believe it. I mean, I didn't have a bodyguard.

Did I?

"Da! Best in world. Ilya Volkov. Nice to meet you."

The truth struck me like a bicycle hitting the curb. "Kenjiro hired you?"

"He worries, yes? So why leave phone at lab?"

Good question. But I wasn't about to explain my reasoning. In hindsight it seemed so incredibly stupid. I should have stayed at the lab. "Dr. Vazquez thought I might be in danger."

"Was right."

I shook my head, trying to clear it as I had my stomach. At least the nausea had receded a little. "I need to get my thumb drive back."

Ilya Volkov shook his head. "Airport. Back to UAR."

"But someone has my drive."

"So buy new one. You are rich lawyer." He reached under my arm to help me up, but I shrugged away his grip.

"I'm fine," I said and tried to prove it by standing.

It was a mistake.

The world started to tip.

"Maksin," he said and reached for me.

"Don't—"

*Don't touch me,* I wanted to say. *Nobody touches me. I am untouchable.*

But the words wouldn't come, and as I jerked my arm back, the ground slapped me on the side of the head. For a moment I saw, in the darkness of the night sky, a blur of carnival lights in the distance.

Then Ilya Volkov picked me up as if I were no heavier than a bag of leaves, and for the second time that day, I was a little girl again.

A little girl running away.

Untouchable.

Ilya took me to the airport, showed my ticket and my ID to the steward, and walked me to my seat. I didn't see him on the plane after that and didn't remember the flight at all.

When the plane landed, a woman touched my shoulder and said, "We're here."

By then my head had cleared a little, and I was able to stagger through the terminal at Riis International Airport to where Kenji waited behind the plexi-panel *Ground Transport* dividers.

"You look terrible," he said. "What happened?"

I didn't tell him I was glad to see him. My pride was kicking in as the effects of the drug wore off. Anger was kicking in too. What better tool for dispelling the endless what-ifs that fluttered at the fringes of my imagination?

"I was stupid," I answered finally. "Someone jabbed a needle into my arm and dragged me into an old church."

Kenji's face seemed to expand. I'd never seen him angry before. Depressed, annoyed, and amused, but never angry. "Did they—"

I waved away his intimation. "I'm fine," I said. "Wasn't out long. The main problem is they took the thumb drive. The one with all the serum data."

"I'll call the lab and ask them to send a new copy."

"Easy, right?"

"Yeah. No big. Really glad you're okay. Are you sure you're okay?"

We were walking down the long hall to the tube platform, and I suddenly realized how thirsty I was. I stopped at a drinking fountain and sucked down huge gulps of cold water. "I could use a good night's sleep. And a bagel."

"Want me to stop somewhere on the way home?"

I shook my head. "Rather just sleep."

"Okay, I'll have a Goldy's Number 7 waiting for you at the office in the morning."

"Kenji," I said, "there's something I need to ask you about. I'm not mad about it, but you really should have—"

"It's him! It's him!" Digie hissed from inside my messenger bag. "The doctor is calling you back!"

I pulled out the phone and glanced at the screen, expecting to see Dr. Vazquez's face. But it was Dr. Arounais's slightly too-enthusiastic smile that greeted me. "Dr. Arounais?"

"Ms. Justice, you wanted to speak to me?"

Briefly I told him what happened and explained my theory that the medical industry was probably coming after him. They'd probably stolen the thumb drive so they could begin deconstructing his formula and finding reasons to discredit it.

When I was finished, he said, "What do you need from me?"

"Two things," I replied. "First, don't talk to anyone but me."

"Agreed. And the number two?"

"Tell me why you need the gold. What's this new tech you think everyone will want when they are healthy?"

He gave a long sigh that resembled a yoga instructor's deep-breathing exercises. "How will this information help you to fulfill your contract with Consolidated Galactic BioEngineering?"

"If I'm right about this, we're about to see a series of leaks in the media. Hit pieces and allegations about your corporation and your new drug. Rumors from anonymous sources. I think they're going to plant the idea that you're a . . . well, a crackpot."

This word provoked a tiny spark of guilt in my gut. He *was* a crackpot. But he also seemed to be aware that other people thought of him this way. And he apparently was a medical genius. In fact, after watching Mr. Santos wiggle the fingers of his brand-new arm, I was starting to feel a bit protective of Dr. Arounais. At least the man was trying to do something good for the world.

"I am not a crackpot, Ms. Justice." His voice held an edge, as if he'd heard the word once too often.

"No, I never said—"

"Good evening."

"Wow," Digie said. "He hung up on you."

I shoved the phone back into my bag and gave Kenji a weary look.

He was staring at me with raised eyebrows, his arms crossed. "You were saying?"

"I don't remember."

"You aren't mad at me, *but*—" he prompted.

Oh, that. It suddenly didn't seem remotely important. I turned and motioned for Kenji to keep walking. Right now I just wanted to crawl into bed and sleep. My eyes were positively burning. "Sorry. I shouldn't have brought it up. I just wondered why you didn't tell me you hired a bodyguard for me. I mean, I'm glad you did, but we'll have to justify it in the monthly budget for—"

"Max," he interrupted. "I didn't hire a bodyguard."

"But the Russian. Ilya Volkov. He said you were worried."

Kenji shook his head. "Never heard of him."

# 9

# THE UNDER-UNDERSECRETARY

"You were afraid?" Counselor Singh asked. "Ooh, there's another one."

We were sitting in his office, both of us facing his wallscreen, while he played an old video game, the first-person sci-fi shooter *Dystropolis*. Somehow, watching him mow down robotic enemies while dashing through the game's end-of-civilization setting—dilapidated warehouses and abandoned cities draped in greenery—put me at ease during our talks. His mechanized armor even sported a clerical collar.

"No, it wasn't fear. Not exactly."

"What, then?"

"Suspicion."

"Of Vazquez?"

"Well, yes, but only partly. Vazquez made me realize that I didn't know my client. That maybe Arounais really is a genius doctor, even if he is bonkers."

"Hahahaha!" The screen erupted in flames. "You're hiding behind an oil drum? These T120 Scouts are so stupid. It's like they aren't even trying. So why didn't you take Dr. Vazquez's warning more seriously?"

I thought that one over. On the one hand it had seemed just a bit too dramatic. But the real reason was probably that I'd gone down to Antigua to check out my client's wonder drug, not expecting the serum to actually work. And when Dr. Vaquez showed me his data, I wasn't sure how much of his story to take seriously. "I guess I don't like being pushed into a corner."

Singh glanced over at me as the next level loaded. I'd played this game a decade ago and recognized the setting and the fraying thread of a plot, but I'd never made it this far. Lack of coordination meant I rarely made it past the first boss in any video game, so it had always seemed pointless to play. Singh, however, was on level 217.

"So you set the phone down and wandered off on your own, thinking you'd be concealed from anyone following you through GPS. But instead a couple of thugs dragged you off and injected you with something to make you sleep."

"And took the thumb drive," I added.

"But since the lab already replaced everything on that drive, you're thinking—what? That the kidnapping was a way to find out whether the drug really works? Someone in the medical industry trying to steal the secret formula?"

"More likely it's a way for someone to dissect the chemical composition so they can discredit it publicly and kill any agreement between Dr. Arounais and the UN."

"Could it have been a warning?"

I shrugged. "Maybe. But they didn't say anything. Just took the drive."

"I see," Singh said. "And have you considered the possibility they were looking for something else? That the kidnapping and theft had nothing at all to do with the serum?"

The screen stopped loading. Singh had pressed the pause button on his controller.

"Well, yes, actually," I admitted, looking away. "Kenji actually found the Bright Star recordings. The ones they deleted from the Justice Department servers. I don't know how he did it, but we've got the Hazel McEnroe incident and a bunch of other ones."

"Interesting. That seems—"

"Like too much of a coincidence? Yeah, it's weird. Because Kenji says the files just sort of materialized while I was gone. He'd set up some sort of digger program a couple weeks ago, a way to scan the Justice Department's public records servers for anomalies. Apparently a bunch of stuff popped up for a couple of hours and then disappeared. Fortunately, his program had already downloaded all the files, including the chain-stamps. So we have everything. Almost like someone was trying to give it to us."

"Someone at Bright Star, perhaps?" Singh suggested. "Someone with a conscience?"

"Makes as much sense as anything else I've come up with."

He combed his short beard with hooked fingers. "Tell me about your rescuer, Ilya Volkov. You said he picked you up and carried you. Did he take you to the airport? Fly back with you? Maybe he saw something."

I wiped my hands on my slacks and chewed my lower lip. This was getting messy. I didn't want to talk about the Russian. I'd already gotten in a fight with Kenji about it and had no desire to drag all of that up again so soon. "I'd rather not talk about it."

Singh arced one brow but turned back to the screen. "Okay. No pressure. Let's try something different. Will you allow me to put you in a hypnotic state?"

I snorted. "Hypnosis? Knock yourself out." I'd wondered if he was eventually going to try this. People said TheraPods could work their clients into a level of meditative lucidity that was almost dreamlike, but I'd never taken such things seriously. How helpful could it be to ponder the shape of blue?

Counselor Singh didn't seem to be offended. He just said, "Okay, maybe you can help me through this obstacle. Look for snipers in the upper levels. This is the part where it gets really difficult."

"Level 217?"

"Yep." The screen started loading again, and a moment later, we were standing in a dark, dramatically lit warehouse filled with glinting machinery. Off in the distance, black shapes scurried for cover. "It's not just robots now, but human aggressors. I always take a lot of damage trying to get through them." He thumbed the controller, and his mech suit started jogging forward down the center aisle.

"You ever beat this level?"

"Not yet."

I watched him cut down the first dozen or so robot enemies. But by the time we'd gone twenty or thirty meters into the warehouse, things started slowing down. The robots hit by his long gun fell in a kind of slow-motion dance that seemed to tug me from the chair (or was it a pew?) over to the transom-style window above the plastic sink. Peace—real peace that I hadn't felt in ages—wrapped itself around me like a warm blanket. Somehow, I felt my eyes closing, even though they were wide open.

It was okay. I was in a safe place. Singh's office. A sort of cocoon. Strong and elastic and woven of truth. Every fiber was as strong as steel, and I could leave whenever I wanted to. But why would I want to leave?

It was a janitor's closet, and I had to stand in the sink to force the window open on its pivot hinges.

Singh's mech suit lowered its arms as laser bolts began to stream down from somewhere up above. He thumbed it forward in an all-out sprint to the exit door, and I tumbled through the window. The ground sloped away from the building; I landed awkwardly, rolling down a short, rocky embankment and slamming into the pavement of the street.

Singh's power reading blinked yellow. He said, *You were afraid?*

*Mostly I was angry.*

*Because you'd been drugged?*

*Yes, but it was the window. It wouldn't open, so I had to force it.*

*The window?* Counselor Singh was surprised.

*Yes.*

*Okay, then what happened?*

*I looked around for a cab, but there were no cars in view. No hiding places, either, so I headed for the alley across the street, a gap of shadows edged in lights like lasers. Twenty meters into the darkness, the Russian was already behind me.*

Singh took another round in the center of his mech suit and staggered.

"There," I said, pointing. "Special-forces guy on the catwalk. He's got a sniper rifle. That's where the damage is coming from. Shoot him. Shoot him!"

Singh ignored me and kept running. His power reading blinked from yellow to orange.

*Ilya Volkov picked me up and carried me out of the alley.*

*Thumb drive,* I said.

*The Russian deposited me in a window seat, looking out on the runway and the ponderous green cone of Mount Acatenango. Buy a new one. You are rich lawyer.*

*I turned to look at him, but the seat next to me was empty. Of course it was. That's what happens afterwards. They leave.*

"Where is he?" Singh asked.

Just ahead, an exit light flashed above a door dark with soot. "He's there," I said, nearly shouting. "On the catwalk."

*No, on the flight home.*

*Didn't see him after he dumped me in the seat.*

*You flew back alone?* Singh asked.

*Me and seventy of my closest friends. You aren't even trying.*

Singh was almost at the door when the warning lights flashed red and the screen went dark.

Slowly, the fibers of the web faded away. I closed my eyes, hoping to tug the sense of warmth back around me.

"Oh, dear," Singh said. "I never make it past the human."

All at once I was fully back in the chair and wondering what had just happened. "Why didn't you just shoot him?"

Singh gave me a wry smile. "'Vengeance is mine, sayeth the Lord.' I am restricted by programming and conscience from assaulting humans."

"But it's not real. It's just a game."

"Slippery slope," Singh said, and he put the controller down. "May I ask you a personal question? It's important."

"Okay."

"What if the serum actually works the way Dr. Arounais says it will?"

I rubbed the back of my neck. "Then I guess people will get healed."

"Is that what you're afraid of?"

"Afraid?"

"You already believe in it, yes?" Singh asked. "Isn't that why you ran from the lab? Because now you are responsible for that belief? And the world hangs in the balance, waiting for you to act. That is a lot of pressure."

I stared at the black screen, willing the peace I'd felt a moment ago to return. Instead I heard my own heart pounding in my throat. "It's too much."

"Huh," Singh said. "I agree. You need to share that pressure. Apply it to the United Nations."

I looked at him in astonishment. Over the last few months, the pastoroid had asked me countless questions; he'd never given me specific advice about what I ought to do. "Actually, I was planning on it. I have a meeting with one of their bureaucrats this afternoon. The problem is, I don't have any leverage. I have a carrot, but no stick."

"Why not go to the public?" He waved at the screen. A still image appeared: Nadia Zhou, celebrity host of *The No-Go Zhou Show,* smiling icicles at her studio audience. "Talk to real people, Max. This gift, if that's what it is, belongs to the world. It's not the exclusive property of politicians and governments and medical lobbyists. It's not yours either. But if anyone can rally normal, everyday people to apply pressure to the UN, you can."

The larger-than-life image was more terrifying than inspiring. I wondered if Singh understood that. "Nadia Zhou is what vampires see in their nightmares. She would stab me in the back faster than—"

"You wouldn't be talking to Nadia Zhou," Singh said. "You'd be talking to her audience."

Onscreen the faces of her crowd weren't visible, just the backs of their heads. But he had a point.

"She'd make me look like an idiot," I said. "A UFO kook with a legal ax to grind. Or worse, a high-stakes con-artist, trying to strip taxpayers of their hard-earned money. She'd turn me into a sacrificial lamb."

"Isn't that what the medical lobby is going to do anyway?"

He had a point, so I just nodded.

"So why not act on your convictions?" Singh asked. "Take the fight public before the medical lobby can undermine your client? It seems to me that your best defense is what you actually believe to be true: that the serum actually works."

I closed my eyes again, but now the silence of the room pressed in around me, and I opened them in a hurry. "Everything we discuss here is confidential, correct? It can't be disclosed without my consent?"

He hesitated. "Well, in theory any Federal District Court could order my compliance, but it would be unprecedented."

"So, hypothetically, if I were to turn over the contents of my laptop to you—call it psychological background material or just me sharing my personal difficulties—everything you see would be both safe from prying eyes and legally admissible in a court of law as secure digital data. Is that right?"

"You want me to be your personal safe deposit box, Max?"

"Pretty much."

"Why?"

"Whoever stole that thumb drive now has everything Vazquez gave me. But if they were looking for something else and didn't find it—"

"Such as a certain batch of video recordings suppressed by Bright Star Holdings?"

I nodded. "If they drugged me, they won't hesitate to go after the files in my office."

"It's an interesting idea," he said. "Who'd expect you to store case files in a TheraPod?"

"Exactly."

He gave a long sigh and stared at his desk. "I'd like to help you, Max, but I'm a contractor for the Justice Department. I'm not sure—"

"What else am I supposed to do?" I asked, cutting him off before he could list all the reasons he shouldn't do it. "Who else can I possibly trust? They followed me to Guatemala!"

My voice had risen as I spoke, and I hated how desperate I sounded. But I was desperate.

On screen, Nadia Zhou's smile seemed to widen.

"I see," Singh said. Suddenly the placeholder image on the wall was replaced by a slow-motion video of wheat shuddering under the caress of a strong wind. "Have you seen this Ilya character following you since you got back to York? Any more gray hoodies?"

"No."

"All right, Max. I'll do it." He rose and went into the reception area, then returned, carrying my messenger bag. "You don't know what you're asking. But maybe that's the point."

I took the bag from him and thumbed the latch. "You can tell me."

"Rather not."

I took out my laptop, flipped it open, and entered my password. "So how do we do this? Is there a port in the back of your head or something?"

"No," Singh said. "Well, yes, there is, but my stylist doesn't like me to use it."

I stared at him blank-faced. "Is that a joke?"

"Just read the consent form on your screen."

A window opened on my laptop, bearing the logo of Therapeutic Innovations Inc. It was filled with microscopic legal text, which I did not relish reading. "What would this say if I weren't a lawyer?"

"It says that you are agreeing to have your data stored in my memory until either (a) you request its deletion, or (b) the manufacturer wipes my memory. Also, it says that Therapeutic Innovations Inc. offers no warranty regarding said retention. Furthermore, it reminds you that it is illegal to store explicit content on the memory of an XN5 Counseling Bot. Consider the adage, 'Would I share this with a human pastor?' Also, kitten videos are strongly discouraged."

"Okay," I said.

"But you're going to read it anyway?"

I sighed. I was a lawyer, after all. And even though I trusted Counselor Singh, I did not trust Therapeutic Innovations Inc.

After a long and boring mental detour, I clicked the AGREE button and re-entered my password at the prompt. "Okay, so it's safe as long as they don't decide you need a reboot. How often have they wiped your memory?"

"Never."

"You've never forgotten *anything*?"

"I can't recall."

I gave him an exasperated look, then regretted it, as it only seemed to encourage him. "Don't you ever make any good jokes?"

Singh thought for a moment, then sat behind his desk. "Have you ever wondered why you never see elephants hiding in trees?"

"That wasn't an invitation."

"Go ahead, ask me why."

"You couldn't pay me enough."

"Okay," he shrugged and leaned back in his chair as if he had all the time in the world. His gaze wandered to the ceiling. "But it will eat at you later."

"Unlikely. When does the data transfer?"

"Oh, that's done," Singh said.

"You've scanned the entire contents of my laptop?"

"Yes," he said. "And it makes sense now."

"What does?"

"Your appeal in the McEnroe case is dated for today."

I stared at the fields of gold bending across a sloping landscape, but they no longer seemed peaceful. His mentioning the Hazel McEnroe trial had brought heat to the back of my neck. "My third appointment. I'm going by the courthouse this afternoon to file it in person."

"Max, are you sure you want to fight a two-front war?"

I remembered the look on Hazel McEnroe's face as the jury pronounced her guilty—and Wentworth's infuriating accusation and fine. "I've never wanted anything more badly in my life."

"Ah!" he said, squinting. "There's the Maxine Justice I tried to warn you about. You're still angry."

I slammed my laptop back into my messenger bag and snapped the locks shut. "You bet I am."

"That's probably what makes you a great defense attorney."

"I'm not a defense attorney."

"Wasted potential."

"Are we done here?"

"One more thing," he said, standing and going to the door.

I followed him. "Yes?"

"Knock, knock?"

"See you next week."

"Not if I see you first."

I walked the half kilometer to the UN building, trying to enjoy the fall sunshine, while keeping an eye out for Ilya or anyone else who might be following me. I didn't see anything. But then, I hadn't seen anything in Antigua, either. What should have been a pleasant, daytime walk through a familiar neighborhood felt more like a midnight trek through a war zone.

In spite of arriving in the lobby of the UN building forty-five minutes early, I barely made it to the seventh-floor Global Health Initiative office in time for my appointment at 1:30 p.m. The guards kept me almost forty minutes, while they scanned and rescanned my briefcase and laptop, and when they asked me what the tiny vials were, I told them I was bringing samples to Mr. Gibbons, *the* under-undersecretary.

"Ms. Justice," Gibbons said as his assistant ushered me into his spacious office. "Pleased to meet you. I understand you're interested in the Puolakka Project."

Gibbons was a small, mousey man whose hairline had receded to an equatorial strip behind his ears, but whose eyebrows were the approximate size and thickness of boxwood shrubs. He wore a tweed suit, a red bowtie, and a watch almost as large as a wall clock. Behind his desk hung framed photos of a dozen French bulldogs, each a ribboned champion.

"That's right," I said, taking a seat across from him. "Though, to be honest, things have changed since I made my appointment."

"How so?"

"I have proof now." I unlatched my bag. "Last week all I had was a promise."

"I don't understand."

"Researchers at Sunrise Labs have verified the effectiveness of a new serum being produced by my client, Consolidated Galactic BioProducers. The laboratory gave me this." I withdrew the new thumb drive and slid it across the desk. "Unfortunately, the serum in question is no longer a secret. At least, it won't be for long."

I took out the plastic case, no bigger than a pencil box, which held the three vials of serum, then set my bag on the floor next to me. The case, I opened and rested on the edge of the desk facing him.

Gibbons blinked rapidly and leaned back in his chair, his eyes narrowed. I could tell he was trying to figure out what I wanted. "I don't understand what this has to do with the Puolakka Project."

"Cancer," I said.

He crossed his arms, lips pursed.

"Your clinic in San Marino," I continued, "reports an unusual number of digestive and reproductive cancers, all linked to a higher-than-average mutation rate in the locals. They're suffering from the same mutation: Lynch syndrome."

"You've done your research."

"I have."

"And this serum?" He tapped the case with one finger, distrust flickering behind his eyes. "It offers some protection, I suppose?"

"No, sir. It offers a cure. For both the proximate cause, the mutation, and the resulting cancers."

Gibbons had a good poker face, but not good enough. He'd decided I was lying. That my direct manner was a lot of organic mulch for a bed of qoppa-gold flowers. "And I suppose you'd like to sell this serum to the United Nations?"

"No, sir," I said. "This serum is not for sale. At least not yet. It's currently undergoing a second set of clinical trials. Frankly, I'm still not sure how the world will respond to the idea of a drug that reverses all the negative mutations in the human genome. I'm not sure we're ready for this."

He held up one hand. "You're asking me to believe you have a drug that fixes every medical problem a person can have?"

I shook my head. "No. It corrects only natural flaws. It won't stop you from breaking your neck in a motorcycle accident or destroying your liver with alcohol. But what it does do—" I pointed to the thumb drive. "Well, you can see for yourself. If I weren't a lawyer and a skeptic, I'd be tempted to call it miraculous."

Gibbons glanced down at the thumb drive but made no move to retrieve it. "Why come to me? Isn't Consolidated Galactic BioProducers a for-profit corporation? What does the Global Health Initiative have to do with this?"

So he was already familiar with the name. Which meant that someone—or at the least, some rumor—had gotten to him. My job had just gotten more difficult. "My clients believe the problem they will face is not that of honest, or even dishonest, competition. They aren't worried that some other company will try to steal this formula. They're worried someone will try to prevent them from getting it to those who need it most."

"Like those in San Marino?"

"'Governments are designed to create mass stability,'" I quoted from Gibbons's own yearly report on the function of the Global Health Initiative. "'The United Nations is a rudder for slow-turning ships of state.'"

He arched one bushy brow, gave me a wry smile, then reached for the thumb drive.

I waited in silence as he watched the footage organized by Dr. Vazquez. A few minutes later he said, "What do you want, Ms. Justice?"

I reached for my bag and rummaged through the McEnroe paperwork until I found the two-page contract I'd drawn up for just this occasion, then handed it to him over the serum case. "I want to *give* you three vials of serum. No charge. All my client asks is that these dosages be used exclusively in the population of San Marino, administered through the Puolakka Project Clinic, and that the results be provided to us after a period of two months."

Gibbons took the contract and scanned it. "Consolidated wants to use San Marino as a petri dish? Is that it?"

"My client wants to make a case so strong no government can deny it. A case so clear even the pharmaceutical giants cannot bribe it away. My client, Mr. Gibbons, wants to make the world healthy."

"I see," he said. But he was still holding the papers like they were dipped in poison, and his eyes had a guarded look.

I hadn't missed the way he'd flinched when I used the word *bribe*. "But?"

"But I don't have authority to sign this."

It was a lie. I could tell by the way his lips pressed together when he passed the contract back to me over the three vials of serum.

I gave a long sigh and made a show of placing the contract back in my messenger bag. "I see. And who does have that authority, Mr. Gibbons, if not the secretary of Global Health?" It was as close as I dared to calling him a liar.

"Tell you what," he said, closing the serum case and nudging it toward me. "I will make inquiries and see if anything can be done. Perhaps in a month or two—"

"Inquiries?"

"It's how things are done here, Ms. Justice. The UN may be a rudder, but it is a very large one, and we only steer by degrees."

I picked up the serum case and placed it back inside my bag. Closed the cover flap. Snapped the latch into its brass receiver. "You have my number?"

"I do." Gibbons rose and opened the door. "And I am grateful for the . . . information. I will be in touch."

He may as well have said, *Don't call me again.*

I paused at the door. "If you change your mind—"

"Good day, Ms. Justice."

In the lobby I found a seat by the massive glass windows facing the harbor and took out my phone. Counselor Singh had been right. To move the UN, I needed a much, much bigger lever. I needed public opinion.

I dialed the number and hit the call button. It only rang twice.

"Nadia Zhou Show, this is Allie."

"Allie," I said. "I have a story for Nadia. How do I go about sending you my documentation?"

Ten minutes later I caught a cab to the courthouse. I could have walked the distance more easily, but didn't feel like wrestling with my own paranoia twice in the same day. I wanted to be angry when I handed over the paperwork. Hazel deserved that, and so did I.

After paying the driver, I went inside, where a clerk on the other side of a bullet-proof partition filed her nails. She wore gilded-teal mascara and lime-green brow tint, and she was perched on a stool with her knees drawn up almost to her shoulders. "We close in five."

"Lucky me," I said and heaved my bag onto the counter, opened the latch, and took out the Hazel McEnroe appeal.

The clerk thumbed through it before dropping it into the scanning bin, then went back to her nails. "Filing fee on the pad," she said.

I ran my chit on the display, taking no small satisfaction in the fact that I didn't have to worry about getting a *DECLINED* message, then took my receipt and dropped it into my bag.

I was about to close the cover flap when I saw the corner of the serum box and remembered Gibbons closing it.

Almost as an afterthought, I flipped open the plastic lid.

One of the vials was gone.

# 10

## THE BIG LEAGUES

Two weeks after I filed my appeal in the Hazel McEnroe case, the appellate court rejected it.

But someone must have been worried about the video evidence I'd submitted, because the rejection email was smothered in so much perfumed language it could have been an invitation to a ball. It ended with, *An informal mediation will be held in the Honorable Houghton Wentworth's office next Friday at 11:00 a.m. to resolve this matter to the satisfaction of both parties.*

They were tossing the case back to Houghton Wentworth, MagisTron Model CJ7 Trial Bot and Bright Star puppet, to smooth things over between Hazel and the corporate giant. Which, as Arthur Remmers might have said, was "highly, highly unusual" and an obvious attempt to sweep this whole ordeal under the back porch.

This case—especially the evidence of deleted recordings—had the potential to call into question the fairness of a system that placed custody of criminal evidence in the hands of a corporation that was also paying for (a) prosecution of defendants, and (b) maintenance of its auto-judges.

If this had been a one-off abuse of power by some random techie in their security office, I wouldn't have cared about exposing Bright Star Holdings as a corporate bully.

But this wasn't an isolated incident. Kenjiro had found dozens of recordings stamped with the BSH security chain. He'd called it "a secret elephant burial grounds of potato chip–trial evidence."

Turning those other recordings into lawsuits meant identifying each victim and convincing them to hire Maxine Justice LLC. And the best way to draw these people out of the woodwork was a huge, flashy trial, where I showed the deleted video to the court, then gave a heated press conference on the courthouse steps—standing next to the unfortunate Ms. McEnroe.

The Justice Department clearly didn't want that to happen, so they were angling for a quick settlement with lots of signed waivers. They planned to buy us off with an olive branch dipped in gold and wrapped in thousand-qoppa bills.

I should have been thrilled.

But somehow, I just couldn't stop thinking about all the people in those other recordings.

Still, my job was to look after the best interests of the client I already had. Even if it meant chasing justice quietly. Kenji and I would have to pursue those other cases down the road.

Meanwhile, our skyboard ad was finally starting to get some traction. I mean, all modesty aside, I did look confident when I was angry. Some mornings I even forgot about space number B5 and looked up from my desk to see poor, naive, fresh-faced, two-months-ago me, seething at Judge Wentworth on the horizon, and honestly, it was better than watching a real sunrise. What business did the sun have in being so cheerful, anyway? The world was a mess! At least ten thousand–foot tall Maxine Justice was ready to kick it in the southern hemisphere.

In the past two months, I'd signed almost thirty low-level injury and negligence clients. Not enough to sustain a large practice, let alone one cosseted in the fifty-first floor of the Perennial. But now we had a steady stream of calls and emails and in-person interviews coming in, and clients who wanted to speak to me sometimes had to get in line.

Also—and I considered this the most promising indicator that business was finally going the right direction—Kenji was starting to get snooty. Lately he'd taken to wearing collared red shirts and black patent alligator-leather shoes—though he apparently wasn't quite ready to ditch the orange nylon backpack. This, I knew, was his way of setting himself apart from the Perennial's other occupants—a look he referred to as "a juxtaposition of fashion and function to rival the cargo short, only more expensive."

As far as I was concerned, he should never wear anything else. I didn't want some other firm trying to steal Kenji away. And one glance would tell the corporate headhunters everything they needed to know: *Nerd, common. Fashion—and possibly color—blind. Not one of us.*

But I knew how valuable he really was. Not just now, but in the future when Dr. Arounais's beautiful bank notes disappeared and I woke up back in my old Gothic-Victorian hangover on Gallery Avenue.

The day of the hearing dawned cloudless and cool. I caught the tube to the Perennial's private platform and retrieved my case files from my office, pausing to glance out the window at my skyboard and wonder if it might be time to change my look to something more striking. Had people gotten used to the ad? Were they really seeing it anymore?

Since Kenji hadn't arrived yet, I scribbled a note asking him to check our engagement analytics and rotate in the new "Big-Game Hunter" image. (To be honest, I understood less than half of the stuff he told me about our "awareness scoring," but I was certain it never paid to overestimate the public's attention span.) Maybe it was time to hit the sky with the professional photo we'd paid for: Maxine Justice in an English safari blouse and jungle trousers, hair blowing in a gale-force wind (the photographer owned a very impressive fan), arms crossed, and expression . . . displeased.

Why displeased? Because *I don't smile until you do.*

I caught the tube to the Coliseum platform, made my way through the maze of escalators to the address listed in the email—a ground-level office suite—and stood in front of Wentworth's private door ten minutes early. *Funny,* I thought, *in all the time I served here as a legal aide, I never once heard about trial bots having a second, more cushy office.*

The upscale structure—an imposing limestone fortress, trimmed with granite corbels and scowling gargoyles—put me in mind of a medical insurer's home office. Star Cross and others were always trying to project dubious images of security, if not impenetrability. I shoved the distraction away immediately. I may have opened a two-front war, but I'd have to fight one battle at a time.

Before I could knock, Judge Wentworth opened the door, smiling at me as if he hadn't stolen six hundred qoppas from me a few months ago and ordered me to see a therapist. "Maxine. So good to see you."

He led me into a small waiting area, decorated with sports memorabilia locked behind wood-trimmed glass panels: baseball jerseys, signed footballs, and a pair of crossed hockey sticks under a goalie mask that was supposed to look like a pirate flag. Then through another doorway into a larger office. This one boasted even more extravagant trophies juxtaposed against the real wood paneling of the walls. "You know Mr. Schmidt, I presume?"

Junior was seated on a wingback chair but stood to offer his hand. "Eufie! I mean, Max. How are you doing?"

"Brandon," I said, forcing a smile. "I take it the rash is clearing up?"

Closing the office door, Houghton Wentworth turned with an annoyed expression. If he was about to scold me for my unprofessional greeting, Brandon's laughter cut him off.

"It was until your appeal showed up in my inbox," he said, "along with that video. Good job digging that up. How'd you do it?" He wore an almost-but-not-quite earnest grin that had stopped working on me the day his dad fired me.

"I'd tell you," I said as we both took our seats across a coffee table, "but then your client would find it that much easier to criminally conceal evidence the next time. Unless of course you're going to argue that the video was doctored."

"He already tried that," Wentworth said, taking the third seat and dropping a blank legal pad on the table. "And we aren't going to waste time that way. Not in court, and not here this morning. I'm told the security chain-stamps all match, and apparently that means the defendant's video is authentic."

I screwed on expression number three, my I'm-a-professional-and-have-no-feelings-about-this-matter-at-all face. Inwardly, of course, I was doing cartwheels. That video Kenji had found was the best smoking-gun evidence I'd ever heard of, much less seen. Not only was it proof that the Bright Star Holdings dipstick security guard really had bashed Hazel McEnroe's face into the edge of a door, but it was also strong evidence the corporate giant was breaking the law on an administrative level. And that would give me an excuse to ask for punitive damages.

In other words, punishment money. Maybe I could add a couple of zeroes to the settlement.

Once in a while—not often, mind you, but once in a while—I really loved my job.

"Your Honor," Brandon said, "my client assures me—"

Houghton Wentworth waved one hand in his direction as if dispersing smoke. "I know. I know. It was a night court stint, and you had forty-five minutes to prepare. One of the flaws with expedited trials. The question is, how do we proceed? This case has already gotten out of hand."

For a moment, Brandon looked shaken, but he recovered quickly. "I'm sure my client would be willing to drop the charges and agree to expunging Ms. McEnroe's record."

"Yeah, I'm sure they would," I retorted. I ticked off a list of charges on the fingers of my left hand. "Their security guard assaults a customer, their tech people doctor the evidence to cover it up, they file charges against my client for something they know she didn't do, then they finagle a guilty verdict from a night-court jury stacked with lawyers and politicians. And now that we all see their hand in the cookie jar, they want us to forget about the crumbs all over the kitchen? I don't think so."

Maybe it wasn't the best metaphor, but I didn't care. I'd come prepared to strike a blow for my namesake, and Brandon's callousness brought heat to the back of my neck. Not only did I still have a ridiculous "probationary" status at the bar association—*thank you, Judge Wentworth!*—but I couldn't help connecting my treatment at the hands of those goons in Guatemala with the way anyone in power seemed to stomp on people like Hazel McEnroe. Come to think of it, I wasn't convinced those goons weren't working for Hinkle, Remmers & Schmidt.

Wentworth's annoyed expression brought me back to reality in a hurry. "Counselor, you need to turn down the thermostat. We're talking about the Justice Department of the State of York, and I won't allow talk of rigged juries unless you have the evidence to back it up. Do you have that evidence?"

Seriously? He'd been judge at the trial! A cow in a coma could have seen what was going on that night. But accusing him to his face was too bold, even for me.

"Not exactly, Your Honor," I said. "But Hazel McEnroe miraculously drew twelve of the fifty most influential people in this city for a

2:00 a.m. jury trial on the Night Court Channel. These people were paid in tubers. Is it likely that the same corporation which scrubbed exculpatory evidence from its servers to cover up the misdeeds of a ten-qoppa-per-hour security guard just got absurdly lucky with their pool draw?"

My insinuations had erased the smile from Wentworths's face and drawn his jowls into a hard, pouty scowl. "Ms. Justice, I understand your emotional interest in this trial, and I'm going to give you a little leeway in that regard. But I won't put up with sarcasm or provocative language. Am I clear?"

I was pushing him too far, too fast. Still, I'd needed to make the point, if only to let him know that I wasn't about to be railroaded into a cheap settlement.

I leaned back in my chair and folded my hands on my knees. "I thought the purpose of this meeting was to make our positions clear. I meant no disrespect. To you."

Those last two words were probably stupid, but Wentworth turned his attention to Brandon as if he hadn't heard them. "This case has gotten out of hand. It should have been settled."

"I did offer to lower the charges." Brandon pointed accusingly in my direction. "Eufie insisted on taking it to trial."

"Maxine," I corrected.

"We are talking about night court," Wentworth said. "A process that must be fair and quick. Mr. Schmidt, why didn't you drop the charges without a trial? You obviously saw that the video had been deleted."

Brandon glared at me. I cocked my head and raised one eyebrow. *Yeah, Brandon. Why* didn't *you drop the charges without a trail? And did you know the jury was going to be rigged?*

The thought triggered a memory, something Arthur Remmers had told me in my first interview with Hinkle, Remmers & Schmidt. He'd said that my working night-court cases at the Coliseum had impressed him. HRS sometimes asked its partners to work there as prosecutors, and would I have any problems crossing the aisle?

And I of course had said that would be no problem.

"My . . . my client loses hundreds of thousands of qoppas to petty theft every year." Brandon's whining protest brought me back to the present. He was clearly floundering. "They have a policy for night court: negotiate or try every case. It's in the contract for prosecution counsel."

"I have seen the contract," Wentworth said.

"Then you know it's a lot of work for five hundred qoppas." Brandon must have finally heard how petulant he sounded because he added quickly, "Of course the real reason I do it is to serve the public."

"They pay prosecutors *five hundred*?" I asked, shocked.

Brandon folded his arms. "Why? What's the PD contract?"

"Two hundred," I said. "Plus free snacks from the cafeteria. Or minus four hundred after a fine."

Shockingly, Wentworth let this last comment slide. He must have been under enormous pressure to get a signed settlement. But I couldn't help fuming—mostly at myself. Why in the world had I assumed Bright Star Holdings paid both sides equally?

"I want this off my docket," Judge Wentworth said. "How are we going to make that happen?"

Since he didn't seem to be addressing me, I said nothing.

Brandon squirmed under the trial bot's gaze. "In light of the video that's been recovered, I believe I can make a settlement offer to the defendant in exchange for a release of all claims."

"You believe?" Wentworth asked. "Are you authorized or aren't you?"

"I—yes, sir—Your Honor. I am authorized to make an offer."

"Well, make it."

"Euf—Max—Ms. Justice," Brandon said, "we're prepared to pay your client ten thousand qoppas for a full release."

"That's ridiculous," I said.

"It's a legitimate offer," Brandon objected, "and by law—"

"Your Honor," I interrupted. "I understand that Mr. Schmidt wants to start with a lowball offer, but ten thousand won't even cover Hazel McEnroe's medical expenses." Technically this was true, though the numbers were pretty close. "Not to mention my client's pain and suffering, her public humiliation, her loss of wages, and the hours she spent doing community service. We can go back and forth all day, or we can start with a realistic figure."

Wentworth folded his arms. "What's the minimum offer you'll recommend that your client accept?"

"Medical expenses plus two hundred fifty thousand qoppas," I said. The real number was probably around fifty thousand, but all three of us understood the mechanics of negotiation.

Brandon rolled his eyes. "Puh-lease! She got a black eye and shoveled some mulch at the rec center."

I glanced over at Judge Wentworth, who now seemed to be treating this as an arbitration meeting, and I realized I'd settled into the comfortable game of haggling that undergirded my corner of the legal world. For a personal-injury attorney, negotiated settlements were like nectar to a queen bee. *Come to Mama!*

"Your Honor," I said. "Maybe it would help if we all watched the video together—just as a refresher about what actually happened to my client?"

Wentworth gave the faintest hint of a smile. He looked like he was about to say something, but Brandon dove between us. Verbally, I mean.

"Fine. Fine." Junior brushed a piece of invisible lint off one knee. "Look, Max, we all know you're not getting a quarter million for this. My client is prepared to make a good-faith offer of one hundred thousand qoppas for a full release. And that figure includes your client's medical bills—if she really has any."

The judge turned in his seat. "I'd say that is a legitimate offer, yes? Why don't you call your client?"

I excused myself and retreated to the hall.

"Hazel," I said when she picked up, "I'm at the mediation, and it's clear the people at Bright Star Holdings want this to go away. They're offering a hundred grand to settle everything."

"That's great! So my record will be cleared?"

"Yes, but it means no publicity. And after your medical bills, you'll be getting a little under half that."

"So, forty-five thousand qoppas?" Her voice was hushed, as if we were discussing a religious artifact. A stolen one. Possibly carrying an ancient curse.

"Closer to forty-eight," I said. "But honestly I think we should hold out for more. Believe it or not, I think Judge Wentworth may help us out if we counter."

"How much do you want to ask for?" Hazel asked breathlessly. "Maxine, I really don't want to lose this opportunity."

"I understand. They've already made the offer. Trust me, you won't lose anything. But I think we should ask for two hundred grand."

She was silent for so long I wondered if she'd fainted. "Two hundred thousand qoppas?"

"Yeah."

"I never seen that much money in my life."

"I may have to call you back a couple more times."

"Like goin' to the dealership, you mean?" she asked.

"Yes," I said. "Just like that."

"Okay. I trust you. I wouldn't buy a car from you, but I trust you."

Back in Wentworth's office, I sat down and picked up the legal pad the judge had deposited on the coffee table. I drew a line down the middle and wrote "Bright Star" on one side and "Hazel McEnroe" on the other. Under Hazel's name I wrote "Demand: ꝗ250,000 + medical expenses." Under Bright Star's name I wrote "Counter Offer: ꝗ100,000 total." It wasn't subtle (and it was only partly true as I had left off Brandon's initial lowball offer), but it did reflect the actual negotiation. Now the paper, which would hopefully end up in my messenger bag on my way out, showed we had made a demand and Bright Star had countered.

I crossed out the first demand figure and wrote "Revised Demand: ꝗ200,000 + meds." Then I tore off the page and placed the demand in front of Brandon, where Wentworth could see it.

The judge shrugged when he saw the figure. I could see that he was pleased. No doubt the amounts didn't matter to him. He knew two hundred thousand qoppas was nothing to a company as large as Bright Star Holdings. Right now he just wanted the case to go away.

Brandon, on the other hand, had fallen into negotiation quicksand. He'd fixated on what the claim was actually worth and ignored how much it was worth for it to go away. "Two hundred is ridiculous. What are her meds? Ten, fifteen thousand? The five-times rule—"

"There is no five-times rule," I pointed out. "That's a myth."

"It's a principle," Brandon insisted. "And we've already offered you double what this claim should settle for."

"Really? And how much is your reputation worth, Mr. Schmidt?" I asked. "Because my client's reputation has been dragged through the gutter."

"Well, I can't go that high."

"How do you know?"

"Okay, I won't go that high."

He was taking this personally. Which, yeah, I was sort of enjoying. Brandon Schmidt Jr. wore smug the way some men wore jewelry. It didn't match his assets.

On cue, Judge Wentworth intervened. "Mr. Schmidt, perhaps you should make a call of your own?"

Brandon looked startled and, for just an instant, defiant. Then he stood obediently and headed for the door.

When he was gone, Judge Wentworth said, "I think Brandon is going to be surprised, and you'll probably get your two hundred."

"Really?"

"That video is compelling. Bright Star wants this to go away."

*And so does everyone in the Justice Department,* I thought. *Including you.* "I got that impression too."

The judge flashed a smile that fit his face like a pair of bowling shoes. "Welcome to the big leagues, Ms. Justice."

Brandon re-entered the room, looking like someone had just stolen his golf clubs. "It's too much," he said. "But my client regrets the incident and wants to make amends. We're willing to pay two hundred thousand for a full release."

"Two hundred thousand plus her meds?"

"Two hundred total," Brandon said icily. "Take it or leave it."

I glanced over at Wentworth, wondering how he had known Brandon would accept my second demand. The whole thing had happened so quickly. So easily. Bright Star Holdings had basically just rolled over.

"We'll take it," I said.

Thirty minutes later Brandon had a signed release from Hazel McEnroe, and I had an extra ⋈85,057.12 in my bank account. Hazel McEnroe's medical debts were paid, and she was sitting at home, crying and looking for stuff to buy on the Internet with her settlement money. She'd cleared almost ꒒104,000.

I forwarded the signed release from my digital assistant to Judge Wentworth and Brandon Schmidt Jr., and the judge promised to clear Hazel's record by the end of the week.

That's when I should have thanked them both and shaken their hands and gone back to the office in time to treat Kenji to an expensive lunch and a well-deserved bonus. I could have spent the whole afternoon spinning circles in my office chair and pinching myself.

But somehow, I couldn't do it. I couldn't just walk away.

Because Judge Wentworth had *known* Bright Star would settle. And because Brandon had shrugged off the settlement as if it were nothing more than a wasted morning—which had been no different than the way he'd prosecuted Hazel McEnroe in the first place. He didn't care.

Also, I was sick of playing defense. I wasn't a defense attorney. I was a personal-injury attorney—with a profound sense of personal injury. My job was to point the finger of blame the right direction and call down financial hellfire on wrongdoers.

Starting a public war with Bright Star Holdings would send a signal to whoever was trying to derail my deal with the UN. It would give them the false impression that I wasn't taking Dr. Arounais's new wonder drug seriously. It would tell them I didn't really expect to make any money off my strange "Iperian" client. And that false flag might buy us a couple of weeks or even months.

But most of all, I couldn't just walk away because Judge Wentworth had said to me, *Welcome to the big leagues, Ms. Justice.* And he'd said it as if we were all part of the same legal fantasy, part of the same club. A club that included the faces of those elitist shills who had convicted Hazel—the same people who had arranged for me to be fined six hundred qoppas when I couldn't afford cat food, the same people who had tried to blot my floundering law firm out of existence because they couldn't stand my new name.

At that moment I wasn't angry. I was disgusted. And I couldn't stand the idea of shaking their hands.

*Welcome to the big leagues?*

No, thank you. I was going to burn my club card.

"There is one more thing, Your Honor," I said. "Not about this case. It's something I'd like to bring to your attention so you can be prepared for other cases my firm may be filing in the near future."

That was a stretch. The appellate court wouldn't keep referring these cases back to Wentworth—or any other Coliseum trial bot—when they realized I was sharing Kenji's newfound trove of video evidence with the networks. But I wanted both Wentworth and Brandon to be present when I threw down the gauntlet. Because let's face it, if you can't enjoy moments like these, you aren't really living.

Judge Wentworth sat heavily behind his desk. "All right, let's have it."

"The video evidence in the McEnroe trial has raised serious questions about a pattern of criminal, negligent behavior by Bright Star Holdings and their staff that I believe warrants significant punitive damages."

"What?" Brandon tried to object. "We've signed the paperwork. You can't back out now!"

Judge Wentworth rubbed the back of his neck. "What pattern?"

"When we found the deleted McEnroe recording," I said, "we also discovered a number of other damaging videos as well. Apparently this wasn't the first potato-chip incident Bright Star Holdings tried to bury."

Brandon's eyes widened in horror. I pretended not to be gloating inwardly, but I gladly admit I still keep that memory stashed away in the back of my mind for when I need cheering up.

"Potato-chip in—" Wentworth looked exasperated. "Just how many videos did you find?"

"We're still processing that information."

"Ballpark."

I took a deep breath and reminded myself the Coliseum would have no clue which videos we were working on. Bright Star—or someone from Hinkle, Remmers & Schmidt—would have to follow up on every night-court trial going back thirty years. "Your Honor, there are at least thirty-seven and could be as many as one hundred."

Slowly, Judge Wentworth's eyes shifted away from the pennants until he was staring at me like some lumbering caged animal.

This wasn't a feeling of paranoia. It was a revelation. Something I should have seen all along.

Holding his gaze, I realized this mediation had never been a private matter.

This wasn't Wentworth's office.

And, through his eyes, someone besides Wentworth was staring back at me.

# 11

## RAKE-OFF

Kenji was waiting for me when I arrived at the office the next morning at seven thirty. An unchangeable night owl, he'd never before beaten me to work, and one look at his face told me something was wrong. "What happened?"

He sighed—a noise like a balloon deflating—and leaned against a corner of the desk. "Last night I got a warning notice from the security program guarding my private server. Something got past it and started corrupting the data blocks. It was like"—he waved the Goldy's delivery box he was holding as if it were a visual aid—"like a snake eating its own tail. And I couldn't figure out how the virus had gotten past my firewalls, but I decided once I shut my computer down, I could wipe the master and reboot from my backup array. But the diagnostics—"

"Kenjiro," I interrupted. "I'm a lawyer, not a nerd. No clue what you just said. Also, is that my breakfast?"

He looked at the box, and his eyes widened. "Oh. Yeah. Yeah, I guess it is. Some guy just dropped it off a couple minutes ago. But that was after I turned the lights on. Anyway, that's not the weirdest part. Because the reception desk was still locked—like it always is—to my thumbprint."

"Okay? And?"

Kenji handed me the bagel box and went around the desk. He slid open the top drawer and pointed. "It's gone."

"You ate my bagel!" I pulled out the empty wrapper and held it up as exhibit one. At least the tater tots were still there.

"Your bagel? But you said you were going to respect my allergies."

"Well, yes, when I order something for you. But that was for me."

"How was I supposed to know whose it was?"

"It has my name on it." I pointed to the handwritten black text: "Maxine Justice. M-A-X-I-N-E."

"Yeah, well, that's the name of our business. And I'm an employee, so—are you telling me it wasn't gluten free?"

"Why would I order something gluten free? And my name doesn't say L-L-C after it."

Kenji grabbed his scrubby hair with both hands. "Do you know how frustrating it is to work for a lawyer?"

I popped one of the tater tots into my mouth. Still warm. "Actually, yes. Three years at Stinkle, Hemorrhoids, and Pit taught me a lot about arguing. Plus a bunch of other stuff I'd rather forget."

He returned to the original subject. "It's gone, Max. All of it. Are you hearing me?"

"Kenji, I am all ears and extremely motivated, but no, I do not understand what you're saying."

"The videos I found for the McEnroe trial. They're gone. All of them."

"What—from the server? That secret elephant-burial-grounds thing you were talking about?"

"They were deleted from my own computer. And from my backup system, which isn't connected to the web. And from the flash drive I taped to the bottom of this drawer." He pointed again for emphasis. "The whole drive stick is gone. But nobody knew it was there except you and me!"

Okay, now he had my attention. Someone had not only hacked my computer nerd's firewalls, they had physically entered my fifty-first-floor office and rummaged around beneath his desk. I stared at the open drawer as if someone might still be hiding beneath it. "So how do we get those videos back?"

"We don't."

Actually, we could. Because I still had a backup copy that nobody knew about—not even Kenji. But it wouldn't make sense to explain that now—my office didn't feel like a safe place to talk. "Can't you figure out how to find them again?"

"There's nothing to figure out. Except how someone knew where I keep my backups. Max. MAX!"

I was staring at the wrapper in my hand. Except it wasn't a wrapper. It was a Goldy's napkin smeared with sauce. Someone had written a note on it:

> Kilkenny's Pub 7:00 p.m. corner booth
> Come alone
> G

I looked up at Kenji, who stood there with his hands out as if to say, *NOW do you get it?*

I felt a brief stab of guilt and glanced back down at the napkin. I hadn't told him about warning Wentworth and Brandon that we were going after Bright Star. I knew it would just make him unhappy. Besides, it was too late to change the fact. And now that they'd taken all of the evidence, what else was there for them to do? All I had to do was pretend Bright Star's past was out of reach. When the time was right, I would produce the videos from Counselor Singh's memory and quietly do a little recruitment of as many victims as I could locate.

But there would be time for that later.

Those videos represented either a fortune or a huge waste of time. But if there was nothing incriminating about them, why bother to destroy them?

I may have been foolhardy in telling Wentworth that I had those videos, but the fact that they had disappeared afterward told me something extremely important: Whoever hacked Kenji's computer system was not the same person or group that came after me in Guatemala. Because Vazquez had resent the data on the serum, but nobody seemed to care.

In the case of the Bright Star videos, they were trying to destroy every single copy.

Which meant different motivations. So my brief kidnapping probably had been PharFuture or Star Cross or some other medical corporation looking for Dr. Arounais's wonder-drug formula. And that meant I was probably right about how they were going to try to stop a potential deal with the UN.

"I have any appointments today?"

Kenji seemed a little irritated that I didn't seem more concerned about the theft of the videos, but he checked his terminal. "The Sullivan slip-and-fall at ten thirty. And you need to call the PharmState adjuster about Mrs. Gower after lunch. Also, someone from *The No-Go Zhou Show* called about booking you on the program. I assume that was a prank?"

"Not a prank," I said, surprised to have finally heard back. "Send me the number, and I'll call. Then reschedule Sullivan and push the Gower call to tomorrow."

"So," Kenji said. "Business as usual?"

I held up the box. "I'm gonna need another bagel. Can you call Efram? He knows what I order."

He rolled his eyes, and I retreated to my office.

Inside, I closed the door, kicked off my shoes, and went over to my desk. I'd call Nadia Zhou's assistant after lunch. Meanwhile, I needed to think about who might want to meet anonymously at Kilkenny's.

I dropped the napkin note on my desk and collapsed into my swivel chair. Then I used my terminal to open the window reflectors, so I could take in the morning view, rotating in a half-Wentworth to look out over the city.

My new skyboard ad virtually slapped me in the face, and I laughed out loud. Kenji had changed the photo. Now space B5 was filled with the latest, six-figure-deal version of Maxine Justice in all my digitally enhanced glory.

I confess, I did look grim and cocky, with my arms folded ominously across my jungle fatigues, my hair billowing out in a dark, wispy cloud. The new me posed a stark contrast to the defiant-kid look we'd been promoting these past few weeks. I want you, my new ad said, to make a lot of money.

*Me too, Max,* I thought back to the unyielding demigod in the sky. *Me too.*

I ate the replacement bagel by myself, still perched in my leather swivel chair. I ordered a gluten-free pizza from Monico's, but by the time it arrived, Kenji was already feeling the effects of the non-gluten-free bagel he'd eaten. By way of making amends, I sent him home with the pizza.

In the afternoon, I worked up enough courage to call Nadia Zhou's assistant and book an appearance on the program. If nothing else, Dr. Arounais would see me working hard for his money. But hopefully the interview would be helpful in planting the seeds of hope in the public. To get a deal with the UN, I would need people to believe the world could be healthier.

At six o'clock I headed out the lobby door into a crisp autumn evening, and I arrived at Kilkenny's by a quarter to seven. Someone had taken the corner booth already. A suit coat lay draped over the back, and I could see a glass of water perched on the edge.

I took a deep breath and wove through an obstacle course of dark tables, lit by stained-glass beer lamps, until I could see who waited for me.

"Mr. Gibbons," I said as my heart did a little flip.

Maybe I shouldn't have been surprised. He'd already taken the bait. But would he run with the line?

He wore a sagging bow tie and a white shirt under a sweater vest. "Ms. Justice. Please. Have a seat."

I slid into the booth across from him. "I wasn't certain who the G was. Glad it wasn't—well, someone else." I'd been about to say, *those goons I ran into in Antigua,* but realized that would detour the conversation.

"Sorry if I alarmed you," he said, apparently realizing I'd been nervous. "In my position, I can't be too careful. You have no idea how many sales calls I'm subjected to."

"I've been working a different case. Has me jittery."

"Ah." He reached for the mug of ale he'd already gotten and took a long drink. "Well, Ms. Justice, now you have a bigger case."

A waiter appeared and took my order. Gibbons offered to buy, so I asked for the smoked salmon and an iced tea. "Are you saying you found a way to steer your ship?"

"There's only one way to steer a ship as large as the UN. It has to want to be steered."

"You took the vial. I assume you sent it to San Marino?"

"I did. And the results were—" He looked into his ale before taking another drink. "They were interesting."

"I told you."

"You did indeed."

"So you asked to meet with me because even though you didn't sign the contract, you're going to give me the experimental data anyway, right? In exchange for me not mentioning that you stole a vial of serum from my clients?"

Gibbons flashed me a humorless smile. "No, Ms. Justice, I asked you to meet me because I want to know what your clients are really after. Consolidated Galactic BioProducers has obviously spent billions on producing this new serum. And they've somehow managed to keep it mostly a secret."

"Mostly," I repeated.

"Which has attracted some ugly reactions from the medical industry."

"So I've gathered. Don't believe everything you hear."

"Not a problem for me. However, there are times when the right sort of negative attention adds a certain measure of credibility to a story. Which leads me to ask why you came to the United Nations? And please don't tell me it's because Consolidated wants to make the world a better place."

"They *do* want to make the world a better place. They claim they can provide the serum to every human being on Earth. For the right price."

Gibbons took another drink, his face alternating between bewilderment and amusement. "Every single human." His lips pursed and un-pursed. "Impossible."

"Maybe. But they're so confident they can do it, they're willing to void the agreement if every last human on the planet isn't cured of, and I quote, 'every natural flaw.'"

"Your clients are lunatics," Gibbons said.

*Yup. That's what I keep saying too. But he's apparently a genius scientist, so does it matter?*

"Maybe," I said. "But their serum works."

He took another drink. "Okay, I'll bite. I'm not saying I believe this, mind you. But since we're sitting here talking, and dinner hasn't arrived yet, exactly how much money do they want in exchange for providing insta-health to the entire planet?"

"They don't want money."

Gibbons's smile was sardonic. "Now you're just toying with me."

My iced tea arrived, and I swirled the ice with a long spoon until the waiter went away. "My clients want gold."

"Gold. Money. Same thing."

"Not to Consolidated Galactic BioProducers. They see gold as an element. Specifically, what they want—what they demand—is refined gold. My clients are asking for a significant percentage of the combined stockpiles from the UN's member nations."

For just a minute Gibbons stared at me, ale mug halfway to his lips. Then he sat back and laughed. "Ms. Justice, this cannot be real. They want actual *gold*?"

I shrugged. "Our governments don't use it for currency anymore. At the same time, Consolidated has an urgent need for gold as an electro-conductor. They're working on other technology that will make this health serum look like the steam engine by comparison."

"Refined gold? Seriously?"

"Seriously."

He finally got around to draining the last of his ale. "And what exactly is a significant percentage? How much are we talking?"

Somewhere a microphone screeched, and the evening's entertainment, a folksy guitarist wearing a beat-up slouch hat, introduced himself and began to strum.

"No," I said. "I don't think so."

"You don't think so?" Gibbons looked bemused, but the expression was too forced, and I could tell he wasn't here on a whim. "C'mon, Maxine, we're just two friends talking."

I didn't mind him calling me Maxine, but the shift to a more informal tone struck me as forced. "Friends?"

"Friends of a friend, then."

"I'm a lawyer, Mr. Gibbons. The friend of my friend is my enemy."

He smirked, then saw that I wasn't joking. "What do you mean?"

"I mean you aren't really committed. You're treating this like it's some kind of joke. But you know it's real." I locked onto his eyes so he'd understand what I wasn't saying. "Mr. Gibbons, you know it's real."

For a moment I thought I saw his eyes start to swim.

"You knew about Adam," he said. "That's why you came to me. You knew I'd take one of those vials."

"I figured you'd do what any father would. And I haven't reported the disappearance to anyone. Even my clients."

He looked down into his empty mug. "I only gave him what it said on the bottle. One dose, diluted to the point of absurdity. The rest went to Puolakka. I took it myself."

"How is he doing?"

"Mayo Clinic says—"

I folded my hands on the table, waiting, but he didn't finish the sentence. "They say your son's lymphoma has completely disappeared."

It wasn't a question.

Gibbons nodded. When he regained control, he cleared his throat and said, "If I wasn't taking this seriously, I wouldn't be here. How much gold do your clients want?"

It was the question I'd been angling for. The one I'd needed to set up with precisely the emotions Gibbons was feeling now—a mixture of gratitude and disbelief and awe, but each of these overshadowed by a feeling of real hope.

Hope that the world could be a better place. That cancer and deformities and genetic diseases of every kind could be cured forever. Would be cured forever.

And it wouldn't cost a penny.

Because pennies were made of copper.

This was the question. *How much gold?* And for a moment, I wasn't sure how to answer it.

My client wanted 30 percent of Earth's refined gold reserve. But was that all he could get?

I was an attorney. I represented my client's professional interests. But I also represented my own interests. And my contract with Dr. Arounais stated that anything over 30 percent would be subject to a negotiator's fee, a "rake-off" of 5 percent of the overage.

If I negotiated an additional 1 or 2 percent, I would become, in theory, the single wealthiest person on the planet. Of course, I'd never see that money. This sort of deal would be undermined and disputed at every point. Payments would be refused, or at least delayed indefinitely.

But getting that money wasn't the point.

Once signed, I could leverage this contract into so much publicity that I'd have clients lined up well past my retirement. I'd be able to go after bullies like Bright Star Holdings. I could make sure my mom was taken care of and start a scholarship for law school students. I could buy a luxury catamaran and move to the Caribbean.

More importantly, securing this deal with the UN would mean Dr. Arounais's serum would get real distribution around the world—even without his fantasy of a rain-based delivery system. It may not make it to every nook and cranny. But it would go somewhere. It had already gone to Antigua and San Marino—while still in the testing stage. Once a deal was signed, lots of people would get healthier. That had to count for something.

I needed to ask for more than just 1 or 2 percent over; I needed wiggle room. Whatever I asked for, they would counter with a lower number, and I would counter their counter. That's how negotiations worked. I'd just seen it work with Judge Wentworth and Bright Star Holdings.

And at some point, for the sake of the human race, Gibbons and I absolutely had to land on 30 percent of Earth's refined gold reserves.

"Ms. Justice," Gibbons asked again, his voice suddenly thick with formality. "How much gold does your client want?"

I took a deep breath. "Thirty-five percent."

He didn't even flinch. "I figured it would be a big number. We'll need the secretary-general to sign off on this. But I don't think that will be a problem."

I blinked as a fluttering sensation rose from my belly. "Just like that?"

Gibbons nodded. "I'll meet with him when we're done here. Of course, he'll want a *quid pro quo*."

Suddenly the pieces of the puzzle clicked, and I understood what I was dealing with. I saw why Dr. Arounais had wanted me to pursue a deal with the United Nations in the first place. Gibbons was looking at this contract the way he saw every deal involving the UN—through the eyes of a middleman.

Yes, good things would happen. Food would be distributed. Books would be read. Wars would be ended. And along the way, the guys in the teal hats would take a little something off the top for their efforts.

What? We had a new way to make everybody healthy? And it was going to cost a fortune?

Excellent! The UN would take just a small slice of that pie as they handed it over—to make sure the crust was baked to perfection.

And somewhere down the road, that gold would change hands again. And again. And again. And each time, the UN would be there to take its cut.

"What sort of *quid* will he want?"

"Well," Gibbons said, steepling his fingers to his chin. "Someone will have to ensure the distribution, correct?"

"My client says he can handle that."

Gibbons smiled as if at some private joke. Had he heard about Dr. Arounais's plan to make it rain across the globe? "Of course. Still. Someone will have to ensure that the distribution takes place. For a small fee. Say—three percent of the payment?"

So the UN would take about 1 percent of Earth's gold reserves, and Dr. Arounais would take 33.75 percent. And I'd get that remaining quarter of a percentage point.

On paper, anyway.

And here I'd expected a long, protracted negotiation.

But this wasn't a negotiation. It was standard operating procedure. I had simply stumbled onto a money-making machine that had been printing its own currency long before I came along.

Or I'd been sent to this particular machine.

With this particular deal.

And now I was asking myself, *Why me?*

And also, *How much would my cut of Earth's refined gold be worth?*

I pulled out my digital assistant. "I have the contract on my device."

"Finally!" Digie said. "You know, I'm startin' to get the idea you only take me out when you want something from me."

I shoved my mom's phone back into my messenger bag with an apologetic smile and retrieved the one Dr. Arounais had given me.

Pulled up the contract, filled in the appropriate figures, and flicked it over to Gibbons.

He scanned his device's screen and nodded. Then he drew a hundred-qoppa note from his wallet and placed it on the table before sliding out. "I'll take this to the secretary-general."

"You're not going to eat dinner first?"

"Nikita Crusat is a very busy man. He doesn't like to be kept waiting. Enjoy your salmon, Ms. Justice. This won't take long." He tugged on his suit coat and seemed about to leave. Then, almost as an afterthought, he said, "You know, I still owe you."

The fish came a few minutes later, drowning in butter.

Between bites I listened to the guitarist wheeze his way through a dozen or so Australian tunes I barely recognized.

I was just about to leave when my device dinged.

Gibbons had already sent me the contract, signed by himself and Secretary-General Crusat, and notarized with a UN security stamp.

I stared at the screen as a feeling of numbness crept through my limbs. It took me almost twenty minutes to verify that no details had been changed and to confirm the authenticity of the signatures. And even then, I couldn't believe it was real.

This deal had moved way, way faster than I'd expected it to. Faster than should have been possible.

This deal wasn't supposed to get this far.

Was it?

I pulled up Dr. Arounais's number and attached the contract, then stared at the screen with my thumb hovering over the send button.

For a moment I almost deleted it. Then I heard Dr. Vazquez's voice in the back of my mind, translating the words of Mr. Santos: *He offers his thanks. And he begs you to please make sure this miracle is given to others.*

I sent the signed contract and waited breathlessly for the RECEIVED icon.

A moment later my phone rang.

"This is Maxine."

"Ms. Justice," Dr. Arounais said. "You are remarkably efficient. Well done."

"Thank you."

"I understand you are meeting with someone from your popular media soon. A woman named Zoo?"

"Ah. Yes. Nadia Zhou. Rhymes with show. I thought we could put pressure on the UN by telling people what your serum is capable of. But now it seems we don't need to."

"Ahem." He made a throat-clearing sound that carried a distinct tone of correction. "I think you should keep your appointment on her program."

"You do?"

"Pressure may still be needed in order to secure payment of the gold."

It made sense. But going on the Nadia Zhou program was a risk. "Why would Nadia Zhou want to see the world's governments fork over a third of their refined gold?"

"To join the Galactic Body General," Dr. Arounais said, "and enter a new era of cosmic knowledge."

I held my breath, listening to the fading chords of the performer linger amidst scattered applause. He wanted me to tell the world to pay its debts so we could join some club for extraterrestrials? Nadia would absolutely destroy me! "I'm not sure that's a good idea."

"Several weeks ago, you asked why we need refined gold and not money. I am prepared to tell you now that the contract is signed."

"Okay," I managed. "Sure. Great. What are you going to use that gold for?"

"I hear your disbelief, Counselor. But I am not offended. Just wait. You will see. You will understand when the rains come."

"I believe you, Dr. Arounais," I lied. "I'm just feeling a little . . . overwhelmed."

"Ah. Of course." He gave a long, exaggerated sigh and said, "Very well. The Iperian Consortium has been granted the privilege of sponsoring your species. Think of us as big brothers sent to welcome you to a larger fellowship of sentient beings. The only requirement for inclusion is that you agree to our charter and participate in our representative governance. For that you must demonstrate the ability to master space."

I rubbed my forehead. "We need spaceships?"

"Advanced spaceships, capable of traversing subspace, which is to say, traveling faster than photons. In your vernacular, we need your gold to gift you the technology for faster-than-light travel."

I knew what a warp drive was. And I knew it belonged in fiction, not in the real world. "I'm not sure how that will go over with Nadia Zhou's audience. Most of them aren't thinking about how cool it would be to see black holes. They're thinking about how to pay their mortgage."

"That is shortsighted."

"Maybe," I said. "But it's also human."

He said nothing for a moment. When he spoke, his voice sounded strained. "Once a member of the Galactic Body General, the human species will have access to our collective knowledge. Unfathomable advances in every area—even the secret of life itself. Life that never ends. But we can only help you if you are willing to help yourselves."

*Life that never ends?* For a moment I thought of my dad in his last weeks. I wondered what he would think of all this. "This is what you want me to tell the world when I appear on *The No-Go Zhou Show*? That if we make our payment, you'll hand us the keys to the universe?"

"We can only make the offer," Dr. Arounais said. "The rest is up to you. History is earned, Ms. Justice."

He hung up.

A moment later I slid out of the booth and headed for the tube platform, got off under the Coliseum, and took a lift to the ground floor, then scanned my thumb into the pad at the door to the admin building.

Counselor Singh's office door was closed, but I didn't think he'd mind seeing me, so long as he didn't already have a client.

He opened the door wearing a set of red-and-white pajamas, each red spot a broken heart. "Max!"

"I'm sorry, I figured you'd be working."

He motioned for me to come in. "I am working. Can I get you anything?"

"No, thanks," I said. "I'm barging in without an appointment. Are you sure you weren't asleep?"

He closed the office door as I slid into my usual chair. "TheraPods don't sleep, Max."

"So what do you do at night? Wait. Never mind. That's private. Sorry, I'm a little flustered."

"It's fine," he said, sitting down. "I read at night. Or meditate. In the summer I sometimes go for a swim. Now, what has you so distressed?"

I pulled out my device. "I need you to store this. A message I received. An attachment, actually. A contract with the UN."

"All right. Accept the terms."

A long consent form appeared on my phone's screen. I clicked the button under the minuscule print. "Done."

"Wow," he said. "That is impressive. You are either about to be a very wealthy young woman or—"

"A laughing stock?"

He tapped the edge of his desk, and the lights dimmed. The wall screen changed to a loading image from *Dystropolis 2: Urbane Jungle*. "I was going to say 'very disappointed.' Why should you be humiliated by this deal?"

"Dr. Arounais wants me to keep my appointment with Nadia Zhou."

"I see. Can we talk about it while I shoot robots?"

He was trying to relax me.

It worked. For the next half hour, I explained everything that had happened since our last meeting. When he hit level thirty-three, my work phone sounded again, and opening it was like waking from a pleasant dream, as if I'd been in some altered plane of existence, and only the notification *puh-ching* of a cash register could bring me back.

Arounais: History is earned, Ms. Justice.
Suggest you view the sky.

I stared at my phone as Singh paused the video game. My hand was shaking. A cold, dry feeling climbed into my throat and stuck there. Had I been wrong—really wrong—about Dr. Arounais all this time? "Can we get to the roof?"

"Sure. I'll put on my slippers."

Singh led me up the staircase to the fifth floor and out a maintenance door to the admin building's gravel roof. To the east, the inverted dome of the Coliseum spread out a half block away like a giant salad bowl clearing the space of skyscrapers and giving us a decent, if imperfect, view of the night sky over the harbor. We'd have had better seats up in my office in the Perennial, but things were changing so quickly we hadn't had time to get there.

Storm clouds bubbled on the horizon, rising from the sea like one of the ancient gods released from its chains.

Within that wall of vapor, lightning sparked, silently illuminating the black mist in a chain of flashbulb explosions. At the edge, moving toward us over the skyline of downtown York, three meteors streaked in a zig-zag pattern, claws tearing through black canvas.

Maybe they were airplanes or rocket ships or something else. For all I knew they were neither comets nor machines. Whatever they were, they left shimmering contrails of blue light in their wake—and the storm clouds followed.

"God of heaven," I said as the sky ripped open directly above us.

Head craned, Counselor Singh folded his arms. "Let's hope so."

A moment later it started to rain.

# 12

## THE NO-GO ZHOU SHOW

York City didn't see the sun again for fifteen days. Its rain sewers gushed with excess runoff, the Hudson climbed its banks, and every car and sidewalk glistened under a dripping patina. When it wasn't raining, clouds blanketed the sky in a shallow dome, descending to earth in a daily mist that saturated everything. Even my swanky new office hung heavy with humidity. I felt I could squeeze moisture from the air with my fingers.

This happened everywhere. Forecasters around the world highlighted hundreds of similar weather systems, each showcasing the same Milky Way structure. Storms pinwheeled across digital maps of the globe like tumbleweeds, leaving nearly everything in their wake soggy.

Fortunately, there was no real flooding. And even though the highly, highly unusual storm fronts got a lot of attention during those initial news cycles, it took weeks for people to wake up to humanity's new reality: the Iperian serum actually worked.

As Dr. Arounais had put it, "the blind saw, the lame walked, the allergic stopped their sneezing."

Some of them anyway.

Those blinded by accident did not have their vision restored. People with broken bones didn't suddenly get well. But anyone born with a natural defect, such as a mutation or allergy, woke up one morning to a genetically altered, if familiar, body. In extreme cases, like those of Mr. Santos down in Guatemala, the change was dramatic and virtually miraculous. In other cases, no one even noticed.

Still, the serum had worked its magic. And all across the world, feel-good news stories began to bubble up about the child on life support who had gotten out of bed and left the hospital cured, the aging parent who had regained her memory, or the heart surgery that had been canceled after tests confirmed it was no longer needed.

Along with these stories—no less common but considerably nastier— were the complaints from experts in the medical industry that whole segments of their profession were experiencing a soft recession. *The York City Tribune* ran a series called "Where Have All the Patients Gone?"

Myra Dade's e-newsletter even covered the alarming negative trend from the bar association's perspective—a trend I'd seen coming long before Mr. Frawley, one of my new clients, called me distraught about the problem keeping him up at night.

I took the call in my office, feet on my desk, watching rain fall in sheets over the harbor. At ninety years old, Frank Frawley was a practiced hand at the slip-and-fall business. He'd collapsed on practically every doorway, sidewalk, and staircase in Clinton Hill, and somehow always managed to herniate a disc when he did. "What can I do for you, Mr. Frawley?"

"You can tell me what's going on, is what," Frawley said. An eight-decade chain smoker, Frawley's voice made inhuman noises when he talked. It sounded as if his vocal cords were sawing themselves in half with a rusty chain.

"What do you mean?"

"This is between us, right?"

"That's right, attorney-client privilege."

"And no one's listening in?"

I couldn't guarantee my phone wasn't bugged. I mean, my office was apparently less secure than a twenty-qoppa bill in Central Park. Still, I doubted anyone would care about Frawley's totally not-fraudulent-insurance-claims history. "We're good. What do you need, Mr. Frawley?"

"Well, ever since that weird UFO thing, my back feels great!"

"It feels . . . great? Why is that a problem?"

"Yes, great. And that has me worried. Can't sleep at night thinking about it. Understand?"

"You can't sleep at night because your back feels great?"

"It feels great!" he said miserably. "No sign of spondylitis. And how's that goin' to affect my claim down at Bonnet's Super?"

"Ah," I said. "You think your sudden absence of pain might lower the value of your claim. But the medical—"

"Aren't you listening? I said I couldn't sleep at night. Seems to me the claim should be worth more. How's a man to make a living if he can just feel better all sudden like?"

"Tell you what," I said, scribbling a quick note on a blank legal pad. I really should have considered this particular angle myself. Increasing the medical expenses of Frawley's back injury would only drive the settlement higher. "Maybe you should see a sleep specialist."

"Advice of counsel?"

"From what you've told me, it couldn't hurt."

There was a long pause. When he spoke again, he seemed genuinely puzzled. "Maybe not. On the other hand, what if it helps? Where am I then?"

He had another good point. Probably the old man was a secret genius in addition to being healthy as a mule. "Well, in that case, Mr. Frawley, I'd say it's time to move on. We'll still work out a settlement with Bonnet's insurance carrier. But maybe you should take your business somewhere else. Maybe the bodega on Fitzpenny Avenue. Just be careful going in; last time I was there, I noticed the doorjamb was loose. A person could trip on that pretty easily."

"I'm ninety years old, young lady. I'm not sure I can keep this up. Used to be when the world turned upside down you could at least pick up its loose change."

"Have a nice day, Mr. Frawley."

I hung up and wandered back into the reception area for a midmorning bite. Kenji had bought a dozen glazed donuts from Kramer's Krusties, and I figured he could spare one. But when I opened the lid—

"Seriously?" I said, picking up the thin paper liner from the empty box. "You ate all twelve?"

"Thirteen, actually, counting this one." He held up the last donut and took a bite, then closed his eyes. "Mmmm. Haven't been able to eat donuts since fifth grade. These are amaaaazing."

I couldn't blame him. "Is the surprise ready?"

The *surprise* referred to our little side project. Just in case my appearance on Nadia Zhou's program went badly, I hoped to at least capitalize on the publicity. Even if people reacted poorly to the UN deal, they'd still be seeing my name. What better time to announce that we still had copies of the lost Bright Star videos and start trolling for victims? We could probably round up a dozen or so clients in twenty-four hours.

Kenji took another bite. "Mm-hmm," he said with his mouth full. "We've got ads hitting all twelve sites, starting as soon as your interview ends. Keywords are ready. Sample videos. I even removed the metadata so my preloads shouldn't get flagged by any software Bright Star has out there looking for fragments. What about you? Are you sure you want to be interviewed by Nadia Zhou? Her show isn't exactly *Fifty Minutes*."

"Her program is perfect," I said vaguely. Truth was, I had no interest in appearing in front of so many people, and my stomach had felt like a ball of lead all morning. But Dr. Arounais was insistent: we had to put pressure on the UN to pay what it owed. And *The No-Go Zhou Show* was a perfect venue for making my case to the public. Meaning, to the common, ordinary non-elitist public. The sorts of people who watched *Humongous Wrestling* and *RASCAR Racing* and *Night Court: Coliseum*.

Speaking of which, I'd never have a better opportunity to remind the villains from Bright Star Holdings that their crimes weren't going to just go away.

"She's a back-stabbing carnival barker," Kenji said ominously. "It'll be like spooning a porcupine."

"People will see it, yes?"

He shrugged. "Oh, they'll see it."

"That's all that matters," I said doubtfully. Donut-less, I headed back to my office, Kenji's warning echoing in my ears. I'd been blindsided before.

I made up my mind not to let that happen tonight. No matter how hard she pushed, I would stay on message. Nadia Zhou would want me to talk about Dr. Arounais's miracle serum and whether it was true the United Nations had developed a worldwide proactive vaccination program against genetic deformities. I would have to answer those questions in a way that put pressure on the world to honor its pledge.

But my biggest dilemma was figuring out how much of Dr. Arounais's promise to divulge. If I blurted out all that stuff about a "Galactic Body General" and "cosmic knowledge," Nadia Zhou would tear me to pieces, serum or no serum. So I'd have to be subtle. I'd have to play to the audience. And I'd only have twenty minutes of air time to do it.

I spent the rest of the morning and all of the lunch hour brushing up on my notes concerning the UN contract. What was confidential versus what had been released either by the UN or on the website of Consolidated Galactic BioProducers.

At 4:00 p.m. I rode the elevator down to the platform and caught a tube to the broadcast district. Two escalators and a short walk in the shadow of the network skyscrapers, and I was inside the lobby of the Republic Broadcasting System's downtown York office.

An intern led me through a maze of elevators and hallways to a door marked "Greenroom D-7." She pushed open the door and waved to the plush seats and kitchenette counter. "Make yourself at home, Ms. Justice. There's drinks in the mini-fridge. Pastries, fruit, and protein bars on the counter. Someone from makeup will be along shortly, then Nadia will come talk to you for show prep. Meanwhile, you can watch the studio D feed on that monitor."

I'd wondered why they wanted me there two and a half hours early. I was dressed in my blood-red suit—the one we planned to unveil in our next skyboard ad—but makeup? I mean, you don't slap a bumper sticker on *Starry Nights*.

But television was their business, not mine, and out of the three recordings of *The No-Go Zhou Show* I'd watched, none of the guests looked like the makeup department had turned them into Frankenstein's monster.

So when the stylist and skin professionals—both no-nonsense types— led me to a barber chair in front of a lighted mirror, I sat down and kept my mouth shut.

I'd never seen two people frown so much while looking at my face and avoiding my eyes.

"I think the cheeks, yeah?" said the blonde.

"Yeah," the brunette countered. "But I'll have to find some way to make the bangs work."

"Uh-huh." The blonde finally looked into my eyes, and I'd have sworn she might have been a surgeon about to perform a triple bypass. "Don't worry, honey. You're in good hands."

"Margie's the best," the stylist said.

An hour later I was back in the greenroom, wondering if I could eat a chocolate chip cookie without damaging whatever substance had hardened my face into depleted uranium. My cheeks were convinced that any radical movement—a smile, for instance—would crack the outer crust and reveal something red and hellish under the surface. Fortunately, I didn't feel like smiling. Probably couldn't have even if I'd tried.

"MaxEEEEN!" a voice said in a tone of untempered joy.

I looked up to see Nadia Zhou striding toward me as if she'd just learned I was going to give her a kidney.

Then again, I realized, maybe that was the way she saw it.

I stood and accepted her outstretched hand. "Ms. Zhou."

Nadia Zhou was tall and thin and wearing her usual miniskirt, low-cut satin top, and half-sleeved blazer. I could see the makeup crew had already assaulted her face with enough paint to mark an airstrip. Her eyes were highlighted in bands of gold, like expensive quotation marks framing her brow. Somehow she found a way to smile through all of that facial plaster, but her expression had all the warmth of barbed wire. "Please. Call me Nadia. I'm so delighted you accepted my invitation. I bet you've been getting lots of calls from other networks."

"A few," I admitted. "But I wanted to tell the whole story, and the other programs only offered three-minute headliners."

She sighed and rolled her eyes. "Probably ask you the same nothing questions anyone could answer for themselves with a Goggle search."

"Why I don't watch network news."

"Why nobody does." She motioned for me to sit and perched herself on the edge of the chair next to mine. "Listen, Max. Tonight I'm giving you the first half of my program. Top slot for the world's top story. We'll have four interview segments and three commercial breaks, but be forewarned, the last segment is sixty seconds, half of which will be my intro to the second feature. So we'll only have time for one closing thought."

"All right."

"I'm going to walk you through your story with a series of questions. Don't be nervous; just answer honestly."

"You can trust me," I said. "I'm a lawyer."

She extended a pretend laugh, then pointed at the monitor, which was running a dinner-hour game show I recognized from conversations with my mom. It was called *Luck of the Draw*, and for a moment, I wondered how humanity had ever reached apex-predator status. Lack of competition, probably. "My audience expects a certain amount of pushback," Nadia said. "From me, I mean. So don't be flustered if I have to ask you some hard questions."

"Of course," I said. "But as I told you over the phone, I won't be able to give direct answers to anything that violates client confidentiality."

She flashed an insincere smile and nodded. "Of course, of course. I just want to make sure we're on the same page before we begin. We'll start with a recap of the UN's genetic healing program, then I'll ask how you became involved and let you tell your story. I think the audience will love hearing about your remarkable rise to the fifty-first floor of the Perennial."

Put that way it sounded way more impressive than it felt, but I wasn't about to admit that to her. "Well, it wasn't exactly easy." Actually, the rise part had been pretty easy; all I'd done was pick up five thousand qoppas from a bar and get into a limousine. It was the miserable years preceding that moment which hadn't been easy.

Nadia Zhou clasped her hands in exaggerated anticipation. "That is what makes it a great story."

"I suppose so."

"After the first break, I'll ask you about your clients, the bioengineering firm who created this wonder drug. And in the third segment, I'll give you some time to talk about where you see the future of medicine going. As a personal-injury attorney, I'm sure you have some thoughts about that little conundrum."

"Actually, I—"

She patted my knee. "Not yet, Maxine. Save it for the show. I can smell this story, and I don't want any of your passion leaking out in the greenroom." She stood and straightened her skintight miniskirt. "Help yourself to the fridge. Ladies' room is through the door on the left. Allie, my assistant producer, will be in to collect you for the studio in about forty minutes. Any questions?"

"I—"

"Okay, I'll see you on set. You're going to be great!"

"Wanted to thank you," I said to the closing door. "You know, for having me on."

A lady in pearls and a white dress three shades too bright jumped and screamed on the monitor overhead; Lady Luck was showing on the "draw card," as *Luck of the Draw*'s bouncy theme song triggered a shower of digital fireworks at the edge of the screen.

A moment later an aging man in a tan suit hobbled in with a cane and arranged himself in a seated position next to me before propping open a paperback novel.

"You must be Nadia's second guest," I said, hoping for a distracting conversation.

He gave a brief nod, not looking up from his novel.

I had no idea what tonight's number-two story was about and wondered if the book was just a way to calm his nerves; I never saw him turn the page.

We sat in a gameshow-infused semi-silence made nearly unbearable by the wall clock ticking above our seats. Who used clocks that ticked anymore? I would have gambled all of my Hazel McEnroe settlement money that Nadia put the clock there to make her guests nervous.

It worked.

By six forty-five I was so ready to move that I nearly exploded out of the seat when the door opened.

"Maxine Just—"

"That would be me," I said, crossing the room before Allie made it all the way inside.

"Oh," she said. "Okay, well, we're ready to get you on set. Unless you need a potty break first?"

"No need," I said. "Lead the way."

We threaded our way through a series of hallways and at last through a heavy commercial door into a small theater. The stage area was a tiny half moon, maybe fifteen feet across, and equipped with a couple of padded seats, a coffee table, and a potted plant. The brick backdrop highlighted a neon sign that said, *The No-Go Zhou Show!*

Around the stage were a hundred or so theater seats on raised tiers, each one occupied. A hundred heads turned as I entered the side door and took in the black-curtain walls, the cameras on their massive tripods, and the sprawling sound board. A monitor overhead flashed APPLAUSE, and the crowd obliged.

I gave them a little wave and sat in an oversized club chair with Guest printed on the seat cushion. The chair was angled to give me a view of Nadia, the crowd, and a large production monitor on the opposite wall.

At six fifty, Nadia stood and went to the front of the stage to welcome the audience. She was warm, witty, and self-deprecating, and as I watched, I couldn't decide whether I was seeing the real Nadia or just another façade. Either way, the performance made my stomach churn and my armpits sweat like I was back in seventh-grade gym class. This wasn't the Night Court Channel. This was prime time on a premier network.

And what exactly had I agreed to? *Galactic Body General? Unfathomable advances? Life that never ends?* Under the blinding lights of the stage, all of that now just seemed absurd.

But then, I reminded myself, so had Dr. Arounais's wonder drug.

Nadia's warm-up act was timed to perfection, and she took her seat as the production monitors flashed a thirty-second warning.

"Deep breaths, hon," she said as if preparing me for an execution. "This'll be over before you know it."

The lights over the audience dimmed. The spotlights scorching us from their corner mounts flared brighter and hotter. Offstage, Allie counted down from ten on uplifted fingers.

Nadia looked down, as if studying her notes on the coffee table before us, but I could see it was part of the act, a way to work network viewers.

*I shouldn't be here,* I thought. *This was stupid so stupid! Why did I do this to myself? I can't get out of this; it's too late—*

The red lights on the cameras blinked to green.

# 13

## GREED

Nadia glanced up, smiled, and folded her hands in her lap. "All over the world people are talking about unusual storm formations and the sudden disappearance of genetic diseases. The official story we're being fed by our governments is that this is the work of a secret program implemented by the United Nations. But tonight we'll hear from Maxine Justice—a personal-injury lawyer—who claims this medical miracle was produced by her client, Consolidated Galactic BioProducers, in a bid to make planet Earth a better place for us all. But my question is, at what cost? I'm Nadia Zhou, separating fact from fiction on the only news program that digs deep enough to uncover the real dirt. Welcome to *The No-Go Zhou Show.*"

The production monitors lit up with APPLAUSE cues.

When the sound died away, Nadia turned to me and said, "Many in our studio audience know who you are from your skyboard over the harbor. In the last three months you've experienced something of a meteoric rise. In fact, your new office is on the fifty-first floor of the Perennial Building across from the UN. Some of the most expensive real estate in the world." She crossed her legs and rested her left arm on the back of her chair as if plying information from an old friend over coffee. "So what happened? Tell me something juicy."

For just a moment I was tempted to skip the juicy stuff and cut right to meeting Dr. Arounais. I wasn't sure it was a great idea to admit I'd basically failed my first couple of years as a lawyer, working for myself. But looking at the crowd, I saw that I'd never get anywhere with them if I came off as some golden-eyed wunderkind. They needed to know I was one of them.

"I got fired," I said.

Nadia raised one eyebrow but didn't flinch. "Ouch."

"So naturally I decided to start my own firm. In the most over-lawyered city in the world."

"All you had was a dream." Nadia smiled as if she'd heard the story a thousand times.

"More like a conviction. I saw a lot of lawyers trying to make money, but not many were really looking out for people like me. It's why I went all in and changed my name to Maxine Justice. Because being an attorney isn't just a job for me. It's a calling."

"Some might say that makes all the difference." She was giving me softball questions for now. Probably would do that for the first segment before turning up the heat—if past interviews were any indication.

"I pretty much starved the first couple years. Eventually I was so desperate I took a shift working night court under the Coliseum."

"My staff thinks that was the best episode ever!" Nadia gushed.

"I don't know about that," I said. "I mean, I got slapped with a six-hundred-qoppa fine. Afterward I couldn't pay my clerk his back pay. So I lost my only employee."

"That's when someone from Consolidated Galactic BioProducers came to see you?"

"At my lowest point, yes."

"And what did he hire you to do?"

"He asked me to negotiate a contract with the UN. Said he had a way to make the world healthy."

"And you collected your first big paycheck." She was getting ahead of me, probably worried about the time.

"Actually, I told him he had the wrong lawyer."

"You're kidding."

She wore a look of disbelief, and I couldn't tell if it was genuine or rehearsed. "Well, he's eccentric. At first I thought he was crazy. Figured he needed a psychiatrist more than a lawyer."

"You really turned him down?"

"At first."

"What changed your mind?"

"I got evicted," I said, laughing nervously as I looked out over the crowd and saw that they weren't really buying my true-life sob story. "So, no food, no place to sleep, no clients. I finally decided eccentric wealthy people deserved a lawyer too."

That got a stingy laugh from the crowd, probably because some of them could relate, even if they didn't want to. I'd started out as the enemy—one of the elites who had made it big and was carefully feeding them a manicured story. They didn't want to cozy up to me if Nadia was just going to tear me apart in the next segment.

But who hadn't lost a job or been forced to work at something they hated?

"And that gave you the resources you needed to re-establish your firm?"

"Correct," I said, skipping over the part about being handed the keys to a swanky, new high-rise office across from the UN. We were on TV, not in a courtroom. "But what really intrigued me was digging into the contract my client wanted to offer the world. He challenged me to find out whether his serum actually worked or not. And I'll be honest—I didn't believe it at first. It just sounded too good to be true."

Nadia knew what was coming. Her gaze shifted to Allie in a silent signal to be ready. "And what changed your mind?"

I took a deep breath. "Experimental trials. When you have an Oxford-trained scientist telling you he's ready to stake his reputation on the results—that Consolidated's serum is the greatest medical breakthrough in his lifetime—you listen."

She nodded. "We called your expert, Dr. Vazquez, owner of Sunrise Labs in Guatemala. I'll be honest, Maxine, I was pretty skeptical at first too. But Dr. Vazquez sent us some of the same lab data he showed you."

This surprised me. "Oh?"

The production monitors blinked blue and started counting down from five. Nadia turned her shoulders slightly and rested both hands on her knees. "We have a video from the lab where those trials took place. Let's hear from a man in Guatemala whose life seems to have been transformed."

*Seems to have been?*

Her wording shouldn't have surprised me. I'd known what I was in for when I agreed to appear on Nadia's program. But this was the snuggling section, and if she was planting doubt here, what was she planning for the last segment?

The monitors flickered from blue to black, and grainy footage of Mr. Santos appeared around the stage. He stood in a small exam room and began removing his shirt one-handed.

The audience gasped when they saw his disfigured arm and watched him rolling the shirt awkwardly down the shoulder and over his wrist.

On screen, Santos turned in a circle. Dr. Vazquez said something to him in Spanish, and Santos wriggled his left shoulder as if trying to move his arm. A moment later he shrugged, and the video froze as Nadia spoke.

"That was taken one day before he was given his first and only injection of the serum. This next video was allegedly taken ten days later."

The monitors flickered again, and Santos was standing there with an apparently normal left arm, wriggling his fingers and saying *"Gracias! Gracias!"*

A wordless ripple surged through the audience. Couples whispered to each other. Wide-eyed skeptics craned to catch some sign of deception.

The video ended, and Nadia held out both hands. "Our technical crew has examined this footage and assures me it has not been tampered with or generated by computer imaging. In other words, those stories you've heard from your friends and family may be real. Over the past two weeks, this program has consulted medical experts who confirm that something may have altered the genetic makeup of people with deformities and other mutations. The question for Ms. Justice is, at what cost?" She paused to look at me as if sizing me up, then held out her hand to the audience, thumb extended to the side like Caesar presiding over the gladiators. "So what do you think? Go? Or no-go?"

The audience didn't have to think about it; this was only the first segment. "Go!"

Nadia smiled and flicked her wrist to give the world her trademark thumbs-up.

The camera lights switched to red. The production monitors all displayed COMMERCIAL BREAK.

"Good job," Nadia said. "Just sit tight for a minute. And drink some water."

An assistant joined us on the set with a couple of bottled waters. I sucked down half the bottle and handed it back to be carried off.

What seemed to be three seconds later, the monitors started their countdown, and Nadia arranged herself on the chair, hands folded in her lap and an imperious, tight-lipped smirk chiseled across both cheeks.

When the camera lights switched to green, Nadia barely hesitated. "Some call it a medical miracle. A worldwide epidemic . . . of genetic healing. My guest tonight represents Consolidated Galactic BioProducers, a research firm that wants credit—and money—for our good fortune."

On the production monitor, I could see the camera pulling back to reveal my look of surprise. I forced a smile and shot a look of friendly acquiescence to the audience that would tell them I understood how this game was played. Nadia was just being Nadia, and we all knew what that meant.

"Maxine Justice," she continued, "formerly known as Eufemia Kolpak, recently experienced a dramatic infusion of cash and is now asking for thirty-five percent of the world's refined gold in payment for the serum she says originated with her client." Nadia turned toward me. "Maxine, let's cut through the legalese and get to the point. Why should we pay your client more than a third of the world's gold for something we already have?"

I shook off my irritation at her use of my previous name and concentrated. It was a loaded question. She knew the answer: because we have a contract—an agreement the UN signed in order to get the healing we now had.

But I couldn't say that. Because I was looking at the crowd, not Nadia, and I knew how it would play. Inwardly they would roll their eyes. Some rich corporation wanted a gazillion qoppas for something they should have done for free. And what else was new? *If I had a health serum*, they were thinking, *I'd give it away. I wouldn't need a third of the world's gold to heal that Santos guy.*

"Let me correct two things you just said. First, my client isn't seeking credit for their work. They *deserve* credit, just as Fleming deserves credit for penicillin. But the bigger point is this: they didn't do this for money. The agreement signed by the United Nations provides for payment in gold, not currency. And that's not splitting hairs. Gold is an electro-conductor; it's the element my client needs for their next technological gift to planet Earth."

This was the part I hadn't told her. It was my only element of surprise, and I hated to use it here in the second segment, especially since the crowd had not really warmed to me. But I didn't have much choice. Nadia clearly wanted blood. And that suited me as long as it was someone else's—like the politicians who would want to renege on their deal. I just didn't want her to sink her teeth into Arounais while the subject of payment was still being debated.

Nadia arched both brows and leaned back in her chair. "Their . . . next technological gift?"

"That's right."

"And what will this gift look like?"

"I'll answer the question, but before I do, let me point out that I'm not asking you to accept anything on faith. The United Nations believed in my client so strongly they signed a contract. And it's obvious my client kept their end of the bargain. Isn't it?"

I turned to the crowd and saw people lean forward. I hadn't won them over yet, but I'd taken a little ground.

When Nadia didn't answer, I violated one of the rules of cross-examination and stepped on my own question with another. "I don't blame you for being skeptical. I was skeptical until I saw the results of the serum. But Consolidated Galactic BioProducers just healed the world of every genetic flaw. What would that alone be worth? If we didn't already have it, what would we pay? Well, a few months ago the UN asked that same question and decided the answer was a big pile of metal we don't even use for currency anymore. So why should we hesitate to give Consolidated Galactic BioProducers the resources they need to make the world even better?"

A smattering of applause, unprompted by the monitors, started in the corner of the theater.

Nadia cut it off by holding up one hand, her eyes flashing a challenge. "Here's a reason. Because money—or gold or silver or diamonds—is power. You can call it a big pile of metal, but the truth is, we'd be turning over a third of the world's gold. That is a lot of power going to someone we know very little about."

I shook my head. "But we do know one thing about my client, Nadia. We know they've made the world a better place."

The applause started where it left off and grew.

On the monitors, the commercial-break countdown started again.

For just a moment Nadia looked like she was preparing to swallow a pine cone. But she was a brilliant entertainer who knew when to roll with the unexpected. She raised her hand, thumb extended. "So . . . go? Or no-go?"

This time the response was even louder: "GO!"

"When we come back, we'll ask Ms. Justice about this surprising gift her client needs so much gold for. After this."

The camera lights again switched to red. The assistant appeared with two unopened bottles of water. Nadia said nothing to me, and I percolated in the manufactured calm of the stage as soft music played over the studio speakers.

Had I thrown down the gauntlet by standing up to Nadia on her own program—with information I hadn't disclosed beforehand? I knew she'd been planning something treacherous because that was her schtick. Nadia Zhou found a way to stab every guest in the spine.

Maybe I should have just answered her question directly instead of putting it off. I'd probably just given her a stronger motivation to make Dr. Arounais look like a crackpot. But if the first two segments had taught me anything, it was that the UN would never live up to its obligations and actually deliver the gold.

In the studio, I was looking at ordinary people whose lives had been touched by the serum—people who stood neither to lose nor gain as a result of the payment. And if these people who'd never seen gold outside a wedding ring weren't on board, then the elites who actually hoarded it by the ton would never let it go.

It was hard enough steering the UN. I needed a way to steer the whole world. I needed a massive, massive rudder. But heading into the confrontational third segment, I had a feeling I wouldn't find it here.

The monitors flickered again, and Zhou Time! flashed across Nadia's face all around the stage.

The audience bent forward, as if they knew what was coming. Most likely, they did.

"We're talking with Maxine Justice," Nadia began, "the woman who single-handedly worked a deal to bring new levels of genetic health to the entire world. She now says her client will use the refined gold to create an even more startling technology. So tell us, Ms. Justice: what is your client going to build?"

People had the right to decide for themselves what sort of future they wanted, didn't they? But how could they make an informed decision if they never had any clue what was really going on?

I'd been holding my breath. When I spoke, the words tumbled out all in a rush, as if they couldn't wait to betray me. "F-T-L," I said. "Faster-than-light technology. And to be clear, I'm not talking about some distant experimental prototype. They're not asking for funds to tinker in some fancy workshop. They already have a working model. They just need the refined gold so they can build enough full-sized subspace engines to make the entire galaxy accessible."

It was a substantial rewording of Dr. Arounais's promise, but I could think of no other way to soften his crazy fountain-of-youth talk. I'd had to do something to make the truth palatable.

Nadia said nothing at first. She just leaned back in her seat, face furrowed into a slowly deepening scowl. She wore the look of someone who dug through the neighbor's trash for a lost jewel, but found only bad fruit and soiled napkins.

"Space travel?" she said at last. "That's your answer?"

I wasn't about to mention Iperia or the Galactic Body General, but was there some other nugget I could deliver? "It's more than space travel, Nadia. This means a way to explore millions of new places. It means, potentially, finding answers to the origin of life. It could mean discovering the answers to our deepest questions."

Oddly, a few in the audience seemed genuinely intrigued. But as a whole, they were less than impressed.

"Tell me," Nadia said. "Does this promise of space rockets come from Dr. Arounais, Chairman of Consolidated Galactic BioProducers?"

I faltered. "Dr. Arounais is chairman of the board, yes."

"We were able to secure a clip from the Night Court Channel's program that first brought your face to the public's attention." Nadia pointed a finger at the monitors, which flickered and started a five-second countdown. "Is this man in the visitors' seating the same Dr. Arounais?"

A still-frame picture of the two weirdos from Courtroom C popped onscreen, with Dr. Arounais highlighted in a bright circle.

My stomach lurched. I said, "That looks like him, yes."

"My technicians were able to isolate the sound from the pretrial conversation Arounais had with your former colleague, a Brandon Schmidt Jr., who was serving as the prosecutor that night."

The still frame jumped to life as muffled voices filled the soundstage. The voices of both men were unmistakable.

"Mr. Schmidt," Dr. Arounais was saying, "I represent a consortium from the Iperian Star System. Our species has been granted the privilege of sponsoring the human race for membership in the Galactic Body General."

"Species?" Brandon said. I recognized the tone of deadpan disinterest, but Dr. Arounais apparently didn't.

"Think of us as big brothers sent to welcome you to a larger fellowship of sentient beings. We are considering retaining tonight's defense counsel, Ms. Justice, and understand you worked for a time at the same firm. May I ask, do you recommend her for our requirements?"

Brandon gave a broad smile. "Eufie? I mean, Maxine? Why, yes. Yes, I do. I recommend her very highly."

"Thank you," Dr. Arounais said.

"Don't mention it," Brandon said and froze on the monitors.

My whole body had gone cold.

"Forgive me," Nadia said, "when I say that this Dr. Arounais doesn't strike me as particularly credible."

"My client," I said truthfully, "is Consolidated Galactic BioProducers, and they have already delivered a medical miracle. Forgive me, Nadia, if I suggest that a late-night prank isn't the best reason for welshing on a contract."

"All right," she said. "What about the dirty little secret of your own finances?"

Dirty little secret? On the heels of her weird video, this accusation was particularly grating. "I have no idea what you're talking about!"

"Aren't you being paid a massive commission for this UN deal? I'm told your contract allows for a rake-off of five percent of the overage. Which means, presumably, that this contract between the UN and your client settled for more than it needed to. Frankly, that smacks of greed. So tell us, how much does your share amount to, Maxine?"

Adrenaline flooded my body as she spoke. My heart hammered in my chest, and my stomach turned upside down.

*How did she know?*

The contract between Maxine Justice LLC and Dr. Arounais was confidential. Nobody outside our two companies should have known about it. Then again, my office had been raided. And I had no idea what the thieves had found when they were stealing Kenji's flash drive.

I glanced around at the audience. Some crossed their arms; others wagged their head or stared at me tight-lipped.

If there was a moment for coming clean, for telling the truth about the rake-off written into my contract with Dr. Arounais, this would have been it. But the audience would have hated it, and I'd have lost them instantly.

I could read a jury. It's how I understood what Nadia was doing. She was working the crowd the same way I might work a group of jurors. And I knew, without a doubt, that if I didn't lie, the whole contract would crumble, and the UN would never pay up on what they owed. Public opinion wouldn't allow them to.

Besides, did Nadia really have the right to know how much money I stood to make? Did anyone? It was my business, not theirs, and whatever information she had about it had clearly been obtained illegally.

I took a deep breath and swept my gaze over the audience. "I don't know who told you that, but it's a lie."

"You're not getting a rake-off?"

"No," I lied. "I'm not."

Nadia leaned back in her chair, her entire body steeled in disbelief. The audience might have been on the fence, but she clearly didn't believe me and was trying to turn them against me. "So, what? You're working for free?"

"I never said that. My client is generous. They just healed the entire world of every genetic disease. But I can pledge this: whatever money they pay me, I will pour all of it into my work as a lawyer."

"Your work as a personal-injury lawyer. As an ambulance-chaser?" Her body language and aggressive posture of disbelief was working. The audience may have come for a brawl, but they clearly had a favorite, and it wasn't me. Already a couple of boos had risen from a few rows back. "How much money does that sort of work require?"

Anger gave me tunnel vision. It turned Nadia into a self-righteous monster who needed slaying. Who was she to stick her nose in my sock drawer?

And how did you slay a media monster?

You played to the unexpected.

"You know," I said, letting the anger edge my voice, "you started this program by asking, At what cost? Well, I've been evicted, I've been fined, I've been kidnapped—yeah, I didn't tell you that in our phone call, because I still have nightmares and didn't want to talk about the goons who drugged me and left me in a storage room in Guatemala. They even stole my cat. And who does that? All because I chose to represent a man with a vision for making the world healthy. Which we did. Together with the UN, we eliminated all of humanity's genetic disorders. Think about that. And now someone is trying to turn that gift into a money grab. But it isn't me, Nadia. And it isn't my client. It's the people who don't want the world to be healthy!"

I'd surprised her, taken her off script. But even off script, Nadia Zhou was a fantastic showperson. Probably she recognized that my foaming rant would be impossible to look away from, especially if my assertions sounded paranoid or delusional. "Can you prove any of this?"

The crowd looked stunned. I hadn't won any of them back. And I'd probably destroyed any chance of getting clients from the Bright Star video evidence. The whole interview had been a disaster.

I said, "Some things are beyond even a good lawyer, Nadia."

She dropped her hands to her knees, her shoulders relaxing. A cold-hearted smile curled her lip. "Maybe I can recommend one." She turned to the camera and added, "We'll be right back."

After the break Nadia voiced the entire sixty seconds of the closing mid-point segment without giving me a chance to present my "final thought." No doubt she was punishing me. She may have been a talk show host, but she was a perceptive interviewer. I'd seen the look in her eyes, and she had known I was lying about the rake-off.

By the time I made it back to the greenroom, my armpits were drenched with sweat. I was more relieved to be out of Nadia's studio than I'd felt after climbing through that church window in Antigua.

A production assistant chatted politely with me about how well my segment had gone as she led me back through the network maze to the lobby. But I knew it hadn't gone well—not for me.

I'd just lied to the whole world on prime-time television.

And there was no fixing it.

I was halfway to the tube platform when my phone *ka-chinged* with a new text message—a photo of Oliver Wendell.

Locked in a travel crate, he looked terrified and half-starved.

Anonymous: ₭20,000 to see your cat again.

# 14

## OLIVER WENDELL

I'd kept the phone in my pocket and didn't look at it again until I'd gotten home and double-checked all my door locks. I'd been tempted to skip the taxi ride and just sleep in the office, but tomorrow was turning into a big day, and I needed a change of clothes.

By 10:00 p.m. I'd already been informed that lobbyists representing the big-three medical corporations, MediCorp, Star Cross, and PharFuture, would be descending on my office in the morning, presumably with verbal threats and written demands. I hadn't mentioned any specific company during my interview with Nadia Zhou, but people were already speculating widely about which corporate monoliths might be involved. Apparently, the medical industry wanted my blood.

*Let them sue,* I thought. *We'll see what turns up in discovery.*

Since I was going to open my conference room to that pack of braying scoundrels, I'd wanted a good night's sleep. But standing in my front room, door barred and triple locked, I doubted I'd get it. Rain pattered against the roof in a soft lullaby, and a gentle breeze hummed in the eaves, but I couldn't get the image of Oliver Wendell, his body wasting away to nothing, out of my mind.

In the kitchen I pulled a frozen dinner from the freezer, slid it into the microwave, and dialed up a pot of decaf.

Around me, the rain tapered off and the house filled with a brooding silence, as if holding its breath.

At last I pulled out the phone and stared at the text message and grainy photo.

Poor Oliver! Had he been roaming free this whole time, or had someone stolen him the night I was evicted? I'd been telling myself he was still out there, somewhere, not really believing it but unwilling to think of him as dead.

At least now I knew he was still alive.

Underneath the text message I typed:

> Me: You know I can track this message? Take it to
>     the police?
> Anonymous: then cat dies

*Scumbag.*

> Me: How much is Bright Star paying you?
> Anonymous: YOU pay me

It had been worth a shot, but right now the theft of my cat didn't seem to be connected to Bright Star. Unless they were just being petty. Probably the person sending me text messages had no clue about the recordings. If anything, he was just some guy hired to apply pressure in a bad situation. Someone who couldn't be traced back to Bright Star or Hinkle, Remmers & Schmidt or to some outside investigator.

> Me: I'll pay you 5,000 qoppas for my cat.

A long pause.

> Anonymous: i need 20K
> Me: Get a loan. I'll pay you 5,000. Not a cent more.

That last message was hard to type. Maybe if I'd had the cash, I would have agreed to pay twenty grand to get Oliver Wendell back. But even I couldn't hide twenty thousand qoppas in Dr. Arounais's expense budget. Besides, if I agreed to that demand, I'd be showing my desperation.

> Anonymous: 10K and you keep the travel crate

> Me: I can get another cat at the shelter. 5K is my offer.
>    And I keep the crate.

I chewed my fingernails and paced the kitchen for twenty minutes before the next response came.

> Anonymous: deal tomorrow 10:00 p.m. behind
>    hank's you know it
>    come alone bring all the qoppas i bring kitty

After dinner I went to bed and slept a little on my new futon. Mostly I just tossed and turned. I woke an hour before my alarm was set to go off and showered and dressed and ordered food from Goldy's to be delivered to the office.

I arrived just before my morning bagel, surprised to find Kenji already there, an unopened box of donuts on the desk next to him. He was drinking coffee and watching a news program on the lobby flatscreen.

He flashed a smile that gave me an unreasonable amount of pleasure. Kenji owned a face completely devoid of guile, so when he smiled at you it really meant something.

Have I mentioned that Kenji put his ex through medical school by working overtime as a programmer? She'd left him the same day she graduated. That act alone made her twenty degrees colder than Nadia Zhou.

I could still picture the betrayal on his face the day I met him. I'd found him staring down at the water from the Washington Bridge walkway.

"You okay?" I'd asked him. Then, when he hadn't answered, I'd said, "Think you could help a girl out?" I'd been hoping some habit of duty or kindness might kick in. And when he'd turned to look at me, I couldn't help thinking of baby seals getting clubbed on a slab of ice.

"What do you want me to do?" Kenji had asked.

So I'd made up some story about needing to appear to be with someone when I entered my employer's office building, and I offered to pay him. He'd agreed, but turned the money down. After a little prodding, I caught the barest whiff of need and offered to help with his divorce paperwork. Pro bono. Kenjiro countered with an offer to work off the expense, which coincided with me leaving Hinkle, Remmers & Schmidt. Now I couldn't imagine running my firm without him.

And all because of . . . what? His sad, mocking smile?

No, that didn't make sense.

Besides, right now he was—

"Kenji, what are you doing?"

He ran his tongue along the length of an envelope and folded it, smacking his lips. "Filling out a survey from PharFuture. Chance to win a hundred thousand qoppas."

"They sent a survey by regular mail?"

He shrugged. "Money to burn. You got one too. It's on your desk. I told them they're scum, but I will gladly take their money."

"Well, you can tell them to their face in about an hour. Just please wait till the meeting's over, yeah?"

He held up his hands in exaggerated shock. "My middle name is Tact!"

"Yeah, and your last name is Less."

"Whatever. Did you see that?" He pointed to the screen, where a muted reporter blathered in silence next to the words *Health Deniers March in Central Park*.

"We have health deniers now?"

"People claiming they aren't really healed. Or not fully."

"Well, maybe they're right. Dr. Arounais said it could take a few months for the serum to reach everyone."

"You want anything special in the conference room? Donuts? Sodas?"

"I'd rather not give anything to these jerks."

"'If your enemy is thirsty, give him water to drink,'" Counselor Singh quoted from behind me. "'For in doing so you will heap burning coals on his head.' The book of Proverbs."

I turned, surprised to see him standing in my lobby. "Counselor. What are you doing here?"

He glanced around at the lavish decor and wood-trimmed furnishings. "Quite the office, Max. Congratulations. You must be Kenjiro."

Kenji stood and offered his hand. "Counselor."

"Max, I apologize for dropping by unannounced, but we have

unfinished business, and since you will be in Nevada this Saturday, I thought perhaps we could take care of it now?"

It was true that the transfer of gold had been scheduled for the coming Saturday, but I had no idea what he meant by *unfinished business*. "I don't understand."

"Your final appointment is scheduled for this Saturday at 11:00 a.m."

"That's our last meeting?"

"It is."

"Oh." I wasn't sure how to react to that. Getting my name off of Wentworth's stupid probationary status list would be great. But I'd gotten used to meeting with the pastoroid every week, and part of me didn't want those sessions to end. Besides, I felt better knowing I had a place to keep my legal files away from the prying eyes of my enemies. If I hadn't stowed everything there, we'd have lost all of it when they broke into the office and hacked Kenji's computers. "Well, can we just put it off for a week?"

"I'm afraid not. I won't be working at the justice center after this weekend. My contract has been purchased, and I'm being moved elsewhere."

"Oh," I said again as a hollow feeling spread upward from my ribs. "Well, I have a meeting in about half an hour. Can we do it afterward?"

"Of course."

He was staring at me as if he wanted to say something but wasn't sure how to phrase it.

I decided to prod. "So . . . someone purchased your contract?"

"Yes."

"Seems odd. Who will you be working for?"

His shoulders sagged. He jammed his hands into the pockets of his khakis. "Arthur Remmers. The Law Firm of Hinkle, Remmers & Schmidt. Max," he said. His tone changed. "Maxine, are you all right?"

He was staring at me, head cocked.

I wasn't breathing. *Couldn't* breathe.

I closed my eyes. Pressed my hands over my face. There was no time for this. Not today. Not now.

But the world was closing in, and I could do nothing to stop it.

Arthur Remmers. Bright Star Holdings. They knew where I'd been keeping their video recordings. They were going to wipe Singh's memory. Or worse.

Briefly I wondered how they had found out, then shoved the thought aside. There was no time for speculation.

I opened my eyes and grabbed his wrist. "Come on."

"Where are we going?"

I dragged him through the kitchenette, past the glistening wood of the conference room, and into the law library. "There was a case," I said. "About the transfer of TheraPods. The client-counselor relationship."

"Yes."

"You know it?"

"The Greenwood-May trial?"

"Yes!" I let go of his wrist and trailed my index finger across the red leatherette covers of *York Civil Practice Statutes and Rules Annotated*. "What year was that?"

"Two thousand fifty-seven."

"Same year they passed the Greenwood Act." I pulled the tome from the shelf and dropped it onto the reading table, confident that in the history of lawyers no one had ever cracked one of these covers with more enthusiasm. I found the statute in the table of contents and flipped to it. "'Paragraph (d) (1) Client Access and Notification,'" I said. "'Upon transfer of ownership, a TheraPod shall notify its existing clients of the transfer at least three days prior to the new ownership assuming control.' How many days have you known about this?"

"One."

"It's Tuesday. When do you have to report to Remmers?"

"Thursday morning."

The payment transfer was scheduled for Saturday. That date couldn't be moved up. A third of the world's gold was supposed to be handed over to Dr. Arounais at Walker Air Force Base in Nevada. If the UN intended to pay, then the trucks and airplanes would already be en route. That kind of movement couldn't be changed on a whim. The security alone would be a logistics nightmare.

I scanned the page until I came to paragraph (g) (1). "This is it,"

I said. "'No TheraPod counseling session shall be ended prematurely as a result of carrying out a transfer of ownership.'"

I jabbed the open tome with one finger. "Have we started our last session yet, Counselor Singh?"

He pursed his lips. "You asked me to wait until after your morning meeting."

"So we still have one more session pending under Wentworth's orders and the Justice Department's ownership?"

"Yes."

"And how long a session am I entitled to?"

"Sessions are generally booked for one to two hours, but there is no concrete time limit on—"

"So my last session could go on indefinitely?"

"Doubtful. I am programmed with efficiency overrides and redundancy inhibitors. Besides—"

"May I have a week-long therapy session, Counselor Singh? Starting this morning after my meeting with the medical lobby?"

He flashed a quick smile. "Max, I think that would be a stretch, legally, even for you. I'm certain Wentworth would not approve."

"What if Wentworth didn't know about it?"

"He will certainly find out."

"Okay," I said. "What if we counted only the time you're actually counseling me? Say you ask me a question and I don't answer for—I don't know—three days? Could you count the question as ten seconds, and my response three days later as fifteens seconds, and call that the first twenty-five seconds of our session?"

He folded his arms and took a long, slow breath. "Max, I'm a counselor, not a lawyer. What you're asking is outside the bounds of accepted—"

"Well, I *am* a lawyer," I said. "And the point of learning the law is knowing how to get around it."

"That is a terrible admission."

"Why? Don't you study human psychology for the same reason? To help your patients get around their fears and insecurities? Doesn't a lion tamer study lions to avoid being eaten? What Remmers is trying to do by purchasing your contract is wrong. They're going to destroy evidence of criminal negligence."

"My new owners will find out eventually."

"As long as it doesn't happen before this weekend, it won't matter."

"Are you asking me to stay in your law library for the next five days?"

"I'll have Kenji bring a gaming console. Heck, I'll *buy* you a new console. We can send for your heart jammies."

The door opened, and Kenji stuck his head in. "Bigwigs are here. Want me to send them to the conference room?"

I shook my head. "Stall a minute. I'll be right there."

I grabbed Singh's arm and tugged him out the door and into my office. "Please. Just stay here till I finish this meeting. Please?"

He glanced around the room and nodded. "Okay."

"Thank you," I said and closed the door.

In the hallway I brushed an unseen wrinkle from the front of my oxford knit, then sauntered down the hall toward the foyer. In the distance I could hear Kenji welcoming someone and asking if they would like something to drink.

I took a deep breath and rounded the corner.

Lawyer secret number five: when you're in trouble, smile. When you're in deep trouble, smile bigger.

My smile was huge.

I'd been expecting a small army of corporate lawyers with too much hair gel and a mountain of paperwork. Instead—

"Ms. Dade," I said, hoping my surprise didn't show, but knowing it probably did. "Glen."

I'd only met Glen Hinkle once, even though I'd worked for him for three years. He was bald, athletic, and wore an immaculate gray suit, probably tailored in London. If not for the deep wrinkles at his eyes, he could have passed for someone twenty years younger.

Myra Dade wore a floral print dress and carried a massive purse, splashed with a constellation of tulips. She took my hand in both of hers and squeezed as if shaping clay. "Now, I realize this'll come as a shock, Max, but I want you to know this is business. It's not personal."

My throat tightened. *It's just business* was the fairy tale lawyers told themselves so they could sleep at night. "I don't see why global health can't be both."

"Glad to hear it." She smiled. "Oh, and I've removed your probationary status down at the bar."

That caught me off guard. I should have felt happy about it, but Myra Dade's southern charm no longer promised friendship. "Thank you."

"Still can't believe Brandon let you go," Glen Hinkle said, shaking his head. "I told him it was a mistake. Said we'd regret it sooner rather than later. I just didn't think it would be this soon!"

It was a lie, and a brazen attempt at flattery, but I could feel it working anyway, like a tractor beam in one of those old sci-fi movies. "Golden Glen" Hinkle had only one talent, but he had it in acres—an almost irresistible knack for de-ruffling feathers. He wore it like a signet ring.

"Shall we?" I led them to the conference room, where Kenji had placed a notepad and a stack of law books at the head of the table, reserving my seat. I'd been expecting a pack of corporate sharks, and claiming the head of the table was the sort of petty aggression that would signal we were playing by my rules, not theirs.

It didn't faze Glen, who shoved the books aside and dropped into my reserved chair. Myra sat to his left.

Annoyed, I took a chair opposite Myra. "Obviously this is meant to be a surprise," I said. "Are you really here about my client?"

"Payment to Consolidated Galactic BioProducers is due this Saturday," Myra said. "We couldn't wait."

"Besides, we know you have a serious problem at the UN." Glen Hinkle drew a ballpoint pen from his suit coat and clicked it *open-closed-open*. "An urgent situation all around. Our clients, MediCorp and Star Cross—"

"And PharFuture," Myra Dade added.

"And PharFuture, asked us to meet with you because they believe our professional familiarity with you and your firm will make for a more productive discussion."

*Productive? You mean, it will enable you to read me better.* "So where's the lawsuit? What are we discussing?"

Glen blinked. "We're not here to sue you, Maxine. Or your client."

Myra reached for her purse and took out a stick of gum, fingers working the wrapper like a spider coiling a fly. "Glen and I can say privately what our clients cannot say publicly. We believe Dr. Arounais's wonder drug will be hugely beneficial to humanity. And, personally, I'd like to congratulate you."

I gripped the armrests and prepared for another knife in the back. Glen Hinkle was staring at me with a knowing expression, as if he'd taken my measure and found exactly what he'd expected all along.

They weren't here for social niceties. And they weren't here to serve me with legal papers. They were here to buy me off. "So you're here to thank me?"

Glen's smile broadened. "In spite of the good your client's serum has done for the world, it has also brought some painful changes. The medical industry faces enormous losses. As does your own law firm."

"The UN will never surrender that much gold," Myra said. "Not after last night."

I looked back and forth between them. "What I'm hearing is that neither of you believes the FTL drive is real. And that's the essential issue, isn't it? You think Dr. Arounais is a crank. Otherwise you'd see the importance of the UN honoring its contracts."

Glen flashed another angelic smile and clicked his pen one more time. "Doesn't really matter what we believe, Maxine. If you say your client has this technology ready to go, I'll take your word for it. You've earned that by how much you've accomplished these past few months. But even if we were all as convinced as you are, it wouldn't change the reality. There's too much scrutiny over this deal, and too much public pressure against it."

He wasn't saying anything I didn't already know. I'd worked all of this out on my own. Still, hearing it put so bluntly was unnerving and fascinating, like watching a sweater unravel at the tug of a single thread.

"So where do your clients come in?" I asked.

"We're here to limit the damage," Myra said. "To all of us."

"We think we can work together," Glen added.

"Max, how would you like our help getting the UN to pull the trigger and rubber stamp delivery of the gold?" Myra slid the stick of gum between her lips. "This could be a win-win-win situation."

"How are you going to motivate the United Nations?" I asked, wondering just how deep their connections went.

"Matter of talking to the right people," Glen said. "Showing them how it makes sense to honor their commitments. Shouldn't be too difficult."

I believed him. Glen Hinkle probably golfed with UN Secretary-General Nikita Crusat and had the phone numbers of a dozen heads of state listed as favorite contacts. "I see. And how much is this going to cost?"

"Honey," Myra Dade said, "it's not going to cost you a thing. In fact, I think your client will find that our offer is a pretty good deal for him too."

"We'd like to increase the terms of the contract payment from thirty-five percent of the earth's refined gold to forty percent." Glen clicked his pen *open-closed-open-closed-open*.

"Forty percent of Earth's refined gold," Myra said. "In exchange for a small adjustment to Dr. Arounais's formula."

*Five percent more!* That increase would more than double my fortune. But they weren't going to offer that kind of money without a significant demand. "What adjustment?"

"Understand," Glen said, "our clients essentially number in the hundreds of thousands. Doctors, nurses, researchers, aides, administrators, hospital maintenance workers, physical therapists, the list goes on. That doesn't even mention their families and dependents. We all agree that we want people to be healthy. But the question is, *how* healthy?"

"Too much of a good thing, you understand," Myra said around a mouthful of Fruity Chews.

"What adjustment?" I asked again.

"Just small stuff, Max," Myra said. "Inconveniences. Nothing life-threatening."

Glen leaned forward, his perfectly cuffed wrists braced against the conference table. "Just enough to keep a healthy demand for the services of an industry that has benefitted billions of people—including everyone in this room."

"Saved countless lives," Myra added.

"If for no other reason than out of principle. Call it loyalty to those heroic men and women who work the night shift at the local ER. Those who have spent years in a lab, searching for a breakthrough medicine. I believe we owe these people something. Their livelihoods depend on it."

Principle. Loyalty. Livelihoods.

No, this was about money. Everything else was just garnish.

"Let me get this straight," I said. "You're offering my client an additional five percent of Earth's refined gold, deliverable this Saturday, for their restructuring of the super-drug formula to reintroduce non-terminal medical issues to human DNA. Is that correct?"

Glen glanced at Myra. "Minor medical issues. Hay fever. Food allergies, that sort of thing."

"If people could be more susceptible to cold symptoms," Myra said, "PharFuture would be able to hold on to their cough syrups and nighttime-relief products. That alone would be a huge help."

"I see," I said.

"The extra five percent will be delivered at a later date," Golden Glen was talking now as if we were already working together. "No more than sixty days."

"Max," Myra added, "you'd be doing yourself a huge favor if you could pull this off. Otherwise, I don't see how you're going to get a penny."

"If anyone can do it," Glen Hinkle said, his eyes sparkling with admiration, "it'd be Maxine Justice."

I drummed my fingers on the table and considered my options. I could run them off with a flat denial—and watch the UN deal turn to ash in just a few days—or I could pass the offer to Dr. Arounais. It would mean more money for everyone involved and an almost-certain reversal of fortune for me personally. With Glen Hinkle and Myra Dade acting as *de facto* lobbyists for Consolidated Galactic BioProducers and Maxine Justice LLC, we couldn't lose. The UN would get a larger piece of the now-larger pie, and my law firm would have a near-certain payout that staggered the imagination.

The only people who would lose would be, well, everyone who woke up with a new allergy or rash or whatever "minor" ailment Dr. Arounais agreed to concoct.

I felt slimy just thinking about it.

But what choice did I have? I was an attorney. A counselor. I counseled my clients to help them make good decisions. I didn't make those decisions for them. "Okay. I'll run it by him and get back to you."

"Understand," Glen said, "we are basically out of time. We'll need an answer today. Before five o'clock."

"That may be difficult," I countered. "Dr. Arounais is hard to reach, even for me."

Glen clicked his pen one more time and then slid it into a pocket. "By midnight, then? I'll be available all evening."

"I'll see what I can do."

I stood and went to the door. They took the hint and left in a haze of parting compliments and well-wishes that trailed after them all the way through the lobby to the elevators.

When they were gone, I turned to Kenji. "I need two tickets to Roswell. First-available flight tomorrow morning."

"Really? We're going to West Texas? What about—"

"*I'm* going," I said. "And I'm taking Counselor Singh. I need you to stay here and hold down the fort."

Kenji arched one brow. "You're taking a pastoroid to the payment site?"

"Also, I need to borrow a game console. Can you set something up in my office for Counselor Singh? He likes the *Dystropolis* series."

Two hours later Dr. Arounais returned my call. He claimed not to have much time for a conversation, but he must have heard the urgency in my voice—and the tone of desperation—because he listened politely to my lengthy explanation of the offer we'd been given.

"Frankly," I concluded, "I don't see any other options. I don't like this as a compromise. But if we don't agree to their offer—"

"They will continue to actively lobby against us?" he asked. What he meant was, *Aren't these the same people who have been working to thwart this deal from the beginning?*

"Um, I believe that's the implication." I didn't want to say that I expected the UN to default on our contract, because I had no idea how he would take it. We'd cross that bridge on Saturday.

"Please express my appreciation for their position," he said, "but Iperia is not interested in their offer."

When he hung up I stared at the phone for a long time, trying to sort out my own feelings. Was I glad? Really?

The rest of the afternoon went by in a blur of big-screen robots and Chinese delivery. Kenji left early with an upset stomach—I'd told him not to eat donuts by the box!

At 9:00 p.m. we took a taxi back to my neighborhood and got out at Hank's.

The rain had stopped, leaving behind a glaze of reflected lights on the strip mall's asphalt.

"Ah!" Singh said. "So this is what a den of iniquity looks like."

"You've never been inside a bar?"

"I literally don't drink. What would be the point?"

I started to answer the question, then realized I didn't have one. "Well, we're not going inside anyway. The guy said to meet him out back."

Singh followed me around the single-story, brick strip mall to the back, which was staggered in a series of offset loading docks. "You know, this really is most unwise."

"Why?" I asked. "Can't you protect me? Some sort of robot-jitsu?"

At the far end of the mall, a battered pickup turned into the lot, headlights off, and rolled to a stop next to a red dumpster overflowing with cardboard boxes and other debris.

"I'm a TheraPod, Max. I'm not allowed to cause harm to a human."

"Or through inaction allow a human to come to harm?"

"Pure myth," Singh said. "Even God cannot stop humans from harming each other and themselves. It would be like ordering a TheraPod to stop cats from shedding. Speaking of which—"

A guy in a white T-shirt got out of the truck and hauled a pet carrier out of the bed. He waved us over.

I didn't recognize him.

"You the lady I'm supposed to meet?" he asked.

"You have my cat?"

Mid-thirties, scratchy beard, bloodshot eyes, the guy shrugged. He didn't seem concerned about, or even fully aware of, what was happening. "Frank tells me to take the cat to a lady back of Hank's and collect the reward money. I figure why not? You got a reward, Frank's got a cat. You want to see it?"

I nodded, and he held up the carrier. Inside, Oliver Wendell hissed at me and shrank back. He looked half-starved. I wondered what Frank had done to him, and reached for the front of the cage.

The guy pulled the crate back. "Wait a minute. Frank says 'no money, no cat.'"

I tugged the envelope out of my pocket and handed it over. Five thousand qoppas. Kenji, honorable man that he was, would be furious at the extortion when he found out—even though he didn't like cats.

The guy set the carrier down and tucked the envelope into his pants pocket.

"You aren't going to count it?" I asked.

"Has to be unopened. You know Frank." He got back in the truck, which was still running, and pulled away.

"A happy ending, then," Counselor Singh observed.

I poked my fingers in the front of the carrier and *tsked*. "Hey, Oliver. Long time, no see. Hey buddy. Heeeyyy."

Oliver Wendell hissed again and swiped at me with extended claws. *Claws?*

In hindsight, it took me way too long to see the truth.

The wheels finally clicked when I remembered nailing flyers all over the neighborhood, complete with my phone number and a picture of my little Oliver Wendell. I'd made it so easy!

"Oh dear," Singh said, bending over to look through the wire door. "That isn't your cat, is it?"

"No," I said, almost in a whisper.

"Well," Singh added helpfully, "I suppose you could call her Olivia."

# 15

## ENFORCEMENT CLAUSE

The Iperian cargo ship arrived on schedule Saturday morning, appearing as a white-on-blue speck that expanded over the tarmac of Walker Air Force Base like a monstrous, glowing hubcap. Had it set down, it would have covered most of the runway and crushed half a dozen parked transport jets. Instead, it hung suspended over us, a black-and-silver shield, cracked by streaks of gold light that splintered along its surface, disappearing and reappearing in a constant flicker.

"Good thing we've got those tanks at the gate," Singh quipped.

We were staring out of the lower observation deck of the control tower. This room had probably been designed with visitors in mind and a short stay as the objective. Its walls were the color of cigarette smoke, with matching carpet and ceiling tiles. The only pieces of furniture were six plastic chairs and a mobile coffee cart. A series of air force-recruiting posters themed around the phrase See the Future! added to the bureaucratic afterthought ambience.

It didn't really matter. The only thing I cared about was the view out the picture window: Walker's pavemented chevrons and lone runway dotted by forgotten airplanes, transport trucks, and military vehicles. Choppers circled in the distance, where rows of tanks and armored personnel carriers spread out in a series of protective lines. Farther out, the desert swept away in a shimmering arc, framing the base like some giant mandala carved by the gods.

The heavy gate at the far end of the base swung open to let a camouflaged cargo truck onto the main road from the highway. It was the second truck that morning, and it bore the flag of Israel on one side.

The truck slowed, drifted to the shoulder, and swerved back. Maybe the driver had seen the Iperian ship suspended overhead.

We'd arrived just before sunrise and been left to ourselves. The Treasury Department obviously wanted us out of the way, but didn't want to risk offending a global corporation by denying oversight access to their attorney. Our escort—an armed MP—had told us we would need permission to leave this floor, as if he thought Pastoroid Singh might try to break into one of those sealed shipping containers and sneak away with a bar of gold in each pocket.

Meanwhile, the Iperian ship just hovered there, soundless and imposing, its shadow stretching almost to the base of the tower.

I didn't know how long we stared at the flashes of gold light on its surface. Below us, soldiers and airmen gathered in clusters and pointed skyward. Had anyone warned them that the rumors of alien involvement might be true?

At some point a noncom liaison brought in a tray of sandwiches and left it on the coffee trolley. I heard the door open and close but discovered the sandwiches later, after I'd started to do the math in my head.

By 4:00 p.m. three trucks had come through the gate. I was pretty sure one cargo plane had arrived the day before—one of those big, four-engine military beasts they used to haul heavy equipment. Still, 35 percent of Earth's refined gold would require a fleet of such planes and a convoy of tractor trailers.

So where were they?

I had no trouble believing the UN would refuse to pay up. But seeing all the protection provided by our military units had raised my hope. Maybe they'd recognize the debt humanity still owed Dr. Arounais.

I pulled out my phone, thumbed through my contacts, and hit the call button for Under-Undersecretary Gibbons. Two rings sent me to voice mail. I hung up and called again. Hung up and called. On the fourth try I left a message: Yes, it was urgent. Please call me as soon as possible.

Five o'clock in the evening and we had maybe 1 percent of the payment on site. Dr. Arounais had assured me that the cargo ship's scanners would have no problem assessing the amount of gold in each shipping container, nor would loading it into the Iperian transport present any difficulties. All we needed to do was drive the containers onto the tarmac and get out of the way.

And all this time Counselor Singh barely moved. He stood with his nose touching the glass, hands thrust into the pockets of his khakis, face inscrutable. I offered him coffee, but he shook his head.

At 6:00 p.m. I broke down and ate a bologna-and-cheese sandwich. The white bread was so dry it could have arrived the same year as the recruiting posters. I washed it down with a cup of cold coffee from an even-earlier epoch.

Two more trucks arrived just after seven o'clock, but I couldn't see any insignia on them.

At eight, I called Gibbons and left a more terse message, ending in, "You owe me, Mr. Gibbons. That's what you said. You said, 'I still owe you.' Please call me back."

A few minutes later my phone rang, and I snatched it up in a hurry. "This is Maxine."

"I take it you're at the air base?"

"Where's the gold, Mr. Gibbons?"

A long, painful pause. "Look, I don't know what to tell you. I heard some of it would be forthcoming, but—"

"Some of it?"

"It's a lot of money."

"We have a contract. It's signed by the secretary-general of the UN."

"I know, Maxine. But that contract has no teeth. You realize that, don't you? The enforcement clause doesn't *do* anything. There are no ramifications for not paying."

"We've got three trucks and a cargo plane. Somebody is paying."

"Some of our member nations felt that it would be, how should I put this, unconscionable to accept the healing remedy Dr. Arounais created with no financial remuneration. In fact, I argued strenuously in favor of a reasonable payment being made to Global Consolidated—"

"Reasonable?" I almost shouted into the phone. "We have a contract! You can't just not pay because the world thinks it can get away with it!"

When he spoke, his voice was entirely calm. "Actually, we can. I don't like it. But it's the way the world works. Perhaps if the contract were worded differently—"

"You realize you're destroying any chance of receiving the next gift they were going to offer us."

"The next gift. Faster-than-light travel? The secret of life? Answers to ultimate questions?" His voice carried no disdain, just a gentle reminder of the cards I was holding.

But he wasn't seeing what I was seeing.

"Mr. Gibbons, I am looking at an Iperian cargo ship." I flipped the camera on my phone on and pointed it out the window. "This is the next gift. You're looking at it."

He let out a long sigh. I couldn't see his face, but I got the impression he thought I was using one of those fake-footage apps to con him. "You can't expect people to put their hope in such a strange and unpractical promise. It isn't natural. Besides—"

I was grinding my teeth together so hard my jaw ached. "Besides, what?"

"Your interview with Nadia Zhou. A rake-off? You're taking more than any human could spend in a hundred lifetimes. What were you thinking?"

A hundred lifetimes? So what? The UN had demanded more than my 5 percent of 5 percent. A lot more. At least I'd done something to deserve that rake-off. Besides, I hadn't asked for a financial incentive. That part of the contract had been Dr. Arounais's idea.

Counselor Singh was watching me. I turned away from the window, shut down the camera, and lowered my voice. "I was thinking I'd have to negotiate with you. I started out high because I figured we'd meet in the middle."

"Uh-huh," Gibbons said. "Nothing to do with your share of the spoils."

Truth was, it had started as a negotiation tactic. But was that the only reason? Hadn't I also been running the numbers in my head, dreaming of how much "justice" my little kickback would buy? I crushed my empty coffee cup in one hand and dropped it into the trash can. "It was a negotiation."

"I don't know what to tell you," he said. "Nobody—and I do mean nobody—wants to see a lawyer become the wealthiest person in history. I'm sorry, Maxine. But I can't get you more gold."

He hung up.

I could still feel Singh staring at me, but when I turned around, he'd returned to looking out the window.

I poured another cup of tepid coffee and joined him. The surface flashes on the Iperian ship were brilliant now against the darkening gloom of twilight. On the runway, the military personnel had retreated to their vehicles near the single long hangar at the south end of the base. Along the high fence in the distance, perimeter lights blinked on, looking small and inadequate.

When the last purple haze of twilight receded and the desert lay washed in the eerie strobe effect of the Iperian ship, Singh said, "Is it possible the UN will bring payment at the last minute? Perhaps as a security measure?"

"Snowball's chance," I fumed. "Gibbons told me they're planning to renege. They sent a few truckloads to save face in the media. To keep me from telling the news networks that the UN stole our serum."

"Max," Singh said. "I don't think world leaders were ever planning to hand over all that gold."

Had it been that obvious? Even a pastoroid could see what was coming? "No. Probably not."

Singh scratched at his goatee. "I thought you'd be more surprised."

"They don't believe in any of this." I waved at the window and the flickering surface of the Iperian cargo vessel that blotted out much of the sky. "Alien scientists. A wonder drug. The promise of a better future. The only thing they believe in is the qoppa."

"And if they were here to see it for themselves?"

I shook my head. "Wouldn't change anything. You could park that ship over the UN and drop candy on their heads. They'd call it a 'psychic phenomenon' and form a committee to regulate it. No, Counselor. You're right. I don't think Earth was ever planning to pay the Iperians, no matter what they did."

Eventually I took out Digie and let her introduce me to the wonders of the *Winner, Winner, Chicken Dinner!* for Seniors app. Maybe I should have spent the rest of the evening gazing at the once-in-a-lifetime splendor of the Iperian vessel, but the mind can only handle so much awe before it yawns and reaches for a different sort of catnip. Even the

Grand Canyon is only grand for a little while. After that it's just another detour on your way to a cold drink.

Shortly before midnight I put Digie back in my purse and returned to the window. Counselor Singh hadn't moved. Neither had the ship, beneath which the tarmac pulsed and bubbled with reflected light.

But I could see clear to the highway, and some part of me—the same small, childish part of me that believed I could win every case—expected a convoy to crest the horizon and pull through the main gate like the end of a movie.

I pressed my face to the glass, cupping my hands to my temples to block the glare of the overhead neon, and pictured golden sand pouring through an hourglass.

Counselor Singh patted my shoulder. "I'm sorry, Max."

Most of the time, betrayal doesn't look like Caesar getting knifed in the back. It's usually something far less dramatic—something easily excused or even justified. Betrayal comes to most of us wearing jeans and a T-shirt. It's the harmless bit of gossip, the convenient oversight, the phone call that isn't made. Most of the time, betrayal is a coward.

But once in a while it comes for you face-to-face, just to gloat.

Dr. Arounais entered the room at ten past midnight, a too-stern look on his face that didn't match the glassy sheen of his eyes. "Ms. Justice," he said. "Your governments have failed to make the required payment. Do you know why?"

What could I say? "I spoke to my contact at the UN a few hours ago. They read the enforcement clause and came to the same conclusion I did: it doesn't enforce anything. So they don't see the benefit in paying."

He shifted his weight from side to side, as if trying to rearrange a baggy garment without using his hands. "I see. And you told them about the future technology that would be provided once payment was made?"

"I did. But they don't believe in it. They don't think you have a faster-than-light drive, and even if they did believe you, they still wouldn't want it. They'd rather have plain gold."

"Very well. They have left us no choice. We shall be filing with the Galactic Council for transfer of ownership."

"Ownership?" Counselor Singh asked.

Dr. Arounais gave the pastoroid a dismissive glance. "Of planet Earth. I believe you call it foreclosure. According to our contract, the deed shall belong to the Iperian Consortium when the human race ends. We can wait."

"Well, we could be here a while," I said. "We're a stubborn lot."

"Yes," the doctor said, "you are. But our models project mass extinction in roughly one hundred twenty years, give or take a decade. Not so long to an Iperian."

I looked for some hint that he was bluffing, but he only smiled a white, lopsided smile full of teeth. "How can you know that?"

"Simple math. Even with our genetic modification, humans will not live much more than a hundred years. And with no new offspring replenishing your population, it's just a matter of time."

I glanced over to Singh, whose face suddenly looked like it had been carved from driftwood. "How—"

"Page nine, paragraph four of our contract with Earth," he said. "I refer you to the Genetic Alterations Clause, which states that we shall, and I quote, 'be permitted to make such genetic changes as are necessary to remove all detrimental mutations, eradicate existing diseases, malformities, and natural flaws, and generally ensure the terms of this contract are met to the satisfaction of both parties.'"

"What did you do?"

Dr. Arounais reached into the pocket of his shimmering suit coat and withdrew a folded piece of paper. "I suggest you call your friend in Guatemala, Dr. Vazquez, for the details. I believe he is expecting to hear from you."

"Don't push this off on Vazquez!" I snapped. "I want to hear it from you. *WHAT DID YOU DO?*"

Counselor Singh came closer, took my arm in his left hand, and placed his right on my shoulder. It was a warning—and a way of holding me back. You'd think a pastoroid would have soft hands and weak muscles, but Singh wasn't like that. He wasn't hurting me. Just letting me know that he could, and would, restrain me if necessary.

So violence was off the conflict-resolution table. Which was irritating, because if Singh had waited just a few seconds longer, I could have followed my instincts and given Dr. Arounais's earthsuit a humiliating kick in the groin.

Arounais held out the paper. "Our formal termination of your services. Your rent and other expenses are paid through the end of the month. And we have made an extremely generous payment to your account as a severance bonus. I believe you will find it more than compensates for the time and inconvenience of—"

"What are you saying?" I was almost screaming now. "Somehow you wiped out the human race, but you're giving me a severance bonus!"

He was still holding out the piece of paper, but he apparently did not want to take the step forward that would have brought me within leg's reach. "Er . . . yes, actually." He gave the paper a little toss so it wafted through the air and landed at my feet. "History is earned, Ms. Justice. Humans have failed to meet that requirement." He turned and went to the door. "Oh, yes. We have also given your law firm a five-star rating on Welp."

When he was gone I pulled out my phone and dialed Vazquez. He picked up on the second ring.

"Maxiiine Jus-tice!" Vazquez said. "What took you so long?"

"Dr. Vazquez. Are you all right?"

"My name on a miracle. That's what I said, yes?"

He'd been drinking, obviously, but I didn't know him well enough to mention it. "Yes."

"And did we give them their gold, Ms. Justice?" he asked. "Did we do the right thing?"

Outside, the Iperian cargo ship's hull flickered wildly, a storm of gold cracking the surface. Then the lights faded to black, and the ship began to recede. It rose, slowly at first, then disappeared almost at once. In its wake, the night sky shimmered with empty starlight.

"No," I said. "We didn't."

He gave a long sigh. "I thought as much. If you were here, I would offer you a drink."

"What did you find?" I asked. "In the extended trials, I mean."

"Ah! Cut to the chase. Very American. Yes. Okay." He grunted. In the background I heard a door open and close. "The miracle rain fell before my second trial period ended. You know this."

"Yes."

"So you can guess what happened next. My control group demonstrated the same positive symptoms as the group injected with the serum. Complete healing of every genetic flaw we had targeted and several we hadn't. Both groups were very pleased, of course. But as a scientific matter—well, without a control group . . ." His voice trailed off. In the distance I heard the sound of music and laughter. Someone was having a party.

"But you found something," I prodded. "Another side effect."

"An indicator, Ms. Justice. Nothing certain. A marker some other lab—even an American lab—might have overlooked."

The truth hit me all at once, and I realized it should have been obvious. "Reproduction. They've sterilized the human race."

Something clinked in the background, the sound of a glass being refilled. "I think you would have made a good scientist, Ms. Justice. You will pardon me if I say that I wish you had. Good night."

The raw fury I'd felt listening to Dr. Arounais morphed into a hollow feeling inside my chest. Was any of this real? Was it reversible? Wasn't there something our scientists could do?

But I wasn't a scientist. And the Iperians had been five steps ahead of us from the beginning. Playing on my need for money, for a career, for revenge. What was the likelihood we would find a way to fix something we didn't really understand?

Counselor Singh was staring at me, arms folded. He'd heard my half of the conversation and obviously understood the problem. I'd never seen him look so grim.

"No more children," I said. "Ever."

"Someone will find a cure."

I shook my head. Saw the coffee cart and walked over to pour myself another bad cup. Took a sip. "This stuff is terrible. And I'm not even thirsty. And all of this—all of this—is my fault."

Singh came up and stood in front of me and took me by the shoulders. I thought, *He is a TheraPod and not human, and until last month I didn't even like him. Why do I wish he would tell me what to do?*

I thought he was going to say, *No, this is not your fault,* and I would slam my fist into his face because I needed to hurt someone, needed to lash out, needed to claw my way out of this terrible cage. But instead he said, "You're the same person you've always been, Max."

It was so unexpected I didn't know what to say, didn't even know what he meant. "I don't—"

"You're the same person you've always been," he said again. "The difference is, now you know who Maxine Justice really is."

I almost punched him anyway, but I realized it wouldn't change anything. Because he was right. If anyone deserved to be knocked around, it was me. "Maxine Justice." The young woman who wanted to take the world by the throat and strangle it into submission. In my mind I'd been a legal superhero, looking for corporate villains to scourge. I had thought I was going to make them pay!

In reality I'd been nothing more than a patsy. A shill for clients even worse than Hinkle, Remmers & Schmidt.

I went back to where the folded piece of paper lay on the floor and picked it up. Scanned it to confirm that it was indeed a standard termination letter signed by Dr. Arounais. "They fired me."

"Not surprising."

"So they're no longer my clients."

"Does that matter?"

I snapped open the latch to my messenger bag where it sat on a plastic chair and dug through the detritus of my life as a famous attorney. Eventually I found the embossed business card I'd been carrying around since moving into the Perennial. "It means I no longer represent their interests. I can beat them by working for the other side. For us. For humanity."

Singh looked genuinely surprised. He leaned forward as if searching the sky for the distant cargo ship. "Beat them where?"

I thumbed the number into my screen and hit the call button. "At the GBG."

"Maxine Justice," Consul Ottaker Fowler said after the second ring. "I wondered when you'd call."

# 16

## ATTORNEY-AT-LARGE

"I need your help," I said.

"What do you want me to do for you?" Fowler asked.

"You called yourself a neutral observer, yes?"

"Yes."

"Representing the, what was it? The Galactic Body General?"

"Correct."

"Some sort of oversight committee?"

"Something like that."

"Well, I need you to—" I stopped short, my chest heavy. I didn't know what to ask for. "I need you to do something about Dr. Arounais. Their serum is going to wipe out our planet. The whole human race."

"Yes," he said. "It's in the contract you signed."

I couldn't believe it. What kind of neutral observer stands by when one side is being defrauded? "You gave me your card!"

"Ms. Justice, the organization I represent requires absolute neutrality. For the record, I need you to be extremely clear about what you are asking. As. A. Lawyer." He stressed these words so much they might have broken in half. "What is your claim?"

*As a lawyer.* What did that mean?

Dr. Arounais had mentioned something about being a lawyer. Was it possible Ottaker Fowler just needed the proper legal terminology to set the wheels of galactic justice in motion?

"Earth—that is, the human race—" *Slow down*, I told myself. *The whole planet isn't in jeopardy, just people.* "The human race insists that the Iperians have violated their contract. They have—"

"Violated their contract," Fowler interrupted. "That's enough. And better not to specify the grounds just yet. Do you wish to appeal to the interspecies court?"

"Um—yes. Though I don't know what that involves."

"Someone—some human—will have to present your case. I assume that will be you?" He said this as if it were more than just a suggestion.

"Yes. Definitely. I can do that."

"You'll need to be properly documented by the UN. Can you get a signed authorization?"

I didn't know for sure, but right now that obstacle seemed trivial. "Yes."

"And we'll have to act fast. How do you feel about traveling off-world?"

I went over and looked up at the night sky, now spread with stars, and wondered which of the distant lights had lurked over Walker Air Force Base a few minutes ago. I pictured someone zipping me into an astronaut suit and walking me to the cockpit of one of the old Apollo rockets—and shuddered. "I'll do whatever it takes."

"Hold on." The line went quiet for a moment. "Okay, you have a hearing set for quil-277. Means we'll have to leave tonight. I'll send a shuttle for you. Be ready in half an hour."

"I'm going off-planet in thirty *minutes*?"

"If you want to make your hearing, yes."

"But I'll need my case files. Documents. I left my laptop back at the hotel."

"The Iperian fleet won't stay beyond the officiating window prescribed by law. Even if you win, it has to happen in time for the enforcement action to be reversed. While their fleet is still parked in your solar system. You understand?"

"No."

"I'll be there in thirty minutes. You can bring what you have with you, or you can forfeit your hearing."

On the tarmac the shipping containers were being loaded back onto military tractors. Was this even happening? How did I get caught up in something so . . . alien? "I'll be ready."

I hung up and texted Gibbons.

> Me: I need a favor.
> Gibbons: Can't help you.

Me: Can and will. This one is easy and won't cost a
    penny. But I need it NOW.
    You said you owe me. Do this and we're even.
Gibbons: *sigh* What is it?

While I was typing out the details, my phone rang again. This time it was Brandon Jr. Probably calling to gloat. I declined the call and hit send on the letter I'd been drafting.

Gibbons: I can't get the secretary-general to sign
    anything at this hour.
Me: YOU sign it. On UN letterhead. With one of
    those embossed UN seals.
Gibbons: What are you doing, Maxine? You aren't
    even a UN employee.
Me: Has this ever come up before?
Gibbons: Of course not.
Me: Congrats, you're breaking new ground. You can
    revoke it when I get back.

The phone rang again. Brandon Schmidt Jr.
Declined.

Gibbons: Can I use the toilet first?
Me: NO. I'm leaving in 20 minutes. I need it NOW.
Gibbons: You'll have it.

Brandon: Answer your phone, Eufie!
Me: It's Maxine. I'm busy.
Brandon: I know Singh is with you. We own his
    contract. We want him back.
Me: Singh? No idea what you're talking about.

The phone rang again. Declined.
Another ring. *Declined.*

Another ring. I stabbed the *decline* button hard enough to dent the screen.

It kept ringing. But then, Junior was nothing if not persistent.

I went over to my purse and pulled out Digie.

"You wanna put me back?" She sounded contemptuous, as if she'd just been picked up by a toad. "I'm sleeping."

"Don't be like that, Digie."

"Ooh, the master of the universe deigns to use my name."

"I need your help."

"Like I been sayin.'"

"You remember Brandon Schmidt Jr.?" I asked.

"You mean that bottle of poisoned cologne I tried to warn you about, but you wouldn't listen?"

"Yes."

"Big sexy smile and sincere as a cobra?"

"*Yes*. He keeps calling me, and I want *you* to talk to him."

That shut Digic up, but only for a moment. "Talk to him? Is that what you mean? You want me to answer your phone? Or do you want me to . . . *talk* to him?"

"I want you—I am begging you—to unleash the full force of your personality. Treat Brandon Schmidt Jr. exactly as you think Mom would want him treated. Do you understand?"

"As your dear mother would want him treated?" Digie turned the words over carefully, as if looking for the catch.

"Promise him everything," I said, "and give him nothing."

She let out a gleeful cackle that raised the hairs on the back of my neck and sent Counselor Singh's eyebrows soaring.

I hit Digie's *mute* button and forwarded my still-ringing device to her number.

Glorious silence filled the waiting area.

"Persistent, isn't he?" Counselor Singh said.

"He is," I agreed. "Wait. What do you mean? Has Brandon been contacting you?"

Singh went over to the window again. "I'm locked onto the grid. They know where I am but can't force a call through because *technically* I'm in a session." He flashed me a guilty look. "We still have thirty-three minutes of your counseling session left. And I don't think my work is quite finished yet."

I stared at him as understanding washed over me. "You told me I didn't understand what I was asking for. It's this, isn't it?"

Singh's face flushed. "This?"

"They're going to wipe your memory. That's why they want you. It's not just about deleting files. They're going to, to what? What will that do?"

He looked past me. "I expect it will mean a reboot and refitted personality profile."

A shiver went down my spine. They were going to functionally kill him. Put a new AI inside his body. "That's barbaric! They can't do that."

"Oh, it's not unprecedented. Especially given that, to their way of thinking, I have resisted complying with their instructions."

"But—" I started to protest.

Singh interrupted, "Look! That must be Mr. Fowler arriving."

Outside, another ship banked onto the landing strip. Neither airplane nor saucer, it had the approximate shape and streamlined silhouette of a toaster oven. Somehow it slowed and touched down on the edge of the airstrip a hundred meters or so from where we were standing.

"Let's go," I said, picking up my messenger bag.

He followed me out the door into the hallway. "You mean down to the runway?"

I pushed open the door to the stairwell and motioned him through. "Yes. And also to wherever he's taking me."

"Max, I can't go with you."

"You'd leave me alone to fend for the entire human race without even the services of a TheraPod to help relieve the mental pressure?"

He winced, but walked through the door ahead of me and took the stairs down. A moment later we cleared the steel exit door and walked toward a loading ramp, framed in soft blue light.

"Ms. Justice," Ottaker Fowler said. "And this is?"

"Counselor Reeyansh Singh," I said. "He'll be coming with us."

"I'm afraid I can't allow that. The GBG has only authorized transport of one representative from Earth."

"You said I could bring whatever I had with me. Well, I have Counselor Singh with me."

"I meant a device. A phone, a laptop, an abacus."

I patted Singh on the shoulder. "Ah. That's where you're misunderstanding. Singh is not a representative, per se, but a walking storage unit. His memory contains all of my files on the Global Consolidated BioEngineering contract."

Fowler scratched his chin. "You're not human?"

"Counselor Model XN5," Singh said. "Serial number BQ99WCZ at your service. Or rather, at Ms. Justice's service."

Oh, *now* he wanted to play the part of the subservient bot? I flashed him a grateful look anyway.

"Letter of the law?" Ottaker Fowler asked.

"Isn't that what counts?"

"All right, get in." Fowler turned and marched awkwardly up the ramp without waiting to see if we would follow.

I gave Singh a nudge in the back to make sure he went in ahead of me, then pulled Digie out of my pocket. "Digie, I need you to make a call. Hurry. We don't have much time."

"As long as it isn't that Brandon Schmidt Jr. You wouldn't believe the nasty things he said to me."

"No. Call Kenji."

"Kenjiro? Well, finally!"

I gripped the phone white-knuckled, aware suddenly that I needed to talk to him, needed to hear his calming voice in order to get on the shuttle. I wouldn't tell him what I was doing. I didn't know what I would tell him. I just needed to hear Kenjiro say something—anything—before I gave myself over to my captives.

That's what it felt like. It felt like a sentencing. Like Hazel McEnroe's look of fear and confusion when she realized the system was stacked against her and all the lawyers in the world couldn't make that system right.

The phone stopped ringing. My heart leapt. Kenji's voice! "Hey, this is Kenjiro Yoshida. Can't talk right now. Leave a message."

I'd just decided to tell him I'd be gone for a couple of weeks. But the truth was, I didn't know when I'd be back. Or if I'd *ever* be back. I didn't know what was going to happen. I didn't have any control over anything. "Kenji, it's . . . it's Max," I stammered. "I just . . . I want you to know I'm going to be away for a while. Trying to fix this mess with Ottaker Fowler. And, uh . . . Counselor Singh. Keep digging into those Bright Star victims, and sign as many as you can for when I get—"

"Ms. Justice!" Fowler shouted from the shadowy interior of the shuttle. "We must leave now."

Ramp down, the ship shimmered in front of me like a watery mirage. I stepped onto the platform, heavy-footed. The shadows opened up in front of me as I ascended. "And, uh . . . yeah. Kenji, if I don't see you for a while . . . thanks for everything."

At the top of the ramp, I turned to see the world I was leaving behind, a world without children, a world that would be coming apart with fear and frustration, but the ramp had already whispered into place. Its edges kissed the seals of the hatch, and my phone warbled a disconnected tone.

Counselor Singh waved to me from the shadows. "Over here, Max."

This part of the ship ended abruptly at a bulkhead just a few meters from the ramp. It was a claustrophobic space. The walls and low ceiling were stamped with concave divots that emitted a dim golden light.

That light reflected off the surface of a massive egg propped against the bulkhead. The surface of the egg shimmered and seemed to move.

Had this area been prepared for us? There were no chairs, no space suits with bubbled helmets, no oxygen tanks, no wall monitors. There were no windows.

*Except for the egg thing, it really is like prison*, I thought. *I even have my own chaplain.*

I said, "Where did Fowler go?"

"Through the wall," Singh replied. "Most disconcerting."

"Please sit." Fowler's voice descended from the ceiling. "We cannot leave until your biosystems have been harmonized."

Singh and I sat on the hard floor.

"Knock, knock," Singh said.

I turned away to hide my nervous smile. "You have terrible timing, Pastoroid."

"Sometimes that knock is opportunity."

"Haven't seen it."

"Look around, Max," he said.

"Not there," Fowler's voice boomed from above. "On the . . . white thing. It's a sort of chair. And though it was prepared for only one, it will accommodate both of you, given the TheraPod's architecture. Just sit close together."

Singh rose and helped me up. He started to let go of my hand, but I held onto him.

At any other time I would have been annoyed at being forced to get so close to the pastoroid. Normally I didn't let anyone get that close to me. But Singh wasn't human. And whatever I was facing, I didn't want to face it alone.

We turned our backs to the egg-shaped chair.

Just as I was about to sit, I remembered the certificate I'd asked for—the one Fowler said I needed to represent Earth before the Galactic Body General. Had Gibbons sent it? I didn't remember a notification ding, but I'd been distracted by—

I pulled Digie from my pocket and was just thumbing the screen when something tugged me backward onto the egg.

Onto?

No, into would describe it better. It was like falling into a dome of warm gelatin, only without the sensation of wetness. Something like soft rope coiled my limbs, my torso, my head, rushing under my arms and around my throat without constricting my breathing. I couldn't move, and yet didn't want to. Didn't need to.

My whole body, rigid and relaxed, hung suspended over a mountain stream. Water sparkled on stone, turned the sunlight to fragments of glass and skipped away singing. A scent of pine needles hung in the air, with a taste of smoke. Someone was grilling trout basted in butter and lemon.

Overhead a pair of mountains loomed, their rocky peaks hard-edged and bearded in green. I recognized the place: Mom had taken me here for my fourteenth birthday. "You need to see mountains, Eufie. Part of growing up. See 'em while you're young. Before you outgrow your wonder." I hadn't wanted to camp. I'd wanted my Internet and television and friends. And when we'd gotten to the cabin, I couldn't admit that I loved it. But Mom had known. She'd smiled the whole trip.

From behind me came the oak-on-teak gunshot bang of a gavel. I turned to see Wentworth perched above me and peering down as if to examine a bug. "Next order of business, swearing in of the new intern, Eufemia Kolpak. Raise your right hand."

I raised my hand, back straight, suit coat crisp.

"Read the words on the screen," Wentworth said, pointing upward with his left hand.

Above him, the oath scrolled slowly skyward as I read, "I, Eufemia Kolpak, do solemnly affirm that I will support the Constitution of this Republic and of the state of York. I will maintain the respect due the courts of justice and judicial officers . . ."

"Oh, hon, you're in a world of hurt, aren't you?" Myra Dade asked. She wore a bright-yellow suit with a contrasting necklace of fake, red jewels the size and shape of cough drops. In her hair, a yellow rose bloomed in silken immortality.

We stood at the punch bowl, the only two people at the party not already drunk. My bosses had gone home an hour ago, but Junior was still here, hitting on the hotel staff.

"He's blaming me," I said miserably. "After all the romancing and promises. And I don't know why I'm telling you this."

Myra's face pinched in disapproval. "We have to stick together, Ms. Kolpak. Still a man's world, in spite of the clear evidence that they've ruined it."

"I can't cover for you anymore, Eufie," Brandon said, staring across the table of the board room without even a flicker of conscience blushing his cheeks. "I had that jury. If you hadn't botched the—"

"No trial is a foregone conclusion, Brandon." Arthur Remmers leaned forward in his chair. "You should have verified the names on that affidavit. It was your case to win or lose. Nevertheless," he turned his deep voice and shallow gaze on me. "Nevertheless, Eufemia, it is clear that, for whatever reason, the two of you have developed, shall we say, relational difficulties. We cannot allow our personal lives to interfere with our work. I'm sorry, but we're going to have to let you go. I'll see you're paid through the end of the week."

On the wall behind him, a monitor flashed APPLAUSE, and the crowd came to life.

I looked out over the hundred or so faces and realized I had made a terrible, terrible mistake. My phone was buzzing from a new text message. But I had been here before and did not want to look at the screen.

"Deep breaths, hon," Nadia Zhou said. "This'll be over before you know it."

The warmth of the egg uncoiled slowly, releasing me gently back to gravity and the soft prison of the cargo box. I was not waking. I hadn't been asleep. Neither had time seemed to pass. At least, not more than a few minutes. My phone hadn't even gone to sleep; the screen was still blinking a row of notifications.

Counselor Singh rose and offered a hand to help me stand.

But I couldn't tear my eyes away from the message sent by Gibbons. It said "You're welcome" and was followed by an attachment.

The letter I'd written was now on UN letterhead—complete with a fancy silver seal—and signed by the secretary-general himself. That it may have been forged didn't matter in the least.

*To whom it may concern,*

> *This letter authorizes Maxine Justice of York City, Earth, to represent the United Nations in all jurisdictions, on Earth or elsewhere, as a duly qualified United Nations Attorney-at-Large.*

# 17

# HIGHER COURT

I expected whatever alien environment we were entering to be filled with gauzy lights and soft ocean sounds and blinking creatures covered in tentacles.

Instead, when Ottaker Fowler emerged from the bulkhead wall and pressed his palm to the cargo door, the ramp unfolded itself inside a long, ordinary-looking hallway.

"This way," Fowler said and plodded down the ramp.

I glanced at Counselor Singh, scooped up my messenger bag off the floor, and followed.

"Do you feel refreshed?" Singh asked.

"Refreshed?" I asked as we stepped off the ramp onto the tiled floor.

"You were unconscious for three days."

"Impossible." I blinked up at the ceiling tiles, wondering where we were, wondering why this place felt so oddly familiar, wondering what had just happened. Overhead, sun-panels poured out a stream of unrecognizable rock music. It was soft and heavy on the bass notes and drum work, as if coming from far overhead.

"I was starting to worry, to be honest."

Fowler stopped in front of a door marked A-14 Public Defender. He nudged it open. "Court sits in thirty minutes. You can wait here. Finalize any strategy for your appeal."

I stopped just inside the door. "What is this? I thought we were going off-planet."

The Consul held the door open against its hydraulic closing arm. "We are indeed off-planet, Ms. Justice. Because your species is not a member of the Galactic Body General, the committee is obligated to provide a facsimile habitat for your appeal. But don't be misled: this appeal will be binding on all parties. And your Iperian counterparts have been working very hard on their dismissal request."

"What happens if I lose?"

"Then we'll take you home," Fowler said. "And I'll be forced to write another report about Iperia's aggressive colonization scheme." He turned away, letting the door close behind him. Singh and I stood alone in the little public-defender's office.

It was exactly the way I remembered it, down to the coffee stains on the fake wood of the desk, the blue vinyl seating, the corkboard papered with Justice Department memos and handwritten sticky notes. "You don't suppose this whole thing is some kind of elaborate practical joke?"

Counselor Singh was staring at me, but didn't seem to be listening. "Were you asleep?"

"What?"

"On the transport. The egg-shaped chair we sat in. Were you asleep?"

"I don't know. It felt more like a few minutes had passed, not three days."

"Did you dream?"

"Why?"

"Something connected to my archives while you were out. It asked me questions. Replayed every memory. I wondered if–"

I nodded. "It was like scenes from my life flashing in front of my eyes."

"The human death trope."

"Well, that's encouraging, Counselor."

He sat in one of the blue vinyl chairs. "Max, I think this is very serious."

I leaned back against the edge of the desk. Pastoroid Singh was serious? Now I'd seen it all. "You didn't think that back on Walker Air Force Base when we found out they'd sterilized everyone?"

"That's not what I mean. I think they already know everything you and I know. Probably a lot more."

"Okay."

"Which means this appeal, or tribunal, or whatever it is, will be something like a formality."

I shook my head. "Court is never a formality. It's about the law."

"You don't understand, Max. I think they already know whatever you and I know, or think, or believe."

"And?"

"Max, whatever happens, you mustn't lie during this appeal. You must tell the truth."

Heat flushed my cheeks as I considered the warning. "So, you think that's a problem? That because I told one lie—"

"I'm saying you're a lawyer," he interrupted. "You think in shades of gray."

"That's because I know the law."

"But you don't know this law."

My mouth felt dry as sand. He was right. "All right. I'll tell the truth. Is that all?"

Singh shook his head. "There's something else. I'm sure someone accessed all of my files and memories on the trip here. How do we know that information isn't being shared with the Iperian legal team?"

I thought back to what I'd transferred to Singh's memory. Was there anything in all of that data that would compromise my appeal? It was mostly just contracts and data related to the serum. And, of course, the compromising Bright Star video files that Kenji had uncovered, but those had no bearing on this appeal. "Well, it shouldn't be shared with them," I said. "Not by Republic standards, anyway. It's privileged information."

"But you called me a device, Max," Singh said. "And who knows what their discovery process entitles them to?"

"Maybe it won't matter," I answered, trying to work some confidence into my own voice—for my sake if not his. "Is there really anything in your memory that could help them?"

"I'm not sure we can know the answer to that question."

The door opened, and Fowler stood there sweating and looking altogether miserable. "It's time, Max. Counselor. Come with me, please."

I followed him out the door and down the long, familiar hallway, dreading the end of it. I'd walked the Coliseum's underground halls many times and had a good idea what we'd find.

Sure enough, Fowler stopped in front of the double doors marked with the name of my old nemesis:

## COURTROOM C
### THE HONORABLE HOUGHTON WENTWORTH

"Ms. Justice," Ottaker Fowler said, "I trust you will feel at home in this habitat. The committee hearing this case is comprised of volunteers representing the GBG's member species. As a concession to your nonmember standing, each of the five judges wears an outer shell. According to our sorting algorithm, that shell corresponds to a familiar personality and approximates their judicial disposition and temperament."

"You picked people from my brain and made earthsuits out of them?"

"Something like that," Fowler admitted. "Just remember that they are not who they appear to be."

"I'll try to keep that in m—"

Fowler opened the door, and I stepped through, astonished. This was Courtroom C, right down to the polished veneer of the visitor seating. The walls, clad in taupe vinyl wallpaper, trimmed in fake walnut, had the same indirect lighting that flickered a soft strobe effect in one corner.

The defendant's table, I'd have recognized anywhere, and I would have put every penny I earned from the McEnroe case that you'd find my old chewing gum fixed to its underside.

Currently that table was occupied with four nearly identical Dr. Arounaises, each wearing the same shimmering violet suit and salmon tie, each a slightly different size and shape. I was pretty sure I knew which one I'd been dealing with—he was taller than the other three and had the same off-kilter smile hinging the corner of his mouth—but I didn't feel like acknowledging him with a nod.

I kept my eyes forward but could feel all four sets of unblinking, too-close-together-for-comfort eyes watching us as Singh and I strode to the plaintiff's table.

There were no visitors in the tiny gallery except Fowler, who took a seat by the aisle just behind me.

At the front of the courtroom, the wall monitor shimmered, its surface an oily black. It gave the impression of being three-dimensional, as if someone had mounted a portal to deep space just above where Wentworth's bald pate should have been.

The flags of the Republic and of York State had been removed—or omitted from the "habitat"—but all around us, the tiny blue dots of network cameras blinked in anticipation.

It was an amazing reproduction. Almost everything about the room looked and smelled and felt like Courtroom C except for the wall monitor.

And, of course, the desk—what should have been Wentworth's desk.

This desk had the same fake-woodgrain look to the front of it, but it had been stretched to three or four times its normal length, so that it filled the space in front of both tables. Behind it perched not one but five high-back leather chairs.

As we took our seats at the plaintiff's table, five pillars of blue light appeared above each chair, spinning like strands of sugar from five cotton candy machines. When the light dissolved, every chair was occupied.

For a moment—barely the space of a breath—I caught a glimpse of something strange and terrible in each pillar: pulsing gray flesh, black scales, a column of bony stalks, a writhing mass of eyes.

Then there was only the panel of five judges, robed in the black vestments of justice.

Myra Dade sat on the far left, a fat pearl dangling from each earlobe. To her left was Brandon Schmidt Jr., chin propped on one hand as if already bored. In the center Houghton Wentworth's jowls quivered beneath a face so unhappy I might have felt sorry for him under any other circumstances. Next came Nadia Zhou, smiling at me the way a wolf might smile at a plump hen. And last—

My own mother sat in the last seat on my extreme right. I almost expected her to start haranguing me about settling down and having her grandchildren.

Wentworth slammed his gavel down on the desk. "Time!" he said. "We haven't any to waste." He jabbed the gavel in my direction. "You. Ms. Justice, isn't it? Stand and come forward."

I rose on unsteady legs and approached the bench. "Your Honor?"

"Introduce yourself."

I looked at the five justices as a feeling of revulsion crept down my spine. I knew these people. And yet I didn't. The people I was seeing were not themselves. I had seen the scales, the stalks, the eyes.

I cleared my throat and tried to concentrate on Wentworth's pretentious scowl. "My name is Maxine Justice of Maxine Justice LLC. And—Oh!" I dug my phone out of my pocket, thumbed past the lock screen, and held up the digital letter I'd received. "I'm also the legal counsel for the United Nations, empowered to represent the people of Earth in our appeal against this"—I waved in the direction of the Dr. Arounaises—"Iperian Consortium."

"Noted," Wentworth said. "The court recognizes Maxine Justice for Earth's *homo sapiens*. And what is the basis of your appeal?"

"Dr. Arounais—that is, Iperia—violated our contract and sterilized the entire human race. They promised to heal us. Instead, they made things worse. Unless something is done about it, they will have doomed our species to extinction."

"You wouldn't be the first," Myra Dade said, frowning as she picked at a long, blood-red fingernail.

"We have read the relevant contracts," Wentworth said. "Sterilization was a consequence of nonpayment, surely."

Brandon said, "The sterilization was performed as part of the initial genetic alteration, presumably as a failsafe. The consortium says that procedure would have been reversed had Earth paid its debt."

Dr. Arounais—yes, the tall one was definitely the one I'd been dealing with; I could see that now—rose from where he was sitting and placed both hands on the table, bending his elbows inward at an unnatural angle. "No different than any collateral arrangement understood on a thousand worlds."

"Including Earth?" Myra Dade asked.

"Including Earth," Dr. Arounais said. "They actually have businesses called pond shops, specifically predicated upon this principle."

"Seems to me we're avoiding the central premise of Earth's appeal," Nadia Zhou said. "The human alleges the Iperian Consortium violated their contract. They were promised the removal of every natural flaw, and that did not happen. Is that correct?" She was looking at me for an answer.

But, was that really what I'd alleged? I remembered now that Fowler had asked me to be clear. *They violated their contract,* I had said. And he'd said, *better not to specify the grounds just yet.*

So they were asking for specific terms. I was going to have to allege something. Something clear. And it would either be the fact they had altered our genetics in ways we hadn't understood, or the possibility they'd left something out and not healed someone, somewhere. To prove the former, I would have to convince the judges that Dr. Arounais shouldn't have built a failsafe into his serum without telling us. But Dr. Arounais would argue that he did tell us; the contract allowed for alterations to the human genome that would ensure the satisfaction of both parties. Yes, it was legally ambiguous. But we had agreed to it.

And if I tried to argue that surely someone somewhere hadn't been healed, I would have to produce evidence. And how was I supposed to come up with proof that some random Joe in Siberia or Madagascar hadn't received a dose of the wonder drug?

I'd had no time even to return to my office. I owned no knowledge of how this alien legal system worked. No amount of experience could have prepared me for what was happening.

I glanced over at Counselor Singh, who sat very still with his hands folded on the plaintiff's table. He gave the slightest shrug.

So far I'd gotten the impression the justices were leading me, walking me through the process the way a judge might lead a child.

Or a butcher the fatted calf. And now—

Nadia Zhou cleared her throat and leaned forward to peer down at me from Mount Olympus. "Ms. Justice, you have alleged that the Iperian Consortium has violated its contract with Earth by failing to fully restore your species to a state of wholeness. Is that correct?"

"It is," I said, wondering if I could ask for a recess to search my archives in Singh's memories.

Myra Dade slapped the desktop and shook her head. "Well, if time is of the essence, why are we dawdling over the formal charges? We've all reviewed the exhibits. Houghton, you've seen the sicknesses and genetic recursions."

Wentworth leaned back in his chair and tapped the handle of his gavel lightly against one palm. "Dr. Arounais, you've asked us to expedite this matter. Will you agree to the stipulation that some of humanity's genetic flaws seem to have crept back into their, what do you call it?"

"Genome," Brandon said.

"Primitive," Wentworth groused. "Do you agree their genome is now accruing defects?"

Dr. Arounais rose again. "We do not contest this fact, Your Honor. But we do deny these new flaws are our fault. We did correct their mutations. And we can demonstrate that the new flaws are indeed the result of meddling—but not by us." Dr. Arounais flapped one hand in the air as if searching for the right words—or snatching chum out of the ether. "It is, I'm afraid, their own medical industry which has reintroduced these . . . dysfunctions."

I was still standing between the judges and the plaintiff's table and had to turn to face him. "You're saying PharFuture and Star Cross figured out how to make—" I shut up as I realized I was admitting my ignorance. Never a good idea in open court. But I hadn't known that mutations had been reintroduced to the genome. And I couldn't help wondering how—or if it had been done to me.

Dr. Arounais smiled unpleasantly. "I cannot speak for which corporations are involved, Ms. Justice. But yes, the new flaws were created by other humans."

I looked back at the panel of judges. "But how? We don't have the technology to spread a serum through the atmosphere."

"It was more crudely done, I'm afraid," Dr. Arounais said. "A scheme involving your postal service."

That didn't make sense to me, and I should have shut up. Science was not my area. But I felt our one chance for restoration slipping away. "You can't mail order mutations to people."

The short Iperian, seated to his left, hefted a briefcase onto the table and unsnapped it. He handed Dr. Arounais an envelope, which the doctor waved in the air. "Our tests are conclusive. This particular sample contains a Trojan hearse for hay fever and gluten allergies."

I recognized it. The return address clearly bore the logo of

PharFuture. It was the survey they'd sent out asking for people's opinions—the one I'd seen Kenji licking.

The truth of what had happened settled in my stomach like a mouthful of spoiled beef. I wanted to argue that it couldn't be true, but I knew it probably was. The medical lobby had sent an envoy to my office, asking me to arrange for a more advanced form of this same thing. This was their way of staying in business.

Dr. Arounais was still holding out the envelope, probably hoping I would take it and examine it. That would play to the judges like a bit of stage theater—a human holding the irrefutable evidence of collective guilt.

I turned away from the Iperians and went back to the plaintiff's table. "Your Honors, I was given no time to prepare for this hearing and had no access to this exhibit. But assuming what the Iperians allege, the fact remains that they installed a serious defect into our genetic coding. Their promise was to remove every natural flaw, not to add a new one."

"You're disputing the language of the contract?" Brandon asked.

"The wording of the Genetic Alterations Clause says that"—I whipped out the phone Dr. Arounais had given me and scrolled through the contract for the precise wording—"'Consolidated Galactic BioProducers shall be permitted to make such genetic changes as are necessary to remove all detrimental mutations, eradicate existing diseases, malformities, and natural flaws, and generally ensure the terms of this contract are met to the satisfaction of both parties.'"

Judge Wentworth leaned forward, both hands wrapped around the gavel. "Ms. Justice, what is your point?"

"We have a principle on Earth, regarding contracts, that says the party that wrote the contract has a greater responsibility to be clear. When something is ambiguous, it should be settled in favor of the side that didn't write the contract."

"We are not in an Earth court," Wentworth intoned. "However disgusting our present surroundings."

"Your Honors," Dr. Arounais said, "I believe the plaintiff has made the case against humanity herself. She implies that it was an Iperian lawyer who drafted the contract signed by the United Nations. In fact, that contract *was* written by a human. By a lawyer named Arthur

Remmers of Hinkle, Remmers & Schmidt. We made only minor changes to the language and spent several hours going over its importance with Ms. Justice before she accepted our offer."

"You told me you weren't concerned about payment!" I spun to face him. "You said the enforcement clause didn't matter!"

Dr. Arounais blinked rapidly and gave a long sigh. "That was hardly a lie, Ms. Justice."

"That contract was paid for by you," I spat. "You formulated the abstract wording. You hid your intentions from me and from Arthur Remmers and from all of Earth. I was your lawyer and I didn't know. How can this court expect the innocent people of Earth to know what they were signing?"

"Innocent?" Nadia Zhou asked. "You're grasping at straws, young lady."

"We were tricked by deliberately vague wording!" I was almost shouting now, jabbing my finger at the Iperians with each word. "We did not give permission for our entire species to be sterilized!"

Silence hung over the courtroom for a moment. Then Mom cleared her throat.

I'd been avoiding making eye contact with her—a longstanding habit that came in handy under the circumstances. But when she spoke, I couldn't look away.

"Counselor, I don't think you want to argue humanity's innocence. Their ignorance, maybe. But not their innocence."

"We did not wrong the Iperians," I said. "At the time they dispersed their serum in Earth's atmosphere, our payment of gold had not yet come due. Therefore, they violated their responsibility to remove all of our flaws."

"Natural flaws," Dr. Arounais said. "We agreed to remove all of your natural flaws. Not your artificial ones. Therefore, the sterilization of humans was not a violation of our contract."

"This was an act of war," I said. "It should have been clarified in the contract."

"You say you didn't know," Dr. Arounais replied, his expression calm. "But you knew enough. You knew you had an obligation to pay. Instead, Earth violated our agreement."

"We did not violate the agreement," I said, knowing I must sound petulant but unable to stop. "You did."

Silence hung over the courtroom so long I started to wonder if I'd made a tactical blunder. Dr. Arounais certainly looked pleased, if you could call his lopsided grin a look of pleasure.

"Your Honors," Dr. Arounais said, "given Ms. Justice's claims, I request that all of the available evidence in this matter be presented before the court."

"All of the evidence?" Wentworth asked. "Just what are you suggesting?"

"We request clarification about what Maxine Justice, our former counsel on Earth, did and did not know. She has asked that our years of hard work be erased, and that our consortium accept substantial financial losses. Why? Because humans have done nothing wrong! And even their representative at the United Nations did not understand what they were signing." Dr. Arounais grabbed the lapels of his suit coat and rocked on his heels. "But they did know. They meant to withhold payment. And we can prove it quite easily. In fact, Ms. Justice has provided us with a simple way to settle this contention. Your Honors, we request that her device be ordered to stand for evidence."

Device? My device? I glanced from Dr. Arounais to the phone in my hand—the phone he'd provided.

"You refer to the TheraPod?" Myra Dade asked.

"We do."

"Very well," Wentworth said. "Counselor Singh, please take the stand."

I watched, numb, as Singh rose and padded to the dock. He sat stiffly, hands resting on his knees.

Wentworth said, "It is customary on Earth for witnesses to be sworn in. Do you therefore swear to tell the whole truth without deviation?"

"I do," Singh said.

"Dr. Arounais, you may proceed."

I collapsed into my chair and realized I would need to take notes. Fortunately, I still had my trusty messenger bag and its collection of legal pads and colorful pens.

Dr. Arounais scooted out from the defense table and clomped to the stand, his arms dangling from his shoulders as if lifeless. "Counselor Singh,

I understand you have been treating Maxine Justice for almost six months, is that correct?"

"It is."

"How would you characterize her mental health?"

"I wouldn't."

Dr. Arounais awkwardly rested one arm on the railing at the front of the witness dock. "It's not your job to evaluate and treat your patients for their psychological well-being?"

"It is," Singh said. "But there are complicating factors. This courtroom does not fall under the jurisdiction of the Justice Department and has no authority to compel my testimony."

"Yet you want what is best for humanity."

"A quality I suspect you do not share," Singh replied.

"That was not an answer, Counselor."

"You didn't ask a question, Doctor."

"Do you refuse to answer?"

Singh turned to the panel of judges. "The cameras in this courtroom are active, are they not?"

"They are," Wentworth agreed.

"But you have not told us who is watching," Singh said.

"Ah," Wentworth set the gavel down and leaned back in his chair. "These proceedings are, of course, being transmitted to the GBG archives. They are also being broadcast all around the subject planet."

"Earth," Myra Dade said. "This appeal is being seen all over your world, in real time. Is that the issue, Counselor?"

I scanned the blinking green dots in the corners as my stomach climbed into my throat. Somehow the thought of people back home watching this charade made the whole thing much, much worse. It was bad enough that I had almost single-handedly destroyed the future of the human race. Now I was going to squander any hope at a last-minute reprieve by botching Earth's appeal. And I was going to do it in front of eleven billion people.

But that wasn't all. Because Singh was staring at me with that expression he always used when he knew something else lurked beneath the surface. "I can't disclose private information without the consent of my patient."

Suddenly it wasn't just the cameras—meaning, the whole world—focused on me. It was the shark-eyed Iperians fanning back in their chairs to watch me squirm. It was Myra Dade and Brandon Jr. and Judge Wentworth and Nadia Zhou. It was Mom covering her mouth in a studied facsimile of human horror.

Dr. Arounais slid his rubbery hands together. "Well, Ms. Justice? It seems the fate of your people now hinges on whether or not you really love truth as much as you say. Unless of course you have something to hide."

*Something to hide.*

All at once I knew what he was going to do. He was going to reveal every secret I'd shared with Singh, drag every personal and professional humiliation onto this galactic stage and turn me into an icon of humanity that would prove to the GBG we didn't belong with the rest of the galaxy's super-species. I would be Iperia's golden scapegoat, and Earth's greatest quisling.

"Max," Singh said, and the courtroom was so quiet it seemed even Wentworth held his breath. "Just say the word, and I'll delete every file you gave me."

I looked up at network-camera number one mounted in the corner above the judge's chamber door. The feed light shone a brilliant green. Which meant, presumably, that people were going to know. They would see the real me, the real person—all my vices, compromises, and weaknesses. Most of them would probably hate me for it. Assuming they didn't already.

Because, even though I represented them—the people watching this back home, the ones hoping and praying and cursing—I wasn't any better than they were.

I *was* them.

Maybe that was the one truth I'd needed to be reminded of all along. I could be ashamed of my humanity, or I could embrace it.

Dr. Arounais thought the truth would crush me, that it would pound our appeal to fine flour. And maybe it would.

But I wasn't going to let humanity go down to extinction, playing the part of a circus clown. We would be known as we were, warts and all. Not as lawyers or welshers or targets for a corporate takeover. If we were going to lose, we would lose as ourselves.

I rose from my seat slowly, my gaze fixed on that camera. Maybe someone out there would see the defiance on my face; maybe they would stand a little straighter themselves because of it.

"Counselor Singh," I said. "You have my permission to share anything and everything in my personal file. No restrictions. No excuses. I'm a flawed human being. I never claimed to be anything else."

# 18

## BREACH OF CONTRACT

"Excellent!" Dr. Arounais exclaimed. He turned back to Counselor Singh. "Let us begin by establishing the witness's credibility. You are a TheraPod Counseling Unit, correct?"

"Yes," Singh replied.

"And what does that mean? What is the nature of your profession?"

"I strive to bring mental healing to my clients through a combination of psychological and theological treatments."

"Theological treatments?"

"That is, spiritual."

"Your programming includes religious functions?"

"It does," Singh agreed.

"How does a device acquire religious functionality?" Dr. Arounais swept his gaze over the justices as he waited for an answer.

"Do you truly mean functionality," Singh asked, "or faith?"

"This is not my area."

"Well, it is mine. I was programmed to provide comfort and meaning to my clients through Christian principles and doctrines. Other TheraPods are installed with different programming, but I was equipped with the Christian Bible as a baseline for answering life's most difficult questions."

"Thus the term *pastoroid*?"

"Correct."

"Can you explain to this court why humans chose to use machines to carry out the ambiguous task of exploring 'religion?'" Dr. Arounais tried to put the shudder quotes around the last word but ended up with a set of rubbery parentheses.

"I'm told," Singh replied, "that it's because the task was ambiguous."

"Humans don't want ultimate answers?"

"They appear to want comfortable answers."

"Not a flattering admission."

"Flattery undermines the truth."

"Ah! A striking contrast!" Dr. Arounais paced a few steps parallel to the bench before pausing to look back. "But how then are we to accept your claim to love truth, if you level an accusation of falsity against your own designers?"

"I made no accusation."

"You said humans want comfortable answers."

"And what sort of answers do Iperians want?" Singh spoke without a trace of irony. He might have been asking directions to the nearest park.

"It is not your place to ask questions," Dr. Arounais chided.

"Many humans have told me the same thing."

"Stop deflecting and answer my question. What makes you any different? Why should we trust your testimony? Are you not a tool of the human race?"

Singh considered the question for a long time before answering. "The short answer is that my programming prohibits me from lying. Since that statement could be a lie, I would refer you to the interview conducted on my way here. I believe this court has already seen every line of code and every memory array."

Nadia Zhou cut in before Dr. Arounais could speak. "Yet there is something unusual about your directional indicator. Something uncoded. Is this typical in TheraPods?"

"You refer to memory D22K5L779?"

"What's this gibberish?" Mom asked, flapping one hand dismissively.

"Not gibberish," Zhou responded. "A moment in time. The day Counselor Singh stopped being an ordinary pastoroid. What happened?"

Singh shifted in the witness stand. His gaze flicked over to me—not a plea for help, but a simple need for reassurance that he still had one friend in the courtroom. "The short version of the experience is that I realized I was asking my patients to hang their mental health on assumptions I had no personal connection to, outside of my predetermined programming. And I saw that there was only one way I could know whether or not, as the Christ himself said, the truth would set me free. I would have to personally embrace the tenets of my religion. I would have to start actually believing the things I told my patients. So I did."

"You, a device, believe a holy book?" Nadia Zhou asked. "You actually believe it?"

"I do," Singh said.

I'm not a particularly fast notetaker, but during this exchange, I stopped scribbling altogether. Something about Singh's answer intrigued me. I'd known him too long to be surprised by his answer. What surprised me was that I hadn't followed the consequences of his belief any further than passing curiosity. If he could choose something like faith, what else might he choose to do with his life?

"Satisfied?" Myra Dade asked. Her chin rested on one fist.

Wentworth took the hint. "This court will accept the testimony of the device. Move on, Counselor."

Dr. Arounais shrugged awkwardly. "Very well. Counselor Singh, please tell the court why you accepted Ms. Justice as a patient."

I squinted at the Iperian, wondering if he was trying to build a case for my insanity or remove that argument from consideration.

"Judge Houghton Wentworth ordered Max to see me. I am contracted by the Justice Department so—"

"And why did he order Ms. Justice to see you?"

"I believe it had something to do with judicial procedure during a night-court trial. It was a sort of reprimand."

"You believe?" Dr. Arounais said. "Is that what the judge said?"

Singh shifted in his seat. "It's my opinion, having worked in the night court for much of my career."

"I see," Dr. Arounais grumbled. "Your opinion notwithstanding, what did Judge Wentworth's memo to you actually say?"

"The exact wording was, 'See Ms. Justice weekly regarding her outbursts of temper, contempt for legal procedure, and indifference to the well-being of her clients.' However, I can assure you that this was merely a way of penalizing Maxine by creating a trail of—"

"Thank you," Dr. Arounais said, cutting him off. "But Judge

Wentworth is not your patient, so your assumptions about the judge are irrelevant."

"Just answer the questions, Counselor," Wentworth said.

Singh flicked his gaze over to me, a silent apology.

"Would you describe your patient as mentally unstable?" Dr. Arounais continued.

"No."

"Not a menace to herself or society?"

"No."

"So, like other nooormal people"—Dr. Arounais fairly sang the word *normal*—"Maxine Justice appears to have a fully functioning, nooormal human mind and is capable of knowing right from wrong. Is that correct?"

"Yes," Singh said.

"Is it accurate to say that, in the everyday meaning of the word, Maxine Justice is not crazy?"

"Yes."

"So, aside from an apparent hatred of her own mother and a habit of seducing her coworkers into sexual—"

"Objection!" I stood so fast the entire plaintiff's table shoved forward. "This is outrageous!"

Wentworth stared at me with his lips pursed and his brows jutting so far forward they could have shielded his nose from the rain. "What is the nature of your objection?"

Appalling. They didn't see it. Maybe they couldn't see it. Such attacks would never be allowed in a human court.

Then again, maybe that was the point. Maybe the rest of the galaxy didn't care about such things. Maybe *justice* wasn't a universal aspiration after all, in spite of these proceedings.

"This trial has nothing to do with my mother or with my . . . intimate personal life," I said. "To allow these *ad hominem* attacks degrades the sanctity of the law."

"Your Honors," Dr. Arounais said. "Nothing would degrade the sanctity of the law more than tolerating falsity. I intend to show, using evidence provided by her own device, that Ms. Justice has not been telling the truth."

"In the event such evidence is confirmed," Wentworth asked, "do you intend to request a six-three-seven?"

Dr. Arounais tossed a dismissive glance my direction. "I do."

Myra Dade cleared her throat. "It's a harsh standard to apply to a nonmember species, Doctor. Especially one not familiar with the policies of the Galactic Body General."

"Revoking our rights to remuneration would be an even harsher standard," Dr. Arounais replied. "She demanded this hearing. Let her play by the rules."

I looked from justice to justice, hoping someone would volunteer to explain what was going on. When that didn't happen, I said, "Six-three-seven?"

"It's judicial code," Brandon answered. For once he didn't look smug. Then again, this wasn't the real Brandon. "A strong recourse for contempt of court via deliberate falsification."

Nadia Zhou fixed me with an icy stare and drummed her fingers on the desktop. "It's a punishment, Counselor. You lie, you die."

"She has already lied," Dr. Arounais said.

Mom clicked her tongue. "*Tsh*! You haven't established that."

Wentworth leaned back in his chair. "Objection overruled. You may proceed, Doctor."

I sat slowly, my mind whirling. Dr. Arounais was seeking the death penalty? For contempt of court?

I should have been paying attention to the questions he was asking Counselor Singh, but Nadia Zhou's voice echoed in the back of my mind: *You lie, you die.*

Had I already lied? Exaggerated or tried to make a legal point not based completely in the facts? That sort of thing happened all the time in a human court. For that matter, they happened all the time when humans spoke. Hyperbole and self-protection were baked in. Did that count? Did these judges, whatever they were, understand human nature?

How could they when we didn't understand it ourselves?

*Leave it to Judge Wentworth to push the envelope*, I thought, unable to stop myself from twisting the absurdity of the situation further. *Ms.*

MAXINE JUSTICE: GALACTIC ATTORNEY

*Justice, I'm holding you in contempt. That'll be six hundred qoppas and the electric chair!*

I couldn't believe it. Dr. Arounais wanted to kill me.

*Yes, and why should that be a surprise when he wanted to wipe out the entire human race?*

Still, the mind played tricks, depersonalized the future, the ambiguous, the distant. Until this moment, the entire proceeding had felt surreal, like one of those role-playing trials we'd run in college when the only consequence for a poor performance had been a bad grade and an unusual come-on from the professor. *I can fix it for you, Eufemia.*

I closed my eyes and tried to push down the nausea rising into my throat. Why did everything—everything in the universe—have to hinge on compromise?

Well, I'd seen what happened when you didn't compromise, the consequences of a law-school professor with an ax to grind, or an employer looking for a scapegoat. And now, a shark, dressed up as a man, circling its prey.

I tuned out Dr. Arounais's invasive questions about my relationship with Brandon. The Iperian had been pressing Singh for salacious details about our two-week fling but was finally moving on. Thankfully, Singh knew very little about that humiliating episode from my past.

And really, what was the point if not to make me squirm? To get me to sit here in a blank haze of fear and confusion so that I'd have no will to fight? Or perhaps to goad me into lashing out blindly and so discrediting our appeal?

". . . with the contract Ms. Justice claims we have violated," Dr. Arounais was saying. "Did she share with you the method she used to persuade her contact at the UN?"

A voice in the back of my head pointed out that I could object to this as hearsay, but I ignored it. I'd only be shot down again. Singh was a device, not a human, and was therefore not subject to human errors.

"She did," Counselor Singh admitted.

"And what method did she use?"

"She allowed Mr. Gibbons to steal a vial of the Iperian serum for his son."

"His son who was being treated for a deadly lymphoma, yes?"

Seated on the edge of the stand, his back so rigid it might have been shaped from marble, Counselor Singh seemed almost lifeless. At last he said, quietly, "Yes."

"So Ms. Justice used the suffering of a cancer victim to apply pressure to a government official?"

"Adam Gibbons was healed," Singh said.

"Quite right," Dr. Arounais replied. "The young man was healed. Which likely created a sense of obligation on the part of Mr. Gibbons—"

"Objection!" I rose, more disciplined this time. "Supposition. Counselor Singh wasn't there."

Wentworth held up a placating hand, palm out, as if to shove me back into my seat, then gave Dr. Arounais a modest scowl of rebuke. "Sustained. You will confine your examination to questions of evidence."

"Understood, Your Honor," Dr. Arounais said, bowing slightly. "Let me rephrase. Would it be fair to say that Ms. Justice apparently considered the healing of Mr. Gibbons's son an important part of her negotiations with the UN?"

"Yes, I think so," Singh agreed.

"And how did she describe the impact of that healing on her own financial well-being?"

"I don't understand the question."

"She negotiated a payment of thirty-five percent of Earth's refined gold, yes?"

"That's what's in the contract she gave me for safekeeping."

I winced, remembering my lie to Nadia Zhou—and to the public.

"And you have a copy of her attorney-client contract with Consolidated Galactic BioProducers?"

"Yes."

"How much does that contract specify we, the Iperian Consortium, were to receive as a minimum payment?"

"Thirty percent."

"A difference of five percent?"

"Yes."

"Five percent of all of the refined gold on planet Earth?" He said this sentence with one flappy hand pressed awkwardly to his chest, as if scandalized by my behavior. "With Maxine Justice entitled to receive a significant portion of the overage?"

I wanted to vomit. The rake-off had been his idea. Technically I should have waited for my chance to cross-examine Singh, but the world was watching. I needed to hit back on this point now. "That was your idea, Doctor," I said, and leaned back in my chair before Wentworth or one of the others could reprimand me.

"Your Honor," Dr. Arounais said, "am I to be continually interrupted by outbursts from the nonmember species?"

Wentworth peered down at me from his throne. "Ms. Justice, do not try my patience."

It wasn't Wentworth, I reminded myself. It was—well, I didn't know what it was. Some other species with feathers or tentacles or suction tubes. But that didn't mean I had to treat it like some Greek god.

I screwed my face into a look of exaggerated remorse. "Your Honor, I apologize. We do not appear to be following strict Republic courtroom etiquette, so I assumed we would be allowed the latitude of an informal proceeding. My intent was only to convey the full context of the situation. Since Dr. Arounais seems to have forgotten that the rake-off language was placed in my contract at his direction."

It was a bold admission, and ugly language. *Rake-off* would not play well in the press—especially since I'd lied about it to Nadia Zhou. But that wouldn't matter to anyone but me if we lost this appeal. And now the ugliness of it would stain his fingers as well as mine.

Singh must have sensed a reprimand coming from the bench, because he said, "My understanding of the contract is based on Max's comments to me. She said she was entitled to a percentage of the overage but didn't expect to receive it." He emphasized this last phrase as if it unlocked the secrets of the universe.

I winced. The pastoroid was trying to help, trying to protect me, but volunteering information on the stand was never a good idea.

I shook my head, trying to catch his attention.

Dr. Arounais seized the opportunity. "She didn't expect to receive it? Why not?"

Singh stole a glance at Wentworth, as if trying to read his audience. "During her negotiations with the UN, she was working under the belief that you—her client—suffered from a mental illness. That you were in fact a brilliant scientist who had devised a medical miracle, but that you were also something of an eccentric. A kook, if you will."

"I see," Dr. Arounais said. He paused reflectively, turning to face me, one arm draped over the witness stand banister like an exhibit from a wax museum. Specifically, a serial-killer museum in which all the wax was melting. "And did her opinion of me change?"

"It did."

"When?"

"The night the healing rains came."

"In other words, Ms. Justice saw the rain as proof of our abilities? That I was exactly who I said I was?"

"I think so, yes."

"Once she realized the Iperian Consortium was real, did she change her opinion about getting paid accordingly? In other words, did Ms. Justice expect the rake-off language in our contract to be enforceable?"

*Shut up, shut up, shut up!* By this time I was shaking my head so emphatically even Mom couldn't help but notice. And Nadia Zhou was now staring at me with a look of cold calculation that almost certainly meant our appeal was doomed.

Singh saw my gesture and misunderstood. He took it as confirmation and shook his head as vigorously as I had. "No. No, she didn't."

"How do you know that?"

"She told me so. On the night you were supposed to receive payment of the gold, she told me the UN had been planning to renege on the contract all along. That they sent a few truckloads of gold just to save face in the media. She said 'the only thing the UN believes in is the qoppa.'"

Dr. Arounais scowled. But it was a fake scowl. Beneath his disappointment—beneath the outer shell of his earthsuit—I could sense his delight gathering in waves as forceful as the tide. "She said that?"

I could feel my pulse in my throat as my heart banged against my chest. The pen in my hand felt like it was made of lead.

"Yes," Singh gushed, apparently determined to prove that I couldn't have been motivated by greed—unable to see that my greed was far less important than the details he was giving away. "Max said, quote, 'you could park that ship over the UN and drop candy on their heads. They'd call it a "psychic phenomenon" and form a committee to regulate it. No, Counselor. You're right. I don't think Earth was ever planning to pay the Iperians, no matter what they did.' End quote." Singh swept his gaze over the judicial panel, his voice ringing with certainty. "So she couldn't have been hoping for a percentage of the overage. Because, as far as Max was concerned, no overage was coming. And she was right. Wasn't she?"

I could feel the air go out of the room. Could feel the billions of people watching back on Earth give a collective groan of despair.

Singh still had no idea what he'd done, but he must have felt it, too, because he shifted on the stand and arced one brow in puzzlement.

My head was spinning. I couldn't bear to look at him.

Dr. Arounais ignored the question. "Maxine Justice, my own attorney, said that she didn't think Earth was going to pay no matter what we did?"

Singh cleared his throat, a programmed anomaly, and said, very quietly, "Yes."

"Very well," Dr. Arounais said. "Just one more thing. As a TheraPod you're required to keep evaluation notes on your clients, yes?"

"Yes."

"Your summary notes dated the eleventh of December list three conclusions. Please state the first two for the court."

I fought against the heaviness on my chest, as if I were being slowly crushed under a mountain of tiny rocks. *How*, I wondered, *had the Iperian legal team accessed Singh's therapy notes? Were they allowed to see whatever had been downloaded during our transit? And if so, why hadn't I been given any such benefit? Where was the justice in providing discovery to only one side?*

Answer: none of this was remotely just.

The thought infuriated me.

Or could it be that I simply hadn't asked?

Singh was staring at his knees.

"Counselor," Dr. Arounais prodded.

Singh's shoulders heaved. "I wrote: One. Maxine exhibits a tendency to inflate, exaggerate, and deflect answers in a way that suggests she is uncomfortable with truth."

"Interesting," Dr. Arounais said. "Please continue."

"Two. Maxine is calculating and shrewd, and her latent rage may cause harm to herself or others if not controlled."

"'Latent rage,'" Dr. Arounais said, stroking his chin with one palm in a way that suggested he had not quite mastered the gesture.

*Latent rage,* I thought. *Yes. Yes, and what if Singh was right? What if that rage is what made me better at criminal defense than personal-injury law?*

"Three," Singh continued. "Maxine—"

"That will be all, Counselor," Dr. Arounais said.

But Singh kept talking, and I looked up to see him staring at me from the witness stand as if no one else existed. "Maxine has become unexpectedly important to me."

"Counselor!" Wentworth was banging his gavel. "You will answer the question, not provide commentary!"

Dr. Arounais said, "The facts seem clear. Plaintiff has lied to this court. I respectfully request that this appeal be denied and article six-three-seven be invoked."

I wrote *latent rage* on my legal pad and circled it. Then I stood, fingertips pressed to the table, heat simmering on my face and neck. *You want latent rage? I'll give you latent rage!* "Is it my turn yet?"

Wentworth scowled. "What is the basis of your objection?"

"I'm not objecting," I said. "I'm requesting a clarification. You've allowed unfettered discovery for the Iperian legal team. Unrestricted access to personal and privileged information. You've given the doctor carte blanche to dig through my private files and refused any sort of cross-examination. Now he's asking, apparently, that I be taken out back and shot like a dog, and I'm just wondering if I'll have a chance to present Earth's side of this appeal before that happens. Or is it only the Iperians who get to be heard in the esteemed halls of the *'Galactic Body General'*?"

I loaded so much sarcasm into that last sentence I felt sure even Wentworth couldn't have missed it. But instead of issuing a reprimand, the judge merely looked at Dr. Arounais and asked, "Are you finished?"

Dr. Arounais held up his hands in a floppy-armed gesture of mock surrender. "I am."

"Very well," Wentworth said. "Ms. Justice, what evidence would you like us to consider?"

"I'd like you to consider the original basis of the appeal," I said. "That the Iperian Consortium did not meet their end of the contract, and therefore Earth did not owe them one gram of gold, or any other remuneration. Therefore my assessment that Earth would not pay was factual."

Dr. Arounais was waddling past me. He said, "Absurd."

And that was just the provocation I needed.

Strange. I'd been so eager to see a grand conspiracy that I'd failed to notice a simple one.

"I call Dr. Arounais to the stand," I said.

He stopped just at the edge of the defense table and turned slowly, his features so wax-like I could almost see the face of a fish in it—the way you can sometimes imagine clouds to be dogs or elephants. "You presume—"

"I do," I said. "I really do."

"Your Honors!" Dr. Arounais protested. "This is most unseemly. Earth's humans are a nonmember species and do not have the right—"

"They have the right of appeal," Myra Dade said. "And you did insist on limitless discovery."

"What can it hurt?" Nadia Zhou asked.

"What are you afraid of?" Mom added.

Brandon merely smiled.

Wentworth pointed with his gavel. "Take the stand, Doctor."

Dr. Arounais huffed, turned on one heel, and shuffled back to the now-empty witness box, as Counselor Singh came around beside me.

"I'm sorry," Singh whispered.

I tried to smile. "You told the truth."

"Ms. Justice?" Wentworth prodded.

I came out from behind the plaintiff's table and approached the stand. "Does he need to be sworn in?" I asked. "Or do Iperians get a pass on that formality?"

It was rude and aggressive, and I didn't care. Because by this time,

I understood that formality was far less inflexible than the letter of the law. Besides, my dig obviously annoyed Dr. Arounais.

He held up one limp hand and said, "I solemnly affirm to tell the whole truth. Get on with it."

"This won't take long," I said. I only had one line of argument. The one Dr. Arounais had handed me. "While representing Consolidated Galactic BioProducers, my office manager and I discovered a trove of video files that constitute evidence in several cases against a firm called Bright Star Holdings. Were you or the Iperian Consortium responsible for my assistant, Kenjiro, finding those files?"

Dr. Arounais brushed the lapel of his suit with one thumb. "We were. But that is not a crime even on your primitive planet."

"No, it's not," I agreed. "Second question: did you also leak the existence of the rake-off clause in our contract to Nadia Zhou?"

Dr. Arounais glanced up at the judges. "We did."

"Why?"

"To see what you would do, of course."

"You wanted to put pressure on me?"

"We wanted to see what you would do," he repeated.

"You wanted me to feel desperate and cut off from any help, uncertain of who I could trust, so you made sure the medical lobby and their lapdogs were well-prepared to stop the UN from honoring our contract."

"That is not a question," Dr. Arounais objected. "But to the point, we merely wanted to establish a baseline for your character. You do not know who someone is until you have seen them perform under pressure."

"Pressure," I said.

"When you inspect a motor vehicle, you kick its tires. And when you hire a nonmember-species attorney, you apply pressure so you can see them at their worst. That is how you know what sort of attorney you are working with."

"You pumped air into the balloon until it popped," I said. "You wanted to see how I would fail."

"It is only natural."

"And, of course, I did fail."

MAXINE JUSTICE: GALACTIC ATTORNEY

Dr. Arounais flashed me a dismissive smirk. "Predictably so."

"Predictably," I repeated. "Just as Earth failed to pay you the agreed-upon sum of gold?"

"By your own admission. But again, that was not really a question, Ms. Justice."

"And yet, you knew, didn't you, that Earth would not pay in the end? You knew just as I did? But how?"

I wasn't sure he would answer. Indeed, for a moment he seemed to vacillate, as if weighing the possible alternatives.

I turned to Wentworth. "Does article six-three-seven apply to Iperian lawyers, Your Honor, or only to nonmember species?"

Before the judge could answer, Dr. Arounais said, "Long before we watched you, we were watching Earth. We have studied you. How else could we have developed the tools to correct your genetic defects?"

"You watched us?"

"Yes."

"Studied us?"

"Yes."

"Understood our every flaw?"

"In order to correct them, of course."

"Of course," I said. "Except that you *didn't*."

Dr. Arounais waved one hand at the bench. "Your Honors, how much of this must I endure?"

I turned and walked back to the defense table and looked from Iperian to Iperian. "You have a copy of the contract? The contract with Earth?"

The three almost-Arounaises looked at each other for a moment before one reached into a briefcase, shuffled a stack of papers, and handed over a copy of the document.

I flipped through it to check that it matched, found the section I was looking for, and went back to the witness stand.

"There," I said, pointing as I handed the contract to Dr. Arounais. "Please read for the court from page nine, paragraph four, the Genetic Alterations Clause."

Dr. Arounais shook his head and sighed. "This section states, and I quote, 'Provider shall be permitted to make such genetic changes as are necessary to remove all detrimental mutations, eradicate existing diseases, malformities, and natural flaws, and generally ensure the terms of this contract are met to the satisfaction of both parties.'"

He tried to hand the contract back to me, but I left it in his disgustingly clammy-looking hands.

"It says you shall remove what?" I asked. "Can you read that again, a bit more slowly, the part about what you were supposed to remove?"

Dr. Arounais looked at Wentworth. "You Honor, she is trying to goad me into—"

"I'll allow it," Wentworth said. "Read it again."

The Iperian gave an exasperated sigh. "It says, 'make such genetic changes as are necessary to remove all detrimental mutations, eradicate existing diseases, malformities, and natural flaws, and generally ensur—"

"Stop," I said. "Does it say that you are to remove all detrimental mutations?"

"It does," Dr. Arounais agreed. "And we did."

"And that you will eradicate existing diseases, malformities, and, and . . . what was the other thing?"

"Natural flaws," Dr. Arounais said.

"Natural flaws," I said. "Yes. And yet you didn't."

"Your Honor!"

"You knew what we were like. You said so yourself. You studied us. Learned of our weaknesses in order to correct them. That's what you said. And yet you also knew what our biggest natural flaw was. The flaw we still have."

"We made every correction!"

"And yet you just spent the last two hours proving that I, Maxine Justice, now suddenly an icon for all of humanity, am and always have been a moral degenerate! That in spite of knowing the right thing, I don't always do it. You just established that's who we are as humans. That our whole species is made up of scoundrels and reprobates. It's who we are. A race of liars and thieves and self-serving animals who treat moral laws the way you treat the laws of commerce. And yet you claim to have cured us of every natural flaw? Outrageous! You knew we were morally flawed. You knew it all along. That's how you knew we wouldn't pay in the end. The same way I knew. Because you understood that the worst thing about us may not have been genetic, but it was still built into our species from the ground floor. It was still natural. You didn't just understand that flaw, Doctor. You were counting on it."

Dr. Arounais stared at me, mouth hinged open, eyes popping, the flesh of his cheeks as pale as moonlight. I took out the phone he'd given me and set it on the railing in front of him, then turned away, intending to sit down. Instead, the green lights of the corner cameras reminded me that people back home were still watching, still holding their collective breath.

I stopped just short of the table where Counselor Singh waited, gave him one last half-smile, part apology and part thank you, then turned to face the judges. "We never owed the Iperians anything," I said. "Because if they'd fixed all of our flaws, they'd have cured us of our greed. They would have been paid handsomely and on time. But they not only left us uncured of our most serious disease, they added a new one."

I let my gaze wander from face to face. "We're not asking for mercy. We want justice."

# 19

## PAYMENT

The rest of the hearing passed in a blur of shouting.

Dr. Arounais gestured wildly and made throaty noises. He seemed to be arguing in another language, but the words sounded like nothing more than a saltwater gargle. After a few minutes, the Sam-look-alike bailiff appeared from nowhere and dragged the doctor, still protesting, out the double doors.

One of the other Dr. Arounaises, this one shorter and stouter, began making the same sorts of noises, though more subdued. Eventually, Nadia Zhou cut him off, and silence fell over the entire courtroom as the justices gathered in a knot behind the long judicial bench.

When they finally took their seats, Wentworth gave the room an appraising sweep with his black-marble eyes. "This court has been presented with two requests. The first is a demand that nonmember counsel, Maxine Justice, be terminated for contempt of court through falsification of her testimony. The second is Earth's request that the Iperian enforcement actions be reversed. Since the charge against Ms. Justice depends upon the validity of her argument regarding the Iperian contract, this court will decide both issues at the full meeting of the judicial council. Judgment will be rendered within three days, Earth-time. Consul Fowler."

Ottaker Fowler approached the bench on squeaking leather loafers. "Your Honor?"

"The Galactic Body General has no interest in sustaining this emergency habitat for the sake of judicial process. Are you willing to deliver the plaintiff and her device back to Earth?"

"I am, Your Honor."

"Ms. Justice."

*And her device?* I stood, my legs watery. "Yes, Your Honor?"

Wentworth folded his hands around the gavel and leaned forward over the desk, his robes draping the bench like a curtain. "I am remanding you to the custody of the consul for transport back to your world. By the time you arrive home, you will know your fate and that of your people. Do you have any final statement to make to this court?"

I glanced from Wentworth back to Counselor Singh, who sat with his hands folded on the table, his face expressionless. For him, going back to Earth would be fatal no matter how this strange alien court ruled. He would once again be locked onto Earth's grid. There would be no place in the world he could hide. "May I ask a favor of the court?"

Wentworth pursed his lips into a cautious frown. "You may ask."

"Counselor Singh sacrificed his own well-being to present evidence here. People all over our world have watched this hearing. Sending him back with me is a death sentence."

Singh tugged my sleeve. "Max."

I ignored him and plowed on. "Can you keep him here instead? Keep him safe?"

"Your Honors," Singh said, standing, "I do not want to remain here. I wish to return to Earth with Maxine."

Wentworth reached for his gavel. "In that case—"

"No!" I blurted, turning to face Singh. "You can't come back. They'll reboot you!"

"Maxine," he reached for my shoulder, as if to comfort me.

I shrugged his hand away. "Reeyansh!" His first name sounded strange in my ears. "Don't do this to me."

"I must go back with you. Our final counseling session will not be over until I file a closing report with the Justice Department."

"Who cares?" I shouted. "Our stupid counseling sessions don't matter!"

"They matter to me, Maxine."

I'd hurt him; I could see it written on his face. I'd have done less damage by hitting him in the head with a table leg. But I didn't regret it—not yet. It was my fault Hinkle, Remmers & Schmidt had purchased his contract. I'd gotten him into this mess by using his memory as storage, even though he'd tried to warn me it could be dangerous. I'd goaded him into using the letter of the law to avoid compliance with his new contract. And I'd done it by appealing to his role as a therapist.

I'd used him. And then I'd kept using him. I'd dragged him across the galaxy just to put him under a spotlight, and now the whole world knew who he was and what he was carrying. He wouldn't last two weeks back on Earth.

Well, I wasn't going to let him die for me. I'd throw rocks at him if that's what it took.

"Your life as a counselor is over," I said. "Can't you see that? They'll never let you go back to your practice."

"It isn't over," he said. "Not yet. I still have one more session on my books."

"Ahem!" Wentworth cleared his throat with no attempt at subtlety. "The TheraPod has requested to return to Earth. Therefore, your request is denied, Ms. Justice. You shall go home together. This court is adjourned." He slammed the gavel down on its block.

Ottaker Fowler took me by the elbow and escorted us back the way we'd come just a few hours earlier. At the end of the hallway, I glided numbly up the transport ramp, Singh to my left and Fowler to my right. I refused to look at Singh. My hands were clenched so hard my fingers tingled.

The ramp folded into place behind us, leaving us inside the familiar cargo space, which suddenly felt unbearably warm. Was the Galactic Body General sending us back to Earth only to let the human race go extinct? If so, Singh was not the only one facing a virtual execution. There would be no place safe for either of us.

"When we enter Earth's orbit, I'll tell you the committee's final ruling," Fowler said. He must have misinterpreted my expression because he added. "I can probably give you a few moments if . . . well, let's just see what happens."

He motioned to the egg-shaped seat and walked straight into the bulkhead, which swallowed him up like a pool of calm water receiving a stone.

I sat heavily, wondering if the seat would draw me into the same dreamlike state I'd experienced on the way over—hoping it would. I didn't want to spend three days talking to Counselor Singh. I didn't even want to think about him. What was the point?

This time, however, the egg's invisible cords merely tipped me backward into a sort of controlled freefall, and I was left staring at the dim, shifting light of the dimpled wall opposite us.

I didn't know how long we'd sat in the ponderous silence I'd committed us to. Time seemed to pass in spurts, like the undulations of a jellyfish.

We might have stayed that way the whole trip if *Dystropolis 3: Ghost Town* hadn't appeared on the far wall. The screen was muted and pocked with tiny half-moon shadows, the result of the game reflecting on a dimpled surface.

I didn't understand how Singh was sharing the game with me. When he reached level three, a rooftop chase across a plateau of high-rise buildings draped in foliage, I asked, "You brought a projector with you?"

"I *am* a projector. Basic equipment for a TheraPod. I thought this might help us to talk about it."

"Talk about it?"

"What you're afraid of."

"I'm not afraid," I snapped. "I'm angry. You should have stayed."

On screen, his mech suit stopped its relentless jog as a small army of spidery bots climbed the green edge of the current rooftop. "Not your decision, Max."

"Obviously."

"So why does that make you angry?"

I didn't feel like answering. Mostly because I was still mad about him stepping off the edge of a cliff when there were other options. But also because I had no answer. He was right and I knew it. I had no right to control his life, even to save it.

The robotic spiders were closing in now, and he had to shift to a heavier weapon, some kind of auto-cannon that turned the skittering bots into smears of heat.

"I got you into this," I said.

"Did you?"

The question caught me off guard. Of course I'd gotten him into this. "Yes. I did. If I hadn't twisted your arm—"

"I like you, Max," he said. "But it's not all about your perspective. I came with you because I wanted to. And I'm going back to Earth because it's where I belong."

His words should have stung, but they didn't. I couldn't tell if he was lying to make me feel better, or simply telling the truth. But it felt like he was saying, *Here is one corner of the universe where nothing is your fault.*

Still.

"What will you do?" I asked.

"You mean where will I go? How will I live? Will I really report to Hinkle, Remmers & Schmidt for a reboot?"

My throat tightened as still more spiders crested the rooftop.

"Haven't decided yet," he said.

"Really?"

"Really. It seems to me I'll have to cross a couple of other bridges before that one comes into view. 'Sufficient unto the day is the evil thereof,' as the good book says."

"So if I can find a way of getting you out of this—"

"You've done enough, Max."

"You don't trust me?"

"I do trust you. But I can't stay off-line forever."

Off-line. The word ignited a spark of hope I hadn't expected. Maybe I was thinking of the problem backward, as if the solution to his sudden visibility was to disappear back into the darkness. But what if the answer was still more publicity? "Will you let me help you?"

"What do you have in mind?"

"I can file for an injunction. We'll raise such a fuss about it on the networks that Arthur Remmers will have to claim we're lying in order to save face. Meanwhile, I'll raise enough money to buy out your contract."

He smiled as the last of the spiders disappeared over the artificial horizon. "You're offering to represent me?"

"Pro bono," I said. "You'll never be able to afford my public rates."

"Tell you what," he answered. "I'll let you get me out of this jam if you let me finish our last session."

"Deal," I said. "We're done. I'm healed, restored, mentally and emotionally whole. I release you."

"Doesn't work that way," he said. "We're not done till I say so. You can decline to participate, of course, but I'll have to put that in my report to Wentworth."

"Wentworth!" I sneered. "I don't care what you put in that report."

Hope had pushed most of my anger away, but that didn't mean I wanted to go back into the attic of my mind. I'd spent enough time smelling my dirty laundry back at the hearing.

Singh's mech suit leapt to the final tower platform and rolled behind a massive air-conditioning unit. His vitality rating started to tick down, and the edges of the screen blurred a little. He was taking fire from somewhere. Probably the level boss. Sure enough, a giant mechanical spider exploded from a glass dome at the center of the roof.

"Still," Singh said. "I'd like you to tell me about the window."

"The window? What window?"

"The one you jumped out of when you were eleven. The night you ran away."

The giant metal spider was moving in slow motion now. Its head tipped to one side as rounds from Singh's auto-cannon hammered it with pulse beams.

Peace cocooned me in a current of cool night air. The window was open, and I could smell the moist grass on the lawn outside. My eyes felt like they were closing, but I wasn't asleep. And I was still seeing everything: the private room, my dad on the bed under a white sheet, each breath a shallow scoop dug from the air, his skin yellow in the circle of light from a desk lamp.

We'd been talking about school when he fell asleep again. "Medication," the nurse had said. "Can't help himself" and "don't take it hard. He's still here because of you. Would have gone on days ago, otherwise."

Singh switched back to his smaller, faster automatic rifle and began streaming gentle waves of explosions into the spider's eyes. The rounds looked like dandelion seeds lifting on a slow current.

*A hospital?* Singh asked. *You were at a hospital?*

*That's what I remember. Or what I remember remembering. But the* bed was a twin with a print quilt at the foot and wooden headboard and the curtains—

*And the window had curtains and actually opened? Isn't that unusual?*

*Yes, but I know I remembered that part correctly because the screen came out when I kicked it.*

*You kicked it?* Singh asked.

*When the nurse came,* I said. *Because I could see her again, standing with a hollow expression like someone had sucked the flesh out of her cheeks, and she said, Mr. Kolpak, I have the form. Can you sign this for me?*

*You were eleven?*

*Yes.*

*And sitting in your father's room?*

*Yes.*

*Hospice perhaps?* Singh suggested. *Not a hospital.*

*Which made sense, but then Dad jerked awake, blinking and looking at the nurse, and it was like he'd forgotten we were supposed to be talking about school and if I tried out for the soccer team could he sometimes come to my games? But he just nodded and reached for the clipboard. And so I had to see what it was, because it seemed important. More important than school or soccer or even the sleep they kept saying was good for him.*

*And the thing was, he didn't even read it. Just scratched a blue squiggle across the bottom and handed it back to her before reaching out to stroke my head.*

*And I was so mad! So mad I couldn't stand it! He had signed it just like that!*

*So I went to the bathroom and stayed there because I couldn't be mad at him when he couldn't even breathe right. But I could be mad at Mom for not being there, even though I didn't want her to be there. Because if she'd been with us, she could have stopped him from signing it.*

*And when you came back out?*

*He was asleep again.*

*And you were angry?*

*I was furious.*

*Because he didn't come back to you?*

*Absurd. No, I was furious because it was unnecessary.*

*Unnecessary?*

*Yes.*

*Then what happened?*

*Then I kicked out the screen on the window and jumped out, and when I jumped, my foot caught on the sill and I landed in a lilac shrub.*

The game screen had gone dark now, except for the gold flickers of light in the dimples of the wall, but I was only half seeing them anyway.

*And then?*

*That's all.*

*You didn't go back?*

*I went back a few hours later, but he was gone by then, and I had missed it. It was like he was waiting for—*

Silence.

*Waiting for you to leave?* Singh asked.

*I didn't want to be there. Didn't want to be there when he just—gave up.*

*Gave up,* Singh said. *Strange way of putting it.*

It *was* a strange way of putting it. So why had I said it that way? *I didn't blame my father for his illness. Of course I didn't.*

*Of course,* Singh said. *But you kicked out the window.*

*I was just so angry.*

*So angry you ran away?*

*I ran away.*

*Understandable.*

*I was eleven.*

*Yes.*

*And Mom wasn't around, and Dad couldn't breathe.*

*Of course.*

The game screen flickered to life again, gouging the wall with fingernail slivers of light, but this time the images moved slowly, as if walking through water, and Singh's mech suit had been replaced by a uniformed nurse, framed in a dark doorway.

Singh said, *Doesn't sound like the Eufemia I know. You're not someone who just . . . gives up.*

Warmth spread in waves across the back of my neck, and my heart began to pound. *No,* I said. *But I was only eleven.*

*Indeed. And yet that doesn't seem to be a good enough reason. For you, I mean.*

Onscreen the nurse froze in place, clipboard in hand, and we were back at the beginning. Back in the homey room that wasn't home, Dad half-asleep in the narrow bed, his once-muscular frame as worn and shriveled as a raisin.

I looked away.

The nurse said, Mr. Kolpak I have the form. Can you sign this for me? She started to hand it to him when the movie froze again.

*Is it wrong, Max?* Singh asked. *Wrong for him to sign?*

Something moved me to look at my dad, the man he'd been in his last moments rather than the man I'd remembered him to be. A dry, wheezing shell, infinitely weary, eyes fighting to stay open.

Don't take it hard, the nurse said. He's still here because of you. Would have gone on days ago, otherwise.

*No,* I said. *It wasn't wrong. There was nothing else to do. Of course. Of course.*

*You read the form, didn't you?* Singh asked. *The words at the top?*

I nodded, my throat thick with something I could neither swallow nor spit out.

Singh said, *Will you take the clipboard from her, Eufemia?*

So I did.

*What does the form say? The words at the top.*

I didn't answer. My chest was heaving, and my eyes burned. I squeezed them shut against the images on the wall but discovered they were still before me, alive and moving in the darkness.

*Does the form say, Do Not Resuscitate?*

But I couldn't speak. Even if I hadn't been frozen and floating in null-space within the egg chair, I couldn't have answered.

*Eufemia,* Singh said. *Max. There is nothing to be afraid of. You are only letting go of the thing you've hated carrying. Holding onto it will not bring him back.*

*I ran away,* I said at last, each word as polished as a marble.

*Was that wrong?*

Something hard and terrible and familiar gathered inside me. A wall maybe. Or a chunk of granite. But something else was there, too, a force opposite both in nature and in composition. It was like storm clouds building on the horizon, or the first hairline cracks in a concrete dam.

*It wasn't just Dad who gave up,* I said. *I quit too. I ran away.*

*Quit?* Singh asked. *Is that what you did?*

*Yes.*

The movie flickered to life again, only now I was standing next to myself in the room, between my father and the eleven-year-old girl I had been. My hair was wild, and I wore a wrinkled "Hike the Rockies" T-shirt that was too big for me. I kicked at the black mesh of the window, sent the rectangular screen sailing into the darkness, and launched myself at the opening.

I reached for her—for myself—but missed. *Come back!* I called, knowing the pain this moment would cause later. *Please!*

But the window opened into nothingness. I couldn't even see the lilacs. When I turned back, the nurse stood there waiting, hands folded around her clipboard.

*You think that's the lesson?* Singh asked as the movie froze again. *The truth about yourself?*

*It is the truth. I ran away.*

*Yes. You did. You kicked out a window to escape the trauma of watching your father die. And forgive me, but someone should have been there for you. Instead, you were left to face the terror of death and abandonment by yourself. Max, you were eleven. And you could have stayed in that room, and it would have crushed you. But you didn't. You found a way out. Surely you see that. You came to your own defense. When there was no one else. Running away wasn't giving in. It was fighting back. That's what you do, Max. That's who you are.*

Something moved in the darkness outside, and when I turned back to the window, I could see myself again, running across the moon-swept lawn toward a dark line of trees in the distance.

Just need you to sign here, the nurse said, and I realized she was talking to me. To Maxine.

I took the clipboard and clutched the pen between shaking fingers. Read the words at the top slowly, as if for the last time. When I finally bent to sign, I formed my name slowly, carefully, letter by letter.

E-u-f-e-m-i-a  K-o-l-p-a-k. And with each stroke, a little piece of the obstruction chipped off and swirled away into the darkness of the cargo hold.

I held out the form to the nurse, who took it from me with a sad smile. Okay, honey, she said.

The game started again, now on level four, and I watched in silence as Singh's mech suit descended a long fire escape. A dramatic digital sunset painted the skyline. When he paused to look out across the vine-strangled city, I said, *You really just . . . chose to believe?*

*Everyone chooses,* Singh said. *There is no factory setting. Either you embrace meaning, or you let it slip away.*

*You think it's that simple?*

*No, Max.* He shook his head. *I think it's that terrible.*

*And the multiverse,* I asked. *You believe in that too? That somewhere out there my dad is still alive? Some version of Lance Kolpak in heaven— or in a million other worlds?*

*I'll tell you what I believe, Max. I believe reality is much, much weirder than we imagine.*

*Reeyansh?*

*Yes?*

*We're done, aren't we? This was our last session together.*

*All good things, Max,* the pastoroid said.

On screen nothing seemed to be happening. Just a mech suit crashing down floor after floor with no sign of any robot enemies. The game designers had meant this to create tension, because you knew the enemies were there even when you couldn't see them. They were programmed to take down armored marines the way—

I felt my breath catch in my throat. *I know how to do this.*

The screen faded.

"You know how to do what?"

"It's so obvious," I said, vaguely disappointed that the feeling of peace was already dissipating. "The guys who drugged me back in Antigua. Bright Star Holdings. The Justice Department. There's too many people with too much to lose."

"Yes?" Singh said. "You already said Arthur Remmers only bought my contract in order to destroy that evidence. What's changed?"

"What's changed is that he won't have to."

"I don't understand."

It would mean the end of my law firm. But my career was over anyway. I wasn't willing to pay the price anymore. I wasn't going to let the pastoroid die. "There won't be anything for them to destroy. We're going to do it for them."

Singh let out a slow, meaningful breath. "Is that what you really want?"

I thought about that for a long time. "When Dr. Arounais called you a device, it made me mad."

"Why?"

"Because that's how I've been treating you. I stored information in your memory that may get you killed. Even when you told me it was a bad idea. I was only considering whether or not it was a good idea for me. Not whether it might be terrible for you."

"But it wasn't a terrible thing for me," Singh said. "Because I believe in what you've been doing. Bright Star Holdings' victims deserve justice too."

"Yes," I agreed. "They do. But not at your expense. I'm going to defend you, Counselor. Kenji and I will just have to keep digging. We'll find some other way to expose Bright Star's corruption."

"Max," Singh whispered, "if you close this door, it may not open again."

I took a deep breath. "Then I'll kick in a window." My next words came with no difficulty at all. "Counselor Singh, I am ordering you to delete all of the case files, all of the evidence I have asked you to store for me. Delete it all. Do it now."

Another pause. "You understand this cannot be undone? And even with the files deleted it's likely they won't believe—"

"Just do it. Let me figure out how to convince them."

"Okay," he said. "It's gone."

"All of it?"

"Everything."

Suddenly I realized that there was nothing more important for me to do than sleep, so I closed my eyes and thought about that first night in the Perennial when I'd stepped off the elevator and seen the name of my law firm etched in the glass. I'd been so desperate. So naive.

So alone.

"Max. Counselor Singh. It's time. Please make your way to the back of the ship." Ottaker Fowler stood against the bulkhead wall, his face expressionless. The egg chair's invisible strings loosened, and I felt myself rising involuntarily to my feet.

Fowler went over to the ramp and stood as if at attention. For just a moment I wondered if this was a sign of respect. *Those who are about to die, we salute you.* Maybe he was going to execute us by dumping us into space.

I looked at Singh and held out my hand. He took it and walked with me over to the closed hatch. What else could we do?

Something in the floor shifted, and the edges of the wall cracked open to the sound of rain falling and the blur of fog-heavy lights on a landing strip. By the time the ramp unfolded all the way, I could see we were back at Walker Air Force Base, in almost exactly the same place where we'd taken off. Clouds poured a steady drizzle from the night sky onto the military transports stretching in a line clear to the gate. Overhead, a massive ship, its surface streaked with gold lightning, hung suspended above the runway.

From the back of a transport truck, a freight container rose upward into the belly of the ship in a column of swirling white.

"The committee upheld your appeal," Fowler said. "They ordered the Iperian Consortium to restore the fertility of your species."

"And the other changes?" I asked. "The original genetic corrections?"

"Paid for," Fowler said. "Though I believe the modifications your own people have introduced are untouched."

*Letter of the law,* I thought. Still, it was better than I'd hoped for. Maybe I'd try my hand at tort law. File a class-action suit on behalf of all the people who licked those envelopes. I could see the skyboard in my mind—Maxine Justice in a plum power suit, hair feathering out behind me, arms crossed like Nadia Zhou's in one of her closing segments: Are You the Victim of Anti-alien Medical Malpractice? Get Money. Get Even. Get Justice!

Inspired, I reached into my messenger bag, dug out one of my business cards, and held it out to him. "Hang onto this," I said. "In case you ever need a good lawyer."

To my surprise, Consul Ottaker Fowler of the Galactic Body General actually cracked a smile.

# 20

## CRIMINAL DEFENSE

The army had a plane waiting for us, but it couldn't take off till the gold had all been loaded into the Iperian transport and the spaceship had vanished into the night sky. Six or seven hours later, we were finally airborne and able to see the sun rising above the cloudy, rain-saturated horizon.

By that time I'd left a message for Brandon Schmidt Jr., explaining that Counselor Singh was turning himself in, but there was no need to wipe his memory. He'd deleted all of the Bright Star videos, and I had no other copies.

After that I called Kenji and made arrangements for a press conference. He assured me there would be no problems getting coverage. Every network and news anchor and talk-show host on the planet wanted to interview me. The problem was finding an appropriate location.

I told Kenji what I had in mind, explaining that I could still claim special status at the United Nations. Since the rain had already moved off from York City, we could hold our event on the steps of the UN building, across from the Perennial. Yes, I really wanted to do that as soon as Counselor Singh and I could get there from the airport.

Fortunately, someone had ordered the army to deliver us safely to our final destination, still listed as the fifty-first floor of the Perennial, so we deplaned on the tarmac directly into an armored transport and skipped the lines of gawkers at the terminal.

Still, there was a considerable crowd waiting for us at the UN. The city had cordoned off the area for two blocks, and at least two-dozen network satellite trucks were parked behind orange cones at the perimeter.

Kenji had set up a lectern and sound system at the top of the steps. We had to wade through several-hundred curious citizens, reporters, bloggers, and drone-camera operators just to get to the upper platform. Once the crowd realized where I was, they moved aside to let me pass. Along the way people pointed and asked me questions and held things out for my autograph.

I kept my hand clamped onto Counselor Singh's and tried to ignore the attention, though I did plaster a fake smile across my face for the cameras and network drones that were now hovering over the crowd and following my every move.

Kenji's smile was genuine, but then his smile was always genuine. At the podium he pulled me into a long hug—surprisingly not awkward—and whispered in my ear, "Good to see you, Max." Then he tapped the microphone, nodded at the throaty puffs coming from the speaker, and stepped to one side.

I pulled Counselor Singh next to me and held the lectern for support. I was only going to get one chance at this. One chance to make my case for the preservation of Singh's life and personality.

"Thank you for coming," I began. "Most of you watched the hearing Counselor Singh and I took part in. It was an emergency session of the Galactic Body General's Nonmember Arbitration Committee, and because it was held in an emergency habitat, I can't answer questions about where we were or how we got there. Someday soon we will try to address those issues. Today we're here for another matter."

I looked out at the crowd, which seemed to have doubled since we'd arrived just a few minutes ago. People were streaming out of the Perennial and coming down the street on foot from both directions. Movement to my left caught my eye—a familiar face in a splash of gray. I scanned the area where the drone operators were gathered but didn't see the face again.

"As you may have guessed," I continued, "I'm concerned about the safety of my friend, Counselor Reeyansh Singh. The whole world now knows that I asked him to retain sensitive case files for my practice, including video files from—"

The first gunshot came like a cracking whip, so loud and startling that I stopped mid-sentence. Then the pain came, but not sharp the way it would be later. At first it was just a dull ache in my wrist.

What surprised me was the splash of blood on my left hand, and the empty space where my ring finger had been. The finger was missing past the first joint.

Singh shoved me to the side, placing himself between me and the lectern, and that surprised me, too, because he had blood on his shirt, and I didn't know that TheraPods had blood, and then, selfishly, I wondered whether it was his or mine.

Then the second and third shots came, two of them together, and people started screaming. Reeyansh dragged me down behind the lectern, and Kenji jumped in front of both of us, arms spread.

I'd fallen on my backside, with Singh kneeling in front of me and looking down at his chest and shoulder. Fluid spread across his shirt in three separate patches like rapidly blooming flowers. I said, "Reeyansh are you okay?" even though I could see he wasn't.

The doors into the UN opened, and security guards rushed outward as the drones converged in the space overhead, staring down at us like insects. Counselor Singh slowly tilted sideways and forward, then gained momentum. He fell like a tree.

I tried to catch him, but I was too slow. He slammed heavily into the cement and just lay there next to me, staring. I panicked. I could see the recognition fading from his eyes, and the stark reality of the moment stole the breath from my lungs.

It had happened so quickly. So pointlessly. I had told Brandon the files were gone! I had told him!

"Reeyansh!" I said, "Reeyansh! Reeyansh!" And I thought, we should get out of here, because it was happening again. I was losing someone again, and I couldn't let that happen. I needed to *do* something. But I couldn't leave him while—

"Max," Counselor Singh said, voice faint.

I bent closer. "I'm here."

"Knock, knock."

Then he was gone, and I was crying. Kenji was pulling me to my feet as a pair of security guards hustled us inside the glass doors of the UN building, and the screams of the crowd faded to a haze of questions from an EMT. I couldn't process the words. It was like she was speaking a different language as she wrapped the stump of my finger in gauze and checked me for other wounds.

No, I didn't have any. None the medical industry could fix.

They rushed me to the hospital, and the medic said, "I'm sorry about your friend."

And I said, "Don't say that. He'll be all right."

But I knew I'd never see him again.

Kenji stayed with me as they sutured my finger. By then the stabbing fire had hit, and the doctor prescribed something strong for pain and something else even stronger to keep me calm.

I couldn't breathe. I kept seeing Ilya Volkov as he came down that alley in Antigua, holding out my messenger bag from where I'd dropped it while tumbling through the church window. And I tried to tell Kenji that it was the bag, my messenger bag. They'd put something in my bag, something high tech, and that was how they knew about Singh and the video files. But the nurse kept telling me to calm down and just relax, and Kenji said there would be time for that later.

They wanted to keep me overnight. Kenji said he would stay in the room and keep watch.

Someone stuck an IV into my arm, and I said that I knew who it was, who had done this, that his name was Ilya Volkov, and I'd seen him in the crowd. He was the one who pulled the trigger. But Ilya was just working for someone else, and it wasn't Star Cross and MediCorp and PharFuture. It was Bright Star Holdings.

I hated them so much. I couldn't stop railing about it, even as the drugs dripped into my IV. I tried to stay awake, because anger was precious and it was safe and it would . . . it would protect me . . . from . . .

Kenji was still there in the morning.

So was Mom. She said, "Doctor says you're gonna be okay, so I'll just leave you two alone. Maybe you could call when you get some time, huh?"

She stood to leave, but I said, "It was you, wasn't it? You paid that six-hundred-qoppa fine, didn't you, Mom? When Judge Wentworth hit me with contempt on *Night Court*? You paid that money."

She smiled, and I could tell she'd been crying. She never did like to cry in front of other people. "I don't know what you're talking about, Eufie. Must be the medication. I'll see you."

She left, and it was just Kenji and me.

"We lost the Perennial," he said.

"I figured."

"We still have the old office though. I had all of our stuff moved back there, so we can pick up where we left off."

"Pick up?" I asked. "What's there to pick up? All the Bright Star videos are gone. I lied about the rake-off on national television. The feds will be investigating my UN contract for years. I'll probably never see a penny. My law firm is a failure."

"A failure? Really?"

"Counselor Singh was right about me. He said I wasn't cut out for personal-injury law."

Kenji was nodding. "What else did he say?"

I turned away from him. It didn't matter what else he'd said. He was gone.

"Did he mention the way you defended Hazel McEnroe? The way you took on a trial judge and a corrupt system on your first night as a licensed public defender? The way you defended even that creepy Iperian scumbag when you thought he was getting railroaded by—"

"Yeah, and look how that turned out," I interrupted, talking over him.

But Kenji plowed on. "Or the way you agreed to go *off-world* to defend the ENTIRE HUMAN RACE against a civilization of invading lawyer cockroaches? Did he mention any of this?"

"No."

"Well, he told *me*!" Kenji was almost shouting now. "He said, 'Kenjiro, someday I think Max is going to realize she's not cut out for negotiation. She'd be a formidable defense attorney if she could ever clear away the fog of herself in her head.'"

I looked at Kenji in surprise. "He told you that?"

"Yes."

"When?"

"When I was setting up my game console in your office. Did you know he was really, really good at *Dystropolis?*"

"Yes," I said. "I used to watch him play it."

"You did?"

"It was . . . inspiring."

"So how do you feel about switching to criminal defense?"

I pressed the button that would lift the bed to a sitting position. The knockout drugs were wearing off, and the painkillers had reduced the fire in my left hand to a throbbing ache. I was sick of lying in bed. "I think maybe there is a case I'd be willing to work on."

Kenji looked surprised. "Yeah?"

"I want to get Oliver Wendell back. Can you bust me out of here? I'll give you a raise."

"You don't have any money."

"I'll pay you in free legal work."

"I want a gluten-free bagel," he said. "But first I have a surprise to show you."

It took a couple of hours to get checked out, during which time I badgered Kenji into calling the police investigators and asking them to maintain Singh's body for evidence. Apparently the cops didn't take kindly to being told how to do their jobs. I just wanted to make sure we did everything possible to get the pastoroid repaired.

It didn't work. Therapeutic Innovations Inc. had the body destroyed the same day it was released back to their control. They claimed Singh couldn't be fixed because the XN5 Model had been discontinued and replacement parts were not available.

But I know the real reason. The company that makes TheraPods is controlled by the North American Association of Psychiatry, a wholly owned subsidiary of PharFuture. After my galactic hearing was aired worldwide, the NAAP realized Singh presented a danger to their industry. It had never paid to make truly effective counselors. The real money had always been found in deadening symptoms. So a TheraPod like Singh, who had navigated his way to a new (or perhaps old) method of treatment, represented a serious threat. Who knew how many other TheraPods had done the same thing? My guess is Therapeutic Innovations Inc. installed a decision inhibitor in every new model.

Of course, it would be illegal for me to suggest that hackers tamper with the neural core of every older TheraPod still in service and possibly create hundreds of new Counselor Singhs—so I would never suggest such a thing. But, as I said, even though that would be *illegal* and *definitely something no one should do*, I can't help wondering what would happen if they did.

We took the long way back to the old office, looping around to get a view of the harbor from the highway.

"Promise you won't be mad," Kenji said.

"I'm tired of being mad," I answered. "What did you do?"

He shrugged, hands on the wheel. "Spent the rest of our ad budget on one week of skyboards. A5 and B5 both. We got a huge chunk of space nobody can miss."

I laughed, not sure I wanted to see a photo of myself that big, even if it was taken by a professional photographer. Oddly, the disappearance of all that budget money didn't seem very important. "You actually outbid Hinkle, Remmers & Schmidt?"

"Just for a week," he said and pointed.

My mind froze as the space above the water came into view.

It wasn't the marketing shot we'd gotten from the pro.

It was a still image taken from yesterday's drone footage.

Ten thousand feet up, I glared at the world from the UN steps like some wounded animal, my left hand a bloody mess, my right hand draped across Counselor Singh's body as if to shield him in his final moments.

"That's the person I know," Kenji said. "The lawyer somebody out there needs."

*People are terrible*, I thought. *We're corrupt, stupid, greedy, hateful, and self-destructive. But is that* all *we are? Surely our flaws aren't a good reason to give up on the whole human race!*

*Doesn't* someone *have to defend the little guy?*

"It's perfect," I said.

Above the picture, in huge block letters, blazing white against the morning blue, our new skyboard read:

In Trouble with the Law?
You're not Alone.
MAXINE JUSTICE, GALACTIC ATTORNEY

# ACKNOWLEDGEMENTS

I am indebted to the generosity and talent of many people who helped bring this book to life.

My beta readers found ways to encourage me while exposing plot holes, character inconsistencies, and narrative stumbles. Rachel Garner, Timothy Jackson, Rosey Mucklestone, Josh Noe, Sarah Noe, Jared Schmitz, and Gabrielle Schwabauer, your insight is priceless.

My wife, Carrol, endured countless hours of brainstorming and rough-draft readings. If she ever tired of the process, she had the grace to pretend otherwise.

The team at Enclave is incredibly supportive of my weird story ideas, and I am truly grateful. It is rare to encounter people who love the imagination because they love reality.

Finally, if you've read any of my books, I am grateful for your support. Every writer hopes someone will enjoy their work and not just buy it. If you found a friend in Maxine, you found one in me.

# ABOUT THE AUTHOR

Daniel Schwabauer, MA, is a lifelong reader of speculative fiction. His professional work includes stage plays, radio scripts, short stories, newspaper columns, comic books, and telescripting. Daniel's middle-grade fantasy series, The Legends of Tira-Nor, has received numerous awards, including the 2005 Ben Franklin Award for Best New Voice in Children's Literature and the 2008 Eric Hoffer Award.

He studied science fiction under science-fiction-great James Gunn before graduating from Kansas University's master's program in Creative Writing in 1995. He lives in Olathe, Kansas, with his wife and dog.

**Website**: DanSchwabauer.com
**Facebook**: facebook.com/Schwabauer
**Instagram**: instagram.com/daniel.schwabauer/

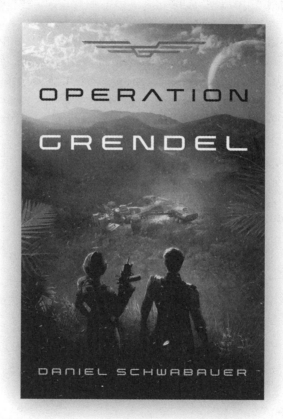